Hard Way
Out of Hell

Center Point
Large Print

Also by Johnny D. Boggs and available from Center Point Large Print:

Mojave
And There I'll Be a Soldier
Top Soldier

**This Large Print Book carries the
Seal of Approval of N.A.V.H.**

HARD WAY OUT OF HELL

The Confessions of Cole Younger

Johnny D. Boggs

CENTER POINT LARGE PRINT
THORNDIKE, MAINE

This Circle Ⓥ Western is published by
Center Point Large Print in the year 2016 in
co-operation with Golden West Literary Agency.

First Edition
December, 2016

Printed in the United States of America
on permanent paper.
Set in 16-point Times New Roman type.

ISBN: 978-1-68324-214-7

Library of Congress Cataloging-in-Publication Data

Names: Boggs, Johnny D., author.
Title: Hard way out of hell : the confessions of Cole Younger / Johnny
D. Boggs.
Description: First edition. | Thorndike, Maine : Center Point Large Print,
2016. | Series: A Circle V western
Identifiers: LCCN 2016032632 | ISBN 9781683242147
    (hardcover : alk. paper)
Subjects: LCSH: Younger, Cole, 1844-1916—Fiction. | Large type
books. | GSAFD: Western stories. | Biographical fiction.
Classification: LCC PS3552.O4375 H365 2016 | DDC 813/.54—dc23
LC record available at https://lccn.loc.gov/2016032632

In memory of John J. "Jack" Koblas.
Thanks for your books, music, friendship,
and the loan of your sofa on those
trips to Minnesota.

"Long is the way
And hard, that out of Hell leads up to light."
—John Milton, *Paradise Lost*

"Blood is contagious."
—John Newman Edwards

Prologue

1913

In the middle of the journey of our life, I found myself within a dark woods; for the straight way was lost.

Thus wrote Dante, a man I have long admired, especially in *Inferno*, his masterpiece, and how brilliantly he described those nine circles of Hell: Limbo, Lust, Gluttony, Greed, Anger, Heresy, Violence, Fraud, and Treachery.

All of those circles, Parson, I have seen. Indeed, I lived in them. Some—Lust, Gluttony, Heresy— I have regretted, but much of the Anger and Violence I would gladly do again. Forgiving is hard, even though you say that I can be forgiven. Am I worthy to walk those Streets of Gold? That question I cannot answer because, honestly, I do not know.

Ma and Pa always wanted me to become a preacher, whilst many of the boys I rode with dubbed me Bishop. For a boy who once only dreamed of being a Christian, who longed to join the Masons, and who desired nothing other than to marry a good woman, and live in peace, I have traveled a hard road. The first five decades proved to be unbearably difficult. Though I rarely dream,

I have wakened from nightmares of unspeakable events that I witnessed, and of horrible crimes that I committed.

It brings to mind William Shakespeare's "Julius Caesar": *The evil that men do lives after them; the good is oft interred with their bones.*

Act III, Scene Two.

Few, I think, will ever forget the evil that I, Thomas Coleman Younger, delivered upon my enemies.

Ask anyone, best friend or the bitterest of enemies, and they will tell you that Cole Younger is an evil man. Bold? Certainly. Loyal? As the noblest blue-tick hound. But wicked. Heartless. Cold-blooded as a timber rattlesnake.

There is no peace, saith the Lord, unto the wicked.

Isaiah, Chapter Forty-Eight, Verse Twenty-Two.

Peace eluded me. Perhaps I avoided living in harmony because the very thought of peace frightened me.

I was, I remain, and I will always be a wicked man, but only because of this sad fact: Almost as long as I can remember, I have been lost in those dark, foreboding woods.

For me, the woods were Missouri. And Stillwater, Minnesota.

PART I

1844–1865

Chapter One

The Missouri River became the River Acheron, and John Brown, instead of Charon, held the job as the master of the ferry. Don't mistake me. I don't hate this fine state. I never cared much for any man, or woman, who disparaged his or her home. I love Missouri. Lee's Summit. Blue Springs and Sni-A-Bar Creek. The woods, and the dogs, and even some schoolhouses I attended. Corn pone, Ma's biscuits, and pig-pickings. And the finest horses and mules you'll find anywhere in this country.

Yet when I was growing up, Parson, and even after I became a grown man, Missouri turned into the worst kind of hell.

Long before you were born, kids everywhere played rolling pins, hopscotch, shuttlecock, quoits, hide-and-seek, and marbles. The most popular game at our house, however, was Old John Brown.

Unless you grew up in western Missouri in the mid-to-late 1850s, that's a game unfamiliar to you. It was pretty simple. On our farm, it usually went something like this.

On account that my baby brothers, John and Bob, were too little to get picked on, Brother Jim got to play the fine Missouri farmer. John, you see, didn't come around till 1851, with Bob trailing two years later. We had a mighty big family, but I always thought we were short a mite on boys. Sadly, all of my brothers would be dead by 1902, and, today, even many of my sisters have gone to Glory.

We young 'uns numbered fourteen, though a fever took sweet Alphae in 1852 when she was but two years old. As the seventh surviving child born to Henry Washington Younger and Bursheba Leighton Fristoe Younger, I joined an already good-size family on January 15, 1844. Laura, Isabella—who everyone called Belle—and Martha Anne came along first, followed by my older brother, Charles Richard, who went by Dick. Dick was the best of the boys, six years my senior. Old beyond his years, he would be the Younger brother that might have amounted to something fine, real fine. Anyway, I don't recollect ever playing anything with him for he kept busy ciphering figures and helping Pa.

After Dick, Mary Josephine—we always called her Josie—and pretty Caroline were born. Caroline got the handle Duck, on account that we usually found her down by one of the ponds as a little girl, quacking like ducks. Sarah "Sally" Ann, Jim, and Alphae followed Caroline and me. John, Emilly, and Robert came after the Almighty took baby Alphae into His arms, and finally baby Henrietta—who everybody knew as Retta—was born.

I remember one neighbor telling Pa: "There's enough of you Youngers to make your own militia." Turns out, history would prove Mr. McCorkle to be practically right.

Getting back to Old John Brown, we would be outside, usually near the barn or corral, and Jim would be making out like he was shucking corn—sometimes, he really would be shucking corn because we Youngers could play and work at the same time—or working a plow behind a mule, just doing the hard, daily work on any farm.

Then out I would stride, all high and mighty, and start preaching blood and thunder, hell and damnation. Jim would stop whatever he had been doing, and yell: "What are you doing here, John Brown? This is Missouri, not Kansas."

Pretending to be Old John Brown, I would tell him something like: "I am what I am, and you are Missouri trash." So we'd get to tussling, and sometimes, in the spirit of things, I'd box Jim's ears. One time, I remember, I must have hit Jim a little harder than I intended. Although Jim wasn't puny, I was big for my age, and because Dick was always busying himself with bookwork, it was left to me to fork the hay, move the sacks, harness the mules, and split the firewood, so I was pretty strong. Anyway, down went Jim, but up he came, catching me with an uppercut that split my lip.

The idea of this game was that Old John Brown would torment a poor Missouri farmer, or a preacher, or just some passer-by. Then the Younger siblings would come to the Missourian's rescue, driving Old John Brown off with pitchforks and hoes, or throwing pecans or dirt clods. They'd pretend the sticks they carried were muskets, or rapiers. Something along those lines, anyhow. One time, they pelted me with the potatoes that we had been tossing into the cellar. They did that until Ma realized what we were doing, and we all got a switching. Even me, who had only been dodging those flying spuds.

Well, the way the game was supposed to be played was that once the neighbors came out to help the poor soul that was being tormented, Old John Brown would hightail it back to Kansas. The good guys, you see, would win.

The time I'm recollecting, I found myself doing what big brothers usually did to their younger siblings. Mouth bleeding, I tossed Brother Jim onto some hay, straddled him, pinned his arms with my knees, and started slapping him this way and that. Then here would come the neighbors, of course—Josie, Caroline, Sally—to drive Old John Brown back to Kansas. Only this time, as Old John Brown, I refused to go anywhere till Brother Jim begged for mercy, or cried uncle. Mad as I was, I'm not rightly sure even that would have stopped me.

So my sisters took to crying and screaming, and within a few minutes hands were grasping my arms, and pulling me off my bleeding, bruised, sobbing kid brother. Still madder than a March hare, I whirled to whip whoever had interfered with my vengeance. I drew back my arm, intending to cave in Dick's face, but a neighbor stepped betwixt us, blocking my punch with his left forearm.

The neighbor was John Jarrette, who, I imagine, would have been around twenty-three years old. Kentucky-born, his family had moved to Missouri right around 1851. His pa was a cabinetmaker, and, like his father, Jarrette had arms like two-by-fours. Still seeing blood in my eyes, I fought to punch him or Dick or Jim, but Jarrette got his hands locked behind my back, and began squeezing the breath out of me, almost crushing my ribs, arms, and backbone.

"Easy there, Old John Brown," I recall him saying in a tight, hoarse whisper.

Now I was big and strong but, being only twelve years old, I could not free myself from Jarrette's clutches.

"Easy there, Cole," Jarrette kept saying over the sobs and shrieks coming from my siblings. "Easy. . . ."

It wasn't John Jarrette who stopped me, though. It was the voice of another.

"'And the Lord said unto Satan, From whence comest thou? And Satan answered the Lord, and said, From going to and fro in the earth, and from walking up and down in it.' So now Satan is walking on my own farm . . . in my own house."

My muscles weakened, and I stopped struggling. John Jarrette released that vise that pinned me, and stepped back, while I stood in front of my mother, head bowed.

"Come here, Coleman," she said, and I obeyed.

I prepared myself to go find a switch, and take my whipping—Pa seemed to be gone most of the time, so punishment usually came from Ma's hands, and I believe her hand was tougher than Pa's. Kentucky-born and bred, and having birthed fourteen kids, Ma was harder than oak. That morning, however, Ma simply turned and walked away from the barn while my two oldest sisters, Laura and Belle, hurried to tend to Jim, who kept sobbing. I followed Ma.

We did not stop until we reached the porch of our farmhouse. Only then did Ma turn, her eyes stern, her countenance firm. "The devil gets ahold of you, Coleman," she said. "You try my patience. You'll never become that preacher if you keep acting like that."

"Yes, ma'am."

" 'Be sober, be vigilant; because your adversary the devil, as a roaring lion, walketh about, seeking whom he may devour,' " she quoted. "Keep this up, and you'll be the one devoured."

"Yes, ma'am."

"Your brothers and sisters be watching, Coleman.

No supper tonight. And you'll go down there and apologize to everyone. Then you'll fetch a switch." She pointed toward the woods, where the brambles could rip off the hide of a rabbit or squirrel. "From down yonder. Don't get yourself bit by no snake, and don't you dare bring me a puny switch."

"Yes, ma'am."

"What was that y'all was playing that let Satan try to steal your soul?"

"Old John Brown."

"Figures," Ma said. "He's the devil, too. 'For we wrestle not against flesh and blood, but against principalities, against powers, against the rulers of the darkness of this world, against spiritual wickedness. . . .' Hurry off, Coleman. I'll be here waiting."

Chapter Two

You're mighty young for a preacher, Parson, so I'm guessing that you were not born till after the War for Southern Independence. Therefore, let me summarize things for you.

John Brown was a fire-eating Yankee Abolitionist, hanged by the neck until he was dead, in Virginia when, in fact, he should have been executed in Kansas for his deplorable acts. Here's what has always eluded my grasp. More than fifty years since he has been, as the song still sung proclaims, "a-molderin' in his grave," he is hailed as a visionary to be celebrated, while men like William Quantrill, Bill Anderson, Frank James, and I are considered murderers who should have been strung up or shot down for committing high treason.

In the 1850s, Brown brought his sons down from New York to Kansas. In 1856, he and his ardent followers set upon the Doyle family, who were living peacefully on Pottawatomie Creek. Yes, the Doyles—and many other Kansans—supported slavery, but in those days, such was their Constitutional right. John Doyle and two of his sons—their names I disremember—did not deserve to be led into the dark and hacked to pieces by broadswords. Had Mrs. Doyle not begged and pleaded for mercy, John Brown would have murdered another of Doyle's boys, a sixteen-year-old. After the butchery, Brown and his felons moved on, yet, bloodlust not sated, the killers then found another Southern home, where they slashed, stabbed, and slayed Allen Wilkinson. Before the night was over, William Sherman was also brutally murdered.

"Bleeding Kansas" certainly ran red.

Yes, Missourians would ride across the border. Certainly Missouri men as well as Kansas red legs would commit wrongs. Free-soilers and border ruffians killed, plundered, and—to my mind—started that ugly Civil War years before the first shots were fired upon Fort Sumner.

The violence I grew up around all started with the Kansas-Nebraska Act of 1854. Residents, according to that new law, would declare a state's slavery status. That sent men like John Brown and other free-soilers streaming into Kansas while Missourians crossed the boundary to support the rights of the South. The Wakarusa War, and battles at Black Jack and Osawatomie followed. A constitution was ratified in Lecompton in 1857, but since it allowed slavery—and was supported by President James Buchanan—the Yankees disallowed the election, called for another vote, and the free-soilers won. When Kansas entered the Union in 1861, it came in as a free state. And Old John Brown? The insane fiend left Kansas for

Virginia, to raid the federal armory at Harper's Ferry, where he was stopped, tried, convicted, and executed—and became a Yankee martyr.

Now, before you label me that unreconstructed Rebel, evil slaver, and butcher, let me lay some facts on you.

Yes, Pa owned slaves, but he was a good man, a Christian, and I never saw any whippings, or abuse of any of the colored servants we had.

Truthfully I didn't think anything much about the slaves we owned. Just took it to be the way things were, had always been, and would always be. When Pa moved from Crab Orchard to Missouri, he set up a little ferry on the Little Blue River near Randolph. He made enough money on that venture to pay back the fellow who loaned him the cash to start up the ferry, and to buy some land in Jackson County, and a few more slaves. One of those slaves, Pa left behind to run the ferry.

All these years later, I regret that part of my family history. But when you're a boy with Southern ties, you didn't think about the wrongs of slavery. It wouldn't be till I ran across a Negro named Erskine Green that my way of thinking changed. That would be in Stillwater. I'll get to Erskine Green directly.

During my growing-up years, I got into some fine discussions about Scripture, hunting, and horses with one of Pa's slaves, a kindly cuss with arms that could have snapped John Jarrette in two. We called him Hardin. And there was Mammy Suse, a plump Negress who helped Ma around the house and took care of us like we were her own young 'uns, especially when Ma came down sick or got worn down.

Yet while Pa was a slave owner, here's something else you should know about him.

Colonel Henry Washington Younger did not hold with Secession. He bled Union red, white, and blue. Ma had similar inclinations, and her father fought with Andy Jackson at New Orleans and was a grand nephew of Chief Justice John Marshall.

A conservative Unionist is how most folks looked upon Pa, which wasn't always a good thing in Missouri, but he fared pretty well. In 1855, he was elected to the Shawnee Mission Legislature, even though he owned no land and never lived in Kansas. He owned maybe thirty-five hundred acres in Jackson and Cass Counties, Missouri—a little more than half of that on our farm near the town of Strother; they would change its name to Lee's Summit in 1865—where we mostly raised livestock. Pa even sold a quarter-section to the county court back in 1852, so the county could set up a poor farm.

In 1859, Josie married John Jarrette, and Pa got elected mayor of the town of Harrisonville and landed a contract with the federal government to deliver mail. That two-hundred-mile run stretched from Kansas City all the way to Neosho. So we moved from our farm to Harrisonville, although Pa spent most of his time carrying letters north or south.

Pa remained loyal to the Union—maybe he did not support Abraham Lincoln and those high-minded, holier-than-thou Abolitionists, but he did his best to stay on the straight and narrow. When our Southern-minded neighbors began bringing up the idea of Secession, Pa—who never strayed from or lied about his convictions—told them exactly what he thought of their views.

"You, sir," I remember him saying as we walked out of the barbershop, "speak of treason."

So, Parson, tell me this . . . why would men who claimed to be fighting for the North abuse a loyal Union man like Colonel Henry Washington Younger?

I speak of the actions of not John Brown, but men like James Montgomery and his Self-Protective Company, Doc Jennison, and Senator Jim Lane. These jayhawkers—nothing more than armed thieves and murderers—crossed the Kansas-Missouri line to hang men with no trial, no jury, just a rope.

Such men were not Abolitionists who I could respect—Frederick Douglass and perhaps even Mr. Lincoln—but brigands. They robbed my father. They stole our saddle mounts, and we had some excellent horses: Morgans, thoroughbreds,

Arabians, and even some Narragansett Pacers, which I don't believe exist any more. Pa liked to crossbreed the Pacers with the Morgans.

Red legs didn't just steal our livestock. They broke into our stables to liberate phaetons, surreys, buggies, spring wagons, hay wagons, buckboards, and farm wagons. At first, they never came to our farm, the house in Harrisonville, or the ferry Pa still owned, but struck the mail stations and other businesses that Pa had a stake in. In one night alone, they robbed us of more than $4,000 in merchandise.

As crimes and war talk heated up, Pa approached me one afternoon while I was mucking out the stables. "Cole," he said softly, "I think it is time you learned how to shoot."

Leaning the pitchfork against a stall, I laughed. "Pa, I've been shooting a gun since I was six years old."

His expression did not change. He did not smile, nor did he blink.

"Son," he said, and the smile vanished from my face, "I speak not of shotguns or rifles." From his coat pocket, he withdrew a .36-caliber Navy Colt, and held it out to me, butt forward.

With some tentativeness, I accepted the revolver, amazed by both its balance and the lightness of weight.

Pa nodded. "It fits your hand," he said, "like you were born with it."

I taught myself to shoot. Bottles, cans, pine cones. Right-handed at first. Then John Jarrette taught me to shoot with my left hand.

"Why would I need to shoot left-handed?" I asked him.

"Because you might get shot in your right arm," he said.

"Shot?" I laughed, until I realized Jarrette was not joking.

Troubled times, certainly, but, like most kids throughout all of history I imagine, I had no idea about how good my life was. Even in those dark days of the Border Wars—since I rarely saw bloodshed or thievery first-hand but only heard Pa, Dick, and Jarrette speak of such crimes— I could hunt, fish. Never did our family go hungry. Ma taught us to read from the Bible, and Pa, a man of letters, would debate—his word—the news of the day with us, for Pa collected news-papers like he owned a Kansas City newspaper stand. Even my sisters would be allowed to voice opinions.

After supper, we might cite Shakespeare, Milton, or Lord Byron. Sometimes we would even bring in Hardin, the slave, to discuss the teachings of Jesus or the letters of Paul.

My parents insisted that their children get a formal education. At one schoolhouse, I got my first taste of the devil.

• • •

His name was Bob Griggs, blue eyed and bald except for the greasy, red hair strands that ran around the sides of his head. A freckle-faced man with a crooked nose, Bob Griggs did not like me—or my brothers or sisters—one iota.

This is how Bob Griggs started every morning, five days a week, in that little one-room schoolhouse.

"Children. . . ." He would be standing behind his desk, which held a few old McGuffey's *Readers*, a Bible, a Webster's Dictionary, and his hat, crown down. He always smiled like some kindly uncle, his hands at his chest, the fingers of one hand spread out and pressing against the fingers of the other hand, highlighting the pointer finger of his left hand that was missing two knuckles. He always ordered all the children—which varied in number between sixteen and twenty-nine, what with the crops and the seasons and the weather, or how the fish might be biting—to come up and draw a number from his hat.

We did that every single day, each of us pulling out a folded piece of yellow paper, and then returning to our seats. After the first couple of weeks of school, the minute he stood behind the desk many of the girls, but even some of the smaller boys, would start crying because they knew what came next.

Releasing his fingertips, he would stare at the

ceiling as if in deep thought, and eventually would look at us carefully before calling out the number. Some unfortunate would come up with the slip of paper with the number he had called, and return it to the hat, and then bend over. Producing an ugly piece of board with holes drilled through, Bob Griggs would arc back his arm and then slam that paddle savagely on the student's backside. Just one slap, and the boy or girl would tearfully walk to the rear left corner, standing there till recess, when perhaps the pain would have lessened enough for that day's victim to sit down again for the afternoon.

Every day.

Four times a week, on average, that unfortunate kid was a Younger since there would have been five of us at school at that time I'm recalling—Josie, pushing sixteen, down to Jim, who was eight.

That day Bob Griggs called out: "Seven!"

My number. This wasn't my first whipping from that sorry old cuss, but it would be my last. From my dinner pail, I pulled out the bullfrog I had caught—my original plan had been to scare my cousin, Nannie Harris, and a real pretty girl named Lizzie Brown—and handed it to Lizzie's brother Tom before I strode up to take my punishment.

Griggs swung hard, the paddle sending spasms of pain racing up my backbone, and I could feel welts rising on my buttocks. But damned if I even flinched.

"What's the matter with you, Younger?" Bob Griggs yelled, and swung the paddle again. I was not expecting a second blow, so, as I was straightening and turning, the paddle caught me on the right hip, and sent me crashing to the floor. At the same time the frog must have leaped out of Tom Brown's hand. Frightened, the girls began screaming, turning the small log cabin into bedlam. That really angered Bob Griggs, who started to take it out on me as I pushed myself up off the floor.

The next swing of the paddle caught my forearm, which I quickly raised to defend myself. The devil, however, had taken hold of Bob Griggs, and the paddle sprained my wrist and left a bruise that eventually stretched from knuckles to elbow. Back came the paddle, catching me on the side of my head. My eyes glazed over. I tasted blood in my mouth. I swore I saw Satan, horns and all, standing over me.

As far as I was concerned that was my punishment for whipping Brother Jim while playing Old John Brown. The devil himself had come to take me straight to hell.

"You uppity piece of trash!" Griggs yelled. "Holier than thou. Richer than God Almighty. Well, I'm about to teach you a lesson you'll never forget!"

As he came at me, I closed my eyes, ready to travel to that terrible place. Something crashed.

A man screamed. I could feel the floor of the school-house trembling as my classmates stampeded outside. They'd tell their parents, I dimly thought. The closest family was the Kelley clan—Doc Kelley had donated the land for the school—but still their house lay three miles southeast, and the Kelley brood always walked to school.

By the time some grown-up came, I would be dead.

So I lay there, practically unconscious, feeling half dead as I tried to remember some good Bible verses.

The Lord is my shepherd; I shall not want.

Train up a child in the way he should go: and when he is old, he will not depart from it.

I went back to the Old Testament, when the earth was without form. I fell into that void, where darkness was upon the face of the deep.

Chapter Three

And God said, Let there be light, and there was light.

Genesis, Chapter One, Verse Three.

My eyes opened. I saw my older brother Dick, whose eyes were rimmed red from tears. Or perhaps rage. His collar had been pulled askew, buttons had been ripped from his shirt, and when he let out that sigh of relief as I returned to consciousness, he lifted his right hand to run through his curly hair. I saw the scrapes on his knuckles.

Dick would have been eighteen on that Friday morning in 1856. Ma and Pa had sent him to Chapel Hill College up in Lexington, but Dick had been riding home for a visit and had decided to stop by the schoolhouse. Why the Lord has always looked over me, I cannot say.

Nor will I ever understand why I should have been blessed with such a kind, sweet, and loving brother like Dick. Neighbors always said we were direct opposites: me the hothead, and Dick the one who sought to reason things out, not turn to fisticuffs.

On that day, though, it took Jack and Tom Brown and Horatio Kelley to pull Dick off Bob Griggs, and even then the schoolmaster had four busted ribs, a shattered jaw, and a nose that had been pretty much flattened.

"Speak to me, Cole," Dick pleaded. "Can you talk?"

My lips parted, and I turned my head to spit out blood.

"Oh, God!" Dick cried.

My head straightened, and I mouthed—"I am all right."—and swallowed.

Nannie Harris came back inside, holding a handkerchief that she had dipped in a well bucket. Kneeling at my side, she began to squeeze the handkerchief, dripping cool spring water into my mouth. That revived me, but still I must have been addled because I asked: "Tom, where's that bullfrog?"

They hauled Bob Griggs back to Strother, wrapped up his jaw, bandaged his ribs. Then the Kelleys and Browns, along with other good citizens, doused his body—naked except for the coverings on his wounds—with hot tar before dumping goose feathers over him. Finally they ran him out of the county. Or at least that's what I heard. I didn't witness any of it, and I never ran into Bob Griggs again—for which Mr. Griggs, if he's not dead, should give thanks every day.

Boosted onto Dick's horse, I slumped in the saddle as my big brother grabbed the reins to lead the blue roan mare through the woods road toward our farmhouse. Sally, Josie, Duck, and Jim followed. When we came to the crossroads and could see our home, Dick stopped, turning to face my brothers, sisters, and me.

"What should we tell Ma and Pa?" Sally asked.

Dick wet his lips. "That Griggs damned near killed Cole. That's all. Hurry down and tell Ma, so she can have hot water and a bed ready. You kids can run faster than I can pull Cole on Frances here."

"I ain't *that* busted up," I said.

"Hush." Dick nodded at the others, and they took off, running, screaming loud enough to alert farms far distant to the south. He watched them run for maybe a minute, and when he turned back, I saw tears streaming down his face.

"Cole. . . ." He was as desperate as I had ever seen him. "Don't tell them, Cole. Please don't tell them what I did to that schoolmaster. Please. . . ."

That was another difference between Dick and me. He had more of Pa in him than I did, and he kept his eye on politics. After he was graduated from Chapel Hill College, he came home—we lived in Harrisonville by then—and opened up a livery business with Will Kelley, who used to freight down the Santa Fe Trail. Dick would become a Mason when the Grand Lodge of Missouri, Prairie Lodge Number 90, started up in 1860. We all figured he was destined for greater things— had life turned out like everyone thought it would.

Me? I was the wild one, the one everyone would have expected to have beaten Bob Griggs so savagely no one could have recognized him.

Over the several miles from the schoolhouse and our home, my reasoning and senses had returned, relatively speaking. It hurt to suck in a deep breath, but that's what I did, holding it for a while before exhaling. My head bobbed. I did not know why Dick should feel ashamed for what he had done to that evil man. Hell, I still don't know. "You didn't do anything," I said. "I whupped Bob Griggs. And I'd do it again," I assured him.

After that experience in school, you might think that I would have shunned education, and joined a bunch of boys like some of the Kelley and Jarrette crew that avoided schoolhouses and books the way Nannie Harris swung wide berths around spiders, snakes, and frogs. Yet, education in the Younger household was considered a privilege, an honor, and a necessity.

We loved our parents, even when Pa was far off in Kansas City, even when Ma was sending us to get a switch to be used on our backsides. We loved the discussions about the world, literature, and the Bible. Yes, I found life beyond books—in the woods where I hunted, on the roads where I rode, during those hours practicing with that Navy Colt. And at the socials, barn-raisings, turkey shoots, and pig-pickings where we ate, danced, sipped of Mr. Jarrette's corn liquor when no grown-ups were looking, once we were teen-agers, or sneaked a kiss from a girl.

Sister Laura married Will Kelley, a widower who had a daughter. Belle wed Richard Hall, a shopkeeper and blacksmith, and they moved into Ma and Pa's first home near Strother. Duck eventually would marry one of Pa's best wranglers, George Clayton. Pa stayed busy, and we prospered, and I returned to school—and loved it.

After we moved to Harrisonville, I got an education from my cousin, Stephen Carter Ragan, and another fine schoolmaster, Stephen B. Elkins, at a fancy school called The Academy. I joked that it was for the brightest kids in the county, but, actually, it was for any boy or girl whose parents could pay the hefty price of subscription per student.

Ragan's ma was Aunt Mary, Pa's sister, and Captain Ragan proved himself to be a mighty fine teacher, who never put a dunce cap on anyone, never made a boy or girl stand in a corner, and never rebuked any kid for giving an incorrect answer. I mean to tell you that, after enduring Bob Griggs for those hellish months, having a cousin for a teacher, and a capable teacher at that, seemed heaven sent. Captain Ragan—he would wear the gray under Generals Kirby Smith, Braxton Bragg, and Joseph Johnston—taught us for two years. Then Stephen Elkins came on the scene.

Elkins was different, but he appreciated my willingness to listen, and learn, and to break up fights—Elkins was not a big gent—when the boys took to rough-housing. One September afternoon in 1859, when every boy in school, including Jim, had gone to the McCorkles' cornfield to shoot doves for supper and the following morning's breakfast, Mr. Elkins called me up to the head of the class. At that time, I don't think Elkins could have been older than seventeen or eighteen, and maybe not even that.

"Don't you like dove meat, Cole?" he asked.

"Yes, sir."

"Well . . ." He glanced out the window, and we could hear the muffled reports of shotguns off the west, where the McCorkles had their farm. "What brought you to school?"

"My older brother Dick," I answered.

"Dick brought you to school." His words always came out a lot different than most folks. He had attended the Masonic College and earned his sheepskin from the University of Missouri over in Columbia, but everyone knew that he hailed from Ohio. He smiled that little wan smile of his, shook his head, and said: "Cole, I didn't ask you who brought you here. I asked you *what* brought you here."

"Same answer, sir," I said. "I'm here because

of Dick. I figure . . . well, if I can be like Dick, then maybe I'll amount to something."

He thought about that before coming close enough to whisper in my ear: "Coleman Younger, I am not a wise old man, but I think I have seen enough in this schoolhouse to know one thing for certain. You, young man, will amount to something."

Chapter Four

Strother lay a tad under twenty miles due north of Harrisonville—an easy ride—so Pa trusted me, now sixteen years old, to make the run with the mail on June 6, 1860. 'Course, I carried the Navy Colt on my hip and the mail in a pouch was secured around the horn of the saddle. I rode the best Narragansett Pacer we had, a fourteen-and-a-half-hand high chestnut stallion, long-necked and high-tailed. I called him Robinson Crusoe, and always rode him at an ambling gait.

The mail I carried included newspapers—the editor of the Harrison *Democrat* had some sort of agreement with the publishers and editors of other newspapers in which they'd send each other that week's papers. The papers made for pretty good reading once I got out of Harrisonville on the northbound route, or Strother when I started back for home. When one editor was finished with a paper or papers, he would mail his batch on up or down the line. Kansas City's *Enquirer* and *Star* . . . Liberty *Tribune* . . . *Border Star* . . . *Occidental Messenger* . . . *Western Beacon* . . . Lexington *Express*. I had plenty to read.

Slowing down Robinson Crusoe that day, I pulled out the *Border Star* from the mail pouch and began reading about the upcoming election.

Pa supported Claiborne Jackson for governor and Thomas C. Reynolds for lieutenant governor. They were running on the Stephen Douglas ticket, and Pa liked them on account they were pro-slavery, but moderate. By 1860, you heard plenty of talk about Secession, but Pa and many others wanted to preserve the Union.

I don't think it mattered much to me one way or the other. I just liked to read.

Besides, it was a hot day, so muggy that I had broken out in a sweat before I had ridden a mile out of town. I didn't want to tax my stallion too much.

Hoofs thudded behind me, forcing me to rein up and look back. The papers also carried news about James Montgomery and Doc Jennison, who kept making off with Missouri property, which they carried back to Kansas. Now, not thinking any red leg would be after me, I didn't even reach for my Colt. What I did do was curse and drop my newspaper, because the roan and rider didn't even slow down till they were about ten yards from me. Then the horse practically slid to a stop, which caused Robinson Crusoe to shy and buck a bit and that sent the Westport weekly into the bar ditch.

"Damn you, Duck!" I shouted, and swung to the ground, holding the reins to Robinson Crusoe and sliding down into the ditch. Rain had been steady that week, the ditch was flowing, and the *Border Star* was soggy. I held up the paper, ink already blurring. "Look what you done!" I yelled.

"No one'll miss one little newspaper, Brother," my older sister told me. "I won't tell Pa. So you won't lose your job . . . or get sent to The Walls."

She meant the state prison in Jefferson City, which had opened back in 1836 and was already considered the "bloodiest forty-seven acres in America". Having seen more than my fair share of bloodshed, I might disagree with that assessment, although I cannot say for certain. I've never been inside any Missouri prison.

After tossing the *Border Star* back into the water, I climbed out of the ditch. Two years my senior, Duck was right. No editor would miss one little newspaper, already a month old, which had been read and passed along by Lord knows how many other publishers. The ink was smeared long before it fell into that bar ditch.

Of all my sisters—actually, of all of my siblings—I felt closest to Duck. Headstrong, pretty, athletic, smart, she could ride like the devil and laugh like a giggling toddler. Her blue eyes always sparkled, and I don't think any of the Younger brood loved life the way she did. She lived for the day, and nothing pleased her more than to spur a horse into a gallop with the wind blowing in her face. Folks in Harrisonville didn't like that she rarely rode side-saddle, but no one had the stupidity to mention that to her, or any of the Youngers.

"What are you doing here?" I asked, both haughty and mad.

"Keeping you company," she said.

"You are not."

"Am, too." She laughed. "Ma said it was all right for me to go and visit Belle and Richard. In her last letter Belle said she finally got that brand-new sewing machine from the I.M. Singer and Company."

I slipped my boot into the stirrup, swung back into the saddle, kicked the chestnut into a walk, saying: "Since when did you ever take interest in sewing?"

Easing her horse alongside Robinson Crusoe, she tilted her head at me and showed her most bewitching smile. "Richard got himself a new shotgun."

We walked about a mile, before Duck got antsy. "C'mon, Cole. I'll never get to try out that new shotgun if we dilly-dally like this." She wore boots. She wore spurs. And the Morgan bolted into a high lope, so I had to follow.

It was miles we rode like that before slowing down to a walk to let our horses cool down. It was long past noon, when I heard some noise a ways up the road. Woods lined both sides of the road, more path than pike, and I pushed back the brim of my hat, leaned forward in the saddle, and listened.

"What was that?" Duck asked.

"I don't know exactly."

Muffled shouts, the breaking of twigs, a horse's whinny all came from the eastern woods. Dogs were barking.

We stopped.

"Sounds like a 'coon hunt," Duck said.

I knew it wasn't. I gripped the butt of the Navy, and eased Robinson Crusoe in front of Duck and her Morgan.

A man burst through the woods, hatless, his clothes ripped by the brambles. He started across the road, but here the ditch had widened to practically a creek, and, panting as he was, both pale and already limping, I guess he knew he could never make that leap across. So he turned and ran north, away from us. So terrified he seemed, I don't think he even saw us.

The blast of a shotgun startled our horses, and pellets rained down among the trees as we steadied our horses. A few seconds later, riders emerged from the trees and briars that grew so thick that they were forced to move slowly, picking their way carefully and cautiously in single file. These men, wearing hats and each carrying a shotgun or revolver, spotted us. One smiled, while another stopped, tipped his hat at Duck, and bowed, before spurring his dun down the road.

Eight men in all. The last one wore a fine morning coat, with a black hat fitted with a purple ostrich plume, one side pinned up. He carried a large revolver in his small hand, which he pointed up the road, yelling: "Stop him!"

They did. Up the road, past the woods in an area where some farmer had cleared the land and planted corn. A big man with a long beard and a buckskin shirt knocked the fugitive down with his dapple horse. Then, quickly, two others dismounted and jerked the man back up to his feet.

When the dainty man with the ostrich plume caught up with them, he cried out: "There!" Then, pointing his big pistol, he yelled: "To that oak! The oak!"

Duck and I could see that one tree remained at the edge of the cornfield, a mighty oak that looked as though it had been growing there for centuries.

"Let's go back," I said, turning my horse around.

Duck blinked. "What's this about?"

"It's none of our affair," I told her as I started walking the pacing horse back toward Harrisonville.

Duck rode toward the clearing, instead. Muttering an oath and pulling the reins, I raced after her.

"Capt'n," the burly man said, pointing at us, and the man with the plumed hat turned toward Duck and me.

Captain? No one in this group wore a uniform, and I couldn't see any chevrons or epaulets on their clothing, yet my newspaper readings and our suppertime discussions with Pa had educated me. During the previous year, the southeastern portion of Kansas had briefly been put under martial law. In Missouri, our legislature had authorized the raising of a militia to put down banditti terrorizing our state, as well as offering rewards as high as $3,000 for the capture of Kansas raiders who crossed the state line to perpetrate atrocities on Missourians.

"What's going on here?" Duck called out as she reined up, watching the captured man, whose hands had been tied behind his back, being pushed toward the oak tree. He was alternating between screaming out in fear and crying out to the Lord.

The big man with the long beard stepped away from the others. An old single-shot pistol remained tucked in his waistband, but he pulled a hatchet and waved it at my sister. "Get out of here, you pryin' little bitch."

A mere second later, he stopped his charge as he stared down the barrel of my Navy Colt.

"You speak to my sister like that again, mister," I said, "and your next conversation will be with Peter at the pearly gates." I actually said that, like I was some character in one of those five-penny dreadfuls that Jim was always reading when he could sneak one into the house without Ma catching him.

The hatchet dropped to the sod, and the man swallowed his tobacco quid.

That got the man with the fancy coat and hat to

44

laugh. He shoved his big revolver into a flapped holster on his left hip and stepped forward, sweeping off his hat and bowing slightly.

"Lankford would apologize, friends," he said as the hat returned to his head, "were he not about to lose his breakfast." Indeed, the man with the thick beard had fallen to his knees and hands, gagging.

Duck could have cared less. "What are you doing to this man?" she demanded to know.

"Why we're hanging him, my dear," answered the fancy man.

His voice sounded more like a girl's, and though I guess he stood maybe five-foot-nine in those high-heeled boots, a good wind would have likely sent him sailing into the cornfield. I doubt if he weighed more than a hundred and forty pounds. His eyes were pale, as was his face, and he had just begun sprouting a yellowish mustache. But his sandy-colored hair was well-groomed, and he carried himself with an easy gait. He didn't look like a captain, more like a schoolteacher, and I don't mean Bob Griggs.

"For what?" Duck demanded.

"He's a damned Kansan!" came a curt shout from a man standing beneath the oak.

The fancy man grinned. "Mister Todd speaks the truth. But more than just a Kansan . . ."—he leaned his head back and laughed—"as I once lived in the fair city of Lawrence myself . . . he foments insurrection. He and others planned to free slaves being auctioned off in Independence, arm them, and sic them on their masters." His voice lowered. "You know what a darky would do to a lovely lass like yourself."

I aimed the Colt at this smooth-speaking gent, but he showed no fear.

Addressing me, he continued: "You know I speak the truth, sir. This rapacious swine would strike you down without remorse, commit the most heinous crimes on you and your family, and would turn western Missouri into a Chicago slaughterhouse."

A number of the other seven men started moving away from the oak tree, their guns in their hands. My palms turned clammy.

Duck looked my way, and for once I saw fear in her eyes.

"It was in the paper," I commented as I holstered the Colt. "The sale of some slaves in Independence."

"If there are no further objections, then," the dandy said, "we shall proceed with our execution." He turned in the direction of the oak, but then stopped and twisted back toward us. "Would you care to watch?"

"No," I said for the both of us. In no mood for any objection from Duck, I took the reins from her and led her Morgan away.

Duck wasn't finished, though. She called back: "Might I have your name?"

Stopping, I turned in the saddle as the man bowed. "But, of course," he said brightly. "I would be honored to have your lips mouth my name. Yet might I first ask to hear yours?"

"Caroline," she said. "Caroline Younger."

Then the fancy man's cold eyes found me.

"Cole," was all I told him. He already knew that Duck was my sister.

"A pleasure to make the acquaintance of both of you." After a quick bow, he walked toward the man they planned to hang, who had dropped to his knees begging for mercy in between his sobs. I didn't think the fancy man was going to tell us his name, or even an alias, for fear we would tell the authorities—though neither Duck nor I ever spoke of that day.

"You may call me Hart!" he called out. "Hart! Charley Hart!"

Charley Hart wasn't his real name, of course. He had been born Quantrill. William Clarke Quantrill.

Chapter Five

I saw my brother Dick in Harrisonville on Election Day, August, 1860, when I rode Robinson Crusoe to the livery he owned with Laura's husband, Will Kelley.

"Come to vote, Bud?" he said, grinning.

Dick was the one who saddled that nickname on me. I never knew why, but it made me laugh. "I'm not old enough to vote, Dick."

"This is Missouri," Dick said. "I bet you *can* vote. Probably two or three times . . . as long as you're voting for the Douglas ticket."

"Thought this was just a city election," I said as I swung out of the saddle and handed him the reins. "Got no interest in politics, Dick," I told him, and gave him a wicked grin. "I just want to see how you shoe a horse."

He took the reins, and led the stallion to the smithy. "I'm a businessman, Bud," he said. "I don't shoe horses. I pay my farrier. Hey, Ned!"

Leaving the Narragansett Pacer with the smithy, Dick led me across the street. I figured we'd be going to some café, though it seemed a mite early for supper, or maybe Pa's mercantile for some new duds because Dick never cared much for how I dressed. But instead, I found myself stepping onto the sawdust and peanut shells that covered the floor of Stricklyn's Tavern.

This being Election Day, the place had drawn a crowd. To make it to the bar took some doing since Dick stopped at any number of tables to shake hands and exchange a few words with the seated men, as well as introduce me. We had to squeeze between two gents in bowler hats who both were using a bar towel to wipe the suds off their mustaches. Once we sidled up, Dick rapped his knuckles on the top of the bar, and when the beer-jerked turned his way, Dick held up two fingers.

"Ma'll raise hell, Dick," I said, not whispering because you had to talk loud to be heard as noisy as Stricklyn's was that afternoon.

"Ma doesn't need to know everything, Bud."

The barman drew two steins of beer, which he slid down the bar one at a time. Dick caught them both, handing the first one to me, grinning. "Don't tell me you haven't been sneaking sips from a jug at the Jarrettes, because, remember, I'm a graduate of Chapel Hill College."

Our mugs clinked, and we drank. Dick borrowed the wet rag to wipe suds from his lips. I used my shirtsleeve.

"You've enrolled, I take it," he said, setting the stein on the bar top. "Like I told you to do."

My head bobbed, yet I sighed as I told him: "I sent in that application, sure."

The stein returned to his mouth. "You don't sound excited."

I couldn't really look at him as I tried to find the words that might lessen his disappointment. "Well . . . I don't see how I can spend two or three years cooped up in some big-ass brick building."

He laughed at that, and pointed at my beer. I drank.

"You and Duck are two peas in a pod," he told me. "You want to spend your whole life guarding mail for Pa? Or hunting and fishing for your supper? Toiling sunup to sundown on some hard-scrabble farm and raising a brood of uppity young 'uns?"

I grinned. "The part about the kids sounds kind of fun." Being in a saloon filled with men, we could make such off-color remarks.

"How about the Army?" he said.

"Huh?" Beer spilled down my chin and shirtfront.

"Bud,"—he put his empty stein on the bar— "you read more than me or our brothers and sisters combined. You know what's happening. War's coming. Even if Stephen Douglas wins the presidency, eventually there will be war. North against South. Fate will not rest until the South becomes its own country."

"Maybe you should run for office," I said, then sipped my beer.

"I intend to, Bud." He was dead serious. "With bigger ambitions than Pa. Jefferson City? Hardly. I'll be in Washington City, or wherever our new Southern nation puts her capitol."

My head shook, but his voice turned firm. "I am serious, Bud, about the Army. I'm thinking of it myself, when the shooting starts. You could make captain easily, the way you ride . . . and how you handle any kind of weapon. Me?" His head tilted back, and he let out a hearty laugh. "I have to think that Colonel C. Richard Younger would be impossible to lose a bid for the senate."

Once I had finished my beer, Dick escorted me out of the tavern, but not before he managed to shake a few more hands. I wouldn't bet against him making it to the senate. We talked a bit more till we had arrived back at his livery.

"Brick buildings are not that bad, little Brother," he told me as Ned led the chestnut stallion out of the stall with four new shoes. "You'd make a fine schoolmaster."

"I'm going to be a Mason, Dick," I told him, and grinned. "Just like you."

"What about preacher?"

I laughed. "After I just drunk a beer?"

We shook hands. I felt good, and not because of the beer.

"I'll see you, Bud," he said.

The next time I saw Dick, he was dead.

I had to escort mail over to Pleasant Hill, which is why I had taken Robinson Crusoe in to be shod. The next day, I made that eleven-mile run northeast, but the Methodists were holding a dance that evening, so I stayed. By the time I got back into town, Dick was dead.

Let brotherly love continue.

Hebrews, Chapter Thirteen, Verse One.

Pa met me on the porch, black band around his white shirt sleeve, redness in his eyes. Of course, I knew something was wrong when I dismounted and saw one of our neighbors, Mrs. McCoy, bringing over a platter full of ham slices. It was the way of things. When a neighbor died, you brought victuals. Yet I suspected it to be one of the little ones, maybe Retta, who then would have been about three years old, or Bob, only six.

"It's Dick," Pa said, and led me inside where Dick lay in a coffin in our parlor, wearing his best suit, with his hands folded across his chest.

I was told how Dick suddenly just took ill, even joking with Richard Kelley that he must have eaten some gone-bad chicken because he had a stomach ache. He was clutching the area around his belly button. He had started for the house he was renting, but then made a beeline for Ma's. By the time he got there, he was doubled over in pain. His right side just hurt like blazes, he told Ma, the pain having shifted over from his middle. When Ma put her hand on his side, he screamed. She got him to bed, and . . . well . . . he never got up. Chills set in. He had to stop drinking and eating because he couldn't keep anything down. By the next morning, he couldn't even move without screaming. Doc Logan arrived, but there wasn't a thing he could do.

Sometime on the morning of August 7th, Dick Younger passed on.

We took his body to the farm near Strother, a grim procession, and laid him in the little cemetery where we had buried sweet Alphae eight years earlier.

"Our Brother, Charles Richard Younger, has reached the end of his earthly toils," said the Grand Master of Grand Lodge of Missouri, Prairie Lodge Number 90, as we gathered near the grave old Hardin had dug. "The brittle thread which bound Richard to earth has been severed, and the liberated spirit has winged its flight to the unknown world."

It was nice of those Masons, for Dick had only been in their fold a few months.

"The cord of silver is loosed." The words still echo in my ears, and I can see myself standing beside Pa, see my ma on her knees, hands clasped, and see the preacher looking stern, gripping the Bible, but nodding every now and then at the words the Grand Mason spoke.

"The golden bowl is broken," he continued. "The pitcher is broken at the fountain. The wheel is broken at the cistern. And, Brothers and Sisters, the dust has returned to Earth as it was." He paused before concluding with the words: "And the spirit has returned to God who gave it."

It was a nice funeral, I guess. The Masons did their part, and the Reverend Ketchum handled the Christian sections and the Amens and the hymns. Lizzie Brown attended, which lifted my heart just a tad. By Jehovah, it seemed like everyone came to say farewell to the best older brother a body could ever pray to have. I have to think that Dick would have enjoyed the turnout, for folks came all the way up from Harrisonville, and a few came down from Lafayette County, where they had taught Dick inside those brick walls of Chapel Hill College.

When it was over, we went inside the house that had become the home of our sister Belle, her husband, and their three-year-old boy. But one thing stands out more than anything else. I can see it just as if it were happening as I write these words.

I held the door open for Ma and Pa, and all the others. The last to come in was Bob. He gave me the most pained look, and his words cut to the quick.

"You'll never be Dick, Cole," he told me. "Don't you even try." He was only six years old, and he was speaking to me like that.

"Don't you trouble me, Bob," I said. "I won't take no guff off you, no matter how old you are."

"You will, Cole," he said, and turned to go inside. "For all your days."

I didn't think anything of it, chalked this up as

some hurting boy who had to vent his pain and anger out at someone, and that someone had to be me.

Bob was right, though. I'd take his guff for the rest of his life.

Chapter Six

Oftentimes I have lain awake wondering how different things might have been had our world not been torn asunder. We Youngers barely had time to grieve for Dick, except for Bob, who never stopped hurting, I guess.

You know what happened. Abe Lincoln defeated Stephen Douglas, and anybody else foolish enough to run for President that year. Southern states began leaving the Union. The men of Charleston, South Carolina, fired on Fort Sumter. Mr. Lincoln called for volunteers to put down this rebellion. War came quickly, especially to Missouri.

The nation divided? Ours was a state divided, and the war fired up Jayhawkers to increase their depredations, especially when that Kansas rapscallion, Jim Lane, was elected to the United States Senate. By May of 1861, men were flocking to Jefferson City to join the Missouri State Guard, if they leaned toward the South, commanded by General Sterling Price. Missourians who supported the Union signed up with "Home Guards". Early that summer, Governor Jackson fled to set up a provincial government in Neosho, and a Yankee captain named Lyon led bluebellies in pursuit. St. Louis had always been pro-Union, and that mealy-mouthed pathfinder himself, John C.

Frémont, was promoted to major general to command the Department of the West. Jefferson City fell in July, so Lyon managed to get Hamilton Rowan Gamble appointed governor. That meant we had two governments, Jackson heading up the South in Neosho, and Judge Gamble sitting on his Northern throne in Jeff City.

Battles—if you could call them that—came at Boonville and Carthage. Then our boys whipped the bluebellies and killed Lyon at Wilson's Creek, and soon forced the Yanks to surrender at Lexington.

In Harrisonville, we heard war talk, but never gunshots. Even when a Yankee captain named Irvin Walley set up a camp in town with a bunch of bluebellies who called themselves the 5th Regiment, Enrolled Missouri Militia, we got along with those boys. Before war came about, we had known many of those new soldiers. I had gone to The Academy with Robert Jefferson, and I had raced horses against two others. To most of us, these soldiers were friends. We did not, however, care much for Captain Walley's big mouth and pushy behavior.

What was I doing during all this excitement? Still escorting mail for Pa, helping Ma—who still had not gotten over Dick's passing—and . . .

"You're still sitting on the fence, Cole?" a voice ahead of me asked.

As I walked down the boardwalk in Harrisonville, glancing with sadness at the livery my late brother used to own, I stopped and found myself staring at my old schoolteacher, Stephen Elkins. He held a grip in his hand, and another sat at his feet. This was near the hotel where the stage-coaches stopped. His eyes did not appear to be friendly, and, remembering that he hailed from Ohio, I figured him to be a Union man.

"It's getting harder and harder to do," I told him. "Jayhawkers raided us three nights ago. Took forty horses. Including Robinson Crusoe. Plus five good saddles, four wagons, and two carriages."

George Clayton, John Jarrette, the Brown boys, and I had trailed them as far as we could, till we lost the trail along West Line Creek near the Kansas border.

"I heard," Elkins said, and his eyes softened, "and I am sorry. Yet the South has men just as callous. I'm sure you have heard of this plunderer named Quantrill?" When I did not answer, he added: "Whether they pledge allegiance to North or South, those are not soldiers, but brigands, and I would not dare join up with men of that ilk. They care not one whit for anything except their spoils. But there are real armies taking the field, with morals, and the will to see to their duties with honor."

I straightened, surprised. "You're joining the fight?"

"I must."

I knew which side he would join, but I held out my hand, and we shook. "Good luck," I told him.

Elkins said: "Do you remember when you bet Jack Brown that he could not walk across the top rail of the corral by the school near Big Creek?"

The memory caused me to laugh. A circus had come to town, and little Jack Brown had been so fascinated and enthralled by the high-wire walker—all the circus had was a bear, a bobcat, two trapeze performers, two high-wire walkers, and a stupid clown—that he kept bragging that he was going to join a circus. So Tom, Jack's brother, and I dared him to try to walk across the top rail of the corral. He almost did it, too, but he slipped about two rods from the finish.

I mean to tell you when he landed on that top rail, you never heard such a wail from a boy or such cackling from the rest of us kids. Once Jack toppled into the dirt, he pulled himself into a ball, and clutched the area between his legs. When the girls began blushing and turned and ran, we boys laughed even harder.

As I recalled the incident, Stephen Elkins said: "That's what happens, Cole, when you try to straddle the fence."

In late September, folks started drifting in from Osceola, a good two- or three-day's ride southeast of Harrisonville. Jim Lane's red legs had raided the town, shot dead a number of fine citizens, looted everything they could, and burned what they couldn't. I had never seen such distraught men, women, and children, and that vacant look in their eyes has remained with me all these years. They'd been cast out of their homes with nothing but the clothes on their backs. They had no town left when Lane took off. Just ashes.

One night Mammy Suse had already started cleaning off the table, Ma had gone to her rocking chair by the window, and the rest of our brood played checkers or were reading books. Only my father and I remained at the table.

"I've written the authorities in Jefferson City and Westport about those brigands," Pa said. "I have asked to be reimbursed for our losses." He looked troubled. His hair used to be blacker than a raven's wing and thick as an eagle's nest. Now it was thin and gray, and he looked pale.

I considered asking him if maybe I should join up with one of those fighting outfits. The Brown boys had. Even George Clayton, our wrangler, kept talking about it. John Jarrette preached hell-fire and brimstone against the Yankee rule. Since Mr. Elkins had left, I felt sometimes that only our family remained loyal to the Stars and Stripes. Seeing Pa, hearing his feeble voice that night, stopped me from saying anything. I helped Mammy Suse with the dishes.

• • •

News came through newspapers and gossips about the fights back East. Talk around Harrisonville and up near Strother suggested that the war would be over by Christmas, and that the South would prevail.

Life went on, and in late October, Brother Jim and I escorted our sisters Sally and Duck to the home of the Mockbees in town. I didn't know Martha that well, but Pa knew her parents, Cuthbert and Sarah, and Duck told me that the Browns were coming, which meant Lizzie would be there.

It was a fine party. Tom Brown secreted some good rye whiskey into the barn. John Jarrette sawed his fiddle. Mrs. Mockbee played the harp like an angel when we slowed down for waltzes. We danced through "Dixie's Land", "Buffalo Gals", "Barbara Allen", "Hey, Betty Martin", and "Old Folks at Home".

Lizzie Brown came up to me when the band struck up "Jeanie with the Light Brown Hair". She curtseyed, and I bowed, handing the cup of spiked punch to her brother.

"This is our dance, ain't it, Cole?" Lizzie asked in that sweet voice.

"Why, Miss Elizabeth Brown," I said with a facetious grin, "I thought you were a Baptist."

Those beautiful brown eyes batted, and she gave me the most devilish of looks. "Not tonight, I ain't."

You would never have known a war was going on what with all the merriment going on at that party as I took Lizzie's hand and led her onto the dance floor—till the bluecoats came in. Oh, like I've said, most Yanks weren't that bad. Tom Brown even handed Robert Jefferson a cup of punch doctored with rye. But Captain Irvin Walley had to join the party, too.

"Pardon me, Lizzie," I said just as we commenced our waltz. Leaving her standing beside Charity McCorkle and Jack Brown, I strode past the table of grub and grog where Captain Walley had a firm hand on a girl's arm. The girl was Duck.

"You mind letting go of my sister," I said. It was not a question.

Walley turned his attention to me, but kept his hand on Duck. "Your sister could learn some manners, Younger."

"He asked me to dance," Duck said, "but I told him that I had betrothed this dance to . . . you, Brother."

It meant I'd have to waltz with Duck instead of Lizzie, but it was just one dance and the night was relatively young. As I reached for my sister's hand, Walley yelled: "She said more than just that!" The bluebelly's ears had turned crimson, and I figured Duck, being Duck, had added on a few choice words in her rejection.

And she still wasn't done. "I didn't know they

62

let pigs in this barn," she said, "did you, Cole?" Although Walley had finally let go of Duck, now he snatched her arm again and pulled her close.

"Let her go, Walley!" I snapped.

Releasing his grip, the red-faced brute turned to me. "You shall address me as Captain Walley, you piece of Southern filth."

My first thought was to break his nose, but there were a lot of bluecoats here, and the flap of Walley's holster remained unfastened. Besides, this was the Mockbee barn, and I meant to cause no trouble.

"There are plenty of ladies here to dance with," I told him, praying he would not choose Lizzie Brown.

"Indeed," my sister Sally said as she stepped up beside Duck. I knew she was just trying to prevent a fight. "I'd be honored to dance with you, Captain Walley." She curtsied as she made her proposal.

The band started into "Old Dan Tucker".

It could have ended there. Should have ended there, but Walley's dander was up, and he saw his men grinning at him.

"Where is Quantrill?" he asked me.

"I don't know where Quantrill is," I told him. "I don't even know who Quantrill is."

Which was true, sort of. The man I had met more than a year ago had called himself Charley Hart, not William Quantrill.

"You are a damned lying son-of-a-bitch."

My fist slammed into his jaw, and he fell backward, and as he tried to climb back to his feet, I sailed atop him. You do not insult a man or his mother, and you do not swear in front of ladies. The music stopped. The women began backing away, a few screamed. Walley and I rolled across the hay until strong hands pulled me off the bleeding, sniveling coward.

"Bud!" Tom Brown yelled, using my nickname and pulling me up and away from Walley. "Settle down, Bud. Settle . . ."

"Drop it!"

Duck and Martha Mockbee gasped at the same time as I heard a noise I would often hear in the years to come—the metallic cocking of a revolver. Quickly Tom and I turned back to see John Jarrette aiming a Baby Dragoon revolver at Walley, who was sitting on the barn floor, his blue uniform covered with hay, his face bloody from a busted nose and split lips. His revolver was pulled out halfway from the holster.

"I'll blow your damned head off, Walley, if you don't drop that pistol," Jarrette said.

Walley shoved the revolver back into the holster, and Bobby Jefferson and another bluebelly rushed up to pull him to his feet. Cursing, the captain pulled away from them. "Back to camp," he snapped, and his left hand reached inside his blouse to withdraw a handkerchief.

As the Yanks hurried out of the barn, Walley turned at the door, pointing at me.

"This is not finished, Younger," he said. "And I'll see you later, Jarrette. I'll see both of you . . . in hell."

Chapter Seven

Pa was fifty-one years old; Ma, forty-five. But they both looked ancient that night as Jim, John Jarrette, and I told them what had happened at the Mockbee barn.

"Hardin!" Pa called, and the old slave appeared. "Saddle the best two mounts those jayhawkers left us with."

"I don't think your son Jim is any danger, Mister Colter," Jarrette said.

"It's for you, John," he said. "You're going with Cole."

"I got a horse, sir."

"One of mine is better." That was one thing few people would deny. We Youngers had more prime horseflesh than anyone in western Missouri—even after that raid by Doc Jennison's sorry lot.

Jim hurried upstairs to our bedrooms, and I figured he just didn't want anyone to see him cry. Ma told Mammy Suse to fill a sack full of jerky, corndodgers, and any leftover food we might have from supper, along with some coffee.

Worry and dread showed on their faces. I wet my lips, but found no suitable words.

"Hide out on the farm in Jackson County," Pa told me. "We'll get word to Belle and Richard when it's safe for you to return. I'll find this

Walley's superior officer. It shouldn't take long."

I hugged my sisters—those downstairs—and told Ma to kiss Retta for me and maybe say good bye to Jim, John, and Bob, even though I doubted if my kid brother would miss me much. It pained me something awful when I shook Pa's hand.

The door opened, and Hardin rushed inside, saying we needed to hurry because he saw torches coming down the road.

That's when Jim ran down the stairs, holding my gun rig with the Navy .36 still holstered.

When I buckled the belt around my waist, Pa objected. "Son," he said, "you know General Frémont's orders. You ride out of here with a weapon, and the Federals can shoot you down for insurrection."

"If he don't takes that gun," Hardin said, "he might gets hisself shot down right here and now. Boys with 'em torches be soundin' right heated."

I didn't have time to kiss Ma farewell.

At the farm near Strother, Pa got word to Belle that Walley had accused me of riding for Quantrill, which Pa denied. That blow-hard of a Yank bragged that he would track me down and see me hanged.

"Pa," Belle told me as tears welled in her eyes, "says you and John should take to the bush." She was clutching her little son in her arms. "It's not safe for you . . . even here."

I felt as if a mule had just kicked me in the stomach.

"It won't be for long, Bud," Belle's husband told me. "War'll be over before you know it."

"They've posted me?" I asked.

Belle shrugged, but Richard said: "Captain Walley certainly has."

"All right," I said as I turned to John Jarrette before turning back to address Richard. "You reckon I can borrow that shotgun of yours?"

We rode east, then west, and took to the bottom-land woods along Sni-A-Bar Creek, where you just about needed a cross-cut saw to get through the brush and brambles, and where the only fish you could eat were carp and gar. I remembered old Hardin telling me a joke about gar a number of years back.

You stuff it with pig dung, then bake it, throw away the gar, and eat the pig dung.

The weather had turned cold, and we sat in what we called tents, a fire between John Jarrette's shelter and mine, Jarrette drinking from a pewter flask, and me taking a liking to tobacco in a long meerschaum pipe.

"What you thinking, Bud?" Jarrette asked.

I blew a smoke ring that the wind smashed into a thousand pieces. "Same thing you are," I answered. Nothing more needed to be said.

The next morning, we rode to an inn along the

road that cut through the thick woods. We ordered ham, eggs, and coffee. And waited.

A couple of men came in, each packing four Colts, two in shoulder holsters and two in their waistbands. They eyed us with intense purpose, and never let a hand get too far from one of their pistols. They spoke only to the innkeeper.

I glanced at Jarrette, but, when he did not acknowledge the men, I remained silent. After our breakfast, we sipped coffee for two more hours. During that time, one other rider came in, but he seemed to be just a farmer, buying a jug. He nodded in our general direction before climbing back onto his mule.

The innkeeper kept glaring at us, but he made no vocal objections to our sitting there. Maybe that had something to do with the fact that a shotgun was lying on the table alongside John's Baby Dragoon. An hour later, horses stopped outside the inn, but we only heard one pair of boots pounding across the porch, and only one man came through the door.

He was big enough, though, for six or seven men, and when he saw me, he pushed back the brim of his battered slouch hat and laughed.

"Howdy, Oll," I said.

Oliver Shepherd, known as Oll, was one of the Shepherd boys—Frank, Martin, Ike, and George being his brothers. Missourians by way of Kentucky, they had settled in Jackson County in the early 1850s. I had seen George and Oll around a lot, though never in school. Their pa had died in '53, so they had been working ever since. Working . . . when not fighting or stealing.

"Frank James and Black Jack Chinn come ridin' into camp, sayin' there's two suspicious gents a-spyin' on Mickey Flannery yonder," Oll said, hooking a big, crooked thumb back toward the innkeeper. "George Todd asks . . . 'What's they doin'?' Chinn says . . . 'Just sittin' and eatin'.' Quantrill then says . . . 'That sounds like the most secretive of spies' . . . so he sends me an' the boys out to kill some spies. But you ain't spies." He shook his head, and laughed, but the laughter faded from his voice when he said: "Saw your pap a while back, Cole."

"How's he doing?" I had not seen Pa in three months.

"Goin' to New York."

That saddened me. Back in September, Pa had told me that I would be making that trip with him. And here I was, in a flea trap along the Sni-A-Bar, staring at one of the biggest cut-throats you'd never wish to meet.

"You know your pap rented a team of matched grays and a buckboard to that damnyankee Walley?" Oll Shepherd asked.

Every muscle in my body tightened. "No."

"Yeah. Figured it would help you out if he done it, I reckon. Can't quite figure out who I hate worser . . . a red leg like Jim Lane, who burns towns, kills anyone he feels like, and plunders all in the name of Kansas and the Union. Or a sneak like Walley, who pretends to be a real soldier and hides behind his blue coat."

"They all hide behind their damned blue coats," I said. "I think you know why John and I are here."

"Reckon I do. Your pap ain't seen that rig or them horses returned yet, by the way." He hooked his dirty thumb toward the door. "Y'all want to ride out of here with me and the boys? Or you wanna just stay here, sippin' cold coffee, gettin' bit by fleas, an' spyin' on that skinflint yonder?"

Deep in the thickets in the Sni-A-Bar, where briars would tangle around a man's feet, arms, or even his neck if he were not careful, Quantrill's camp didn't seem that much different than where John and I had been wintering. His men lived in a ravine, some sleeping in caves and some in tents that had been stolen from bluebellies.

Quantrill stepped out of the largest tent as Oll Shepherd led John and me into camp, reining up a few feet short of the leader, and telling Jarrette and me to dismount. Men—not much more than two dozen—rose from their fires, their dice games, or their bedrolls. Each man carried maybe eight to twelve pounds of weaponry.

71

As I studied Quantrill, I realized he had changed a bit. The hair was longer, the face more chapped and bronzed by sun, wind, and cold. His mustache appeared a little fuller, but he had not packed on any weight. The boots remained shining black with built-up heels, but a tan slouch hat had replaced the fancy plumed one, and, instead of a fine coat, he wore only a woolen shirt and corduroy pants. He carried a brace of revolvers, tucked inside a green sash.

"You," he said, nodding in my direction, "I remember." He raised a finger to his lips as if trying to think. Then his blue-gray eyes brightened. "Ah, yes. How is your charming sister?" Before I could answer, he said: "Still spunky, I take it."

"Some might say so."

His head bobbed slightly as he turned to Jarrette.

"But you . . . you I do not know."

"Jarrette. John Jarrette."

"My brother-in-law," I said.

"Please," Quantrill said as he looked back at me, "say that this brute did not take lovely Caroline's hand in marriage."

Hell, he even remembered Duck's name.

"Another sister," I said. "I got plenty."

"Indeed." His face brightened.

"Indeed." I glared.

Quantrill slapped his hands together. "Well,

since Oll did not hang, stab, shoot, or decapitate you, I take it that you are not spies for the Yankees. Since he brought you here, might I presume that you are here to ride under our black flag." He gestured behind him.

I saw no flagpole.

I can tell you, Parson, we rode under no black flag. We took no blood oath. Put our right hands on no Bible. All John Jarrette and I did was answer one question.

"Will you follow orders," Quantrill asked, "be true to your fellows, and kill all those who serve and support the Union?"

"Yes," we said simultaneously with both hands at our sides.

Quantrill grinned and shook our hands. "The only other thing I ask of you, is that should you be killed, die game." His face hardened. "The enemy shall give you no quarter, and he shall be granted none from us."

We never marched, rarely drilled, and orders came out more like suggestions. I came to join an army, but can't say that I did.

"Chinn!" Quantrill called out to a lean, pock-marked man. "Take the horses. But, Chinn, try not to steal them." He nodded at Oll Shepherd. "Oll, show Private Jarrette around camp." He made "private" sound like some sort of joke. Then Quantrill looked around before pointing a long finger at one of the men standing. I recognized him. He had been in Flannery's inn when Jarrette and I had first arrived.

"And, Buck, would you be so kind as to lay down the law to Private Younger here?" Again . . . that feel of a joke.

Instead of saluting, this tall drink of water turned his head to spray a river of tobacco juice on a rock before walking over. He stood maybe six feet tall, a bit taller than me, though I outweighed him by maybe forty pounds. Although slender and trim, he walked with a quiet, confident ease. His face was long, his forehead square, and coarse whiskers covered his fair face. His eyes were set deeply in his head, and his black hat was pulled low over his sandy hair.

"Name's Frank," Frank James told me, "but folks call me Buck."

That was his introduction, and he led me around camp, introducing me to other bushwhackers. It was a quick introduction, and when we were back where we started, I asked: "How long have you been sitting here in camp?"

I was eager to do something. I did not join Quantrill to hide in these dark woods where my brother-in-law and I had already been hiding.

Frank James shifted the quid of tobacco from one cheek to the other and cited a passage from Shakespeare, which caused me to stare at him harder.

74

There is a tide in the affairs of men.
Which, taken at the flood, leads on to fortune;
Omitted, all the voyage of their life
Is bound in shallows and in miseries.
On such a full sea are we now afloat,
And we must take the current when it serves,
Or lose our ventures.

When he finished, I said: " 'Julius Caesar'." This caused him to stare at me more intently. I went on: "Brutus is telling Cassius that if we wait, our power lessens, while the enemy's grows. You seem to agree with me, I take it."

Again he spit. "Get your bedroll and possibles and pitch them in my tent. Don't have many men in camp with whom I can have an educated discussion about the Bard. But don't you worry about fighting. Or killing. You'll get your fill."

Chapter Eight

Killing became a specialty of mine. I did it often. I did it well.

But, Parson, let me contradict one shameless falsehood that has dogged my path since the war. Never did I line up eight, ten, fifteen—the number always varies—Yankee prisoners in single file and test a liberated Enfield rifled musket to see how many bodies one bullet could penetrate. I did not say: "This Yankee gun ain't nothing more than a popgun." Nor did I draw my revolvers and dispatch the surviving prisoners one by one. Yes, I killed, but never murdered.

The smell of bacon and coffee wafted in the cold air, but I remained underneath my blankets, though I had been awake before the coals had been fed with fresh tinder. It was a lesson my new friend taught me.

"Don't be the first up, Bud. You don't want to be getting the fire going and cooking breakfast, especially when it's cold as it is now. Let some other boy do those chores."

Frank James had experience in the army. Having joined the Missouri State Guard, he had been at Wilson's Creek, although he said he saw no action. Taken sick with the measles, he had been captured by the Yankees, which might have been a good thing. The doctors treated him, and paroled him. He took the oath, and returned to his farm in Clay County. Frank could be a hard one to figure out. Maybe he got sick and tired of all the misery bluebellies kept inflicting on peaceful farmers. Perhaps he just got bored. After the war, I came up with yet another theory: That he broke his parole to get away from his mother. I never met a woman as mean as Frank's ma.

The fire crackled now, and I could smell coffee. So could Frank James.

"Time to get up, Bud," he said as he rolled out of his bedroll. "Let's join the boys."

And most of us were exactly that. Boys. Frank was nineteen. I had just turned eighteen. William Gaugh and Little Archie Clement were sixteen; Jim Cummins, seventeen; Billy James and Clell Miller only fourteen. Black Jack Chinn might have been thirteen years old, but he could handle his jackknife with that seven-inch blade better than Jim Bowie could use a Bowie knife—and that boy knew horses better than Hardin, Pa, or even me. Bill Anderson was twenty-two, and I don't think Quantrill had been on this earth more than twenty-five years. We called Hiram George Old Man because he was twenty-eight.

As time passed, more boys kept joining our ranks. When I first found Quantrill, he had had maybe twenty-five men. But now our numbers were fast approaching fifty.

"We don't get up now," Frank advised on this morning, "we'll be hungry for the rest of the day."

Salt pork had started frying.

"Suspect you're right," I sighed as I got to my knees and began rolling up my bedroll on the frozen ground.

Next thing I knew I was on my back, unable to hear a thing, but smelling smoke that came from no campfire. Shaking my head, I blinked back the astonishment and reached for my Navy Colt. Frank was crouched beside me, and now I could make out the sound of guns firing, hear the zip of bullets through the air. My hearing had returned, to my eternal regret.

"Mama . . ."

"Oh-God-oh-God-oh-blessed-Jesus-I-am-kilt."

Screams.

I tried to find a target, but saw only four or six of our boys lying in a blackened crater in the center of our camp.

Quantrill swore savagely as he yelled: "The Yanks have a cannon!"

Another ball fell in the woods behind us, splitting timbers as it exploded, showering us with flaming branches, twigs, and shrapnel.

A sea of blue charged from the other side of the clearing, and we answered with Rebel yells, buck and ball, and pistol shots. They must have outnumbered us three-to-one, but those blue-bellies came from cities. Most of us were farm boys who had grown up hunting, and all that pistol practice I had done to help protect Pa's mail served me well.

"God A'mighty, Bud," Frank said as he reloaded his Remington revolver. "That Yank was sixty yards away."

Another cannonball landed near the cook fire, but failed to explode, and our steady, accurate fire drove the bluebellies back into the woods. My mouth felt dry. Sure, we had driven the Yanks back on their first charge, but I knew we were in a fix.

A man slid beside me, and I turned to see William Gregg, a Jackson County man maybe twenty-four years old, already sweating despite the cold. "Quantrill wants to see you," he said.

"Huh?" I fitted the last cap on the Navy's cylinder.

"Now," he snapped, and did not wait for any response. Crouching as the Yanks began peppering us with musketry, I lowered the hammer on the revolver and hurried after the man. Gregg weaved his way back to Quantrill's tent. I just made a beeline, thinking that if a bullet was meant to hit me, no amount of dodging around would stop it. I made it to Quantrill's tent without a scratch.

"I am told you know this country, Younger,"

Quantrill said as he pulled on one boot and smoothed his pants leg before he rose from the camp chair and picked up his hat from a traveling desk.

"Well . . ."—I holstered the Navy—"a little."

"So how do we get out of this embarrassment?"

I thought for a second, then tilted my head down the trail that cut through the woods. "There's a farmhouse not far from here. Had a bunch of cattle penned up when Buck, Cummins, and I passed by yesterday. If we could hold those bluebellies to a standstill till nightfall, then . . ."

A bullet snapped the canvas and blew apart the shaving cup near Quantrill's bed.

"I do not think we have till nightfall," Quantrill stated.

"All right," I said. "Y'all get ready." Without waiting for any order, I stepped away from Quantrill and his adjutant, drew the Navy, and waved it in the general direction of the little woods road. "Buck!" I shouted. "John! Oll!" I didn't really expect anyone to follow me, and I started running toward the road. Bullets dug in the earth in front of me, snapped branches in the woods to my right. I popped one shot toward the Federals, or Jayhawkers, or whoever they were, and did not stop running.

Once I reached the woods and followed the little track, the shooting at me stopped. Footsteps sounded behind me, and I glanced back as I continued to run. Lo and behold, Frank James, John Jarrette, and Oll Shepherd were right behind me. And behind them? Little Archie Clement, who stood five feet tall if he wore high-heeled riding boots, Jim Cummins, and Clell Miller.

Frank James, the fastest, caught up with me.

"We're . . . horse . . . soldiers . . . ," he reminded me. "Not damned . . . infantry."

"Horses up ahead. And cattle."

It wasn't long before we could see a man and his wife standing in front of the dogtrot cabin, staring in wonderment toward the battle beyond their farm. Spotting us, they ran inside, slammed the door, and pulled in the latchstring. When Clement aimed a Dragoon pistol, I snapped at him: "We've no quarrel with those folks."

He pulled the trigger anyway. "That'll remind 'em," he said, adding, "Bishop."

"No time for saddles," I said as we reached the corral. I counted four plow horses, a mule, maybe twenty-five steers. "Some of you'll have to ride double, or walk." I grabbed the halter to the biggest of the horses.

No one asked me what my plan was. And if they had, I don't know if I could have told them. I leaped onto the big dun's back, and, as Clell opened the gate, I loped out to the pen that held the cattle. Frank followed on a brown nag, and we opened that gate. Then I rode back behind the cattle, already prancing and bawling, acting skittish. I fired the Navy twice, and the steers took off.

John Jarrette, on another brown mare made for the cornfields, and Frank took the point, guiding the stampeding beef toward the woods road. Little Archie Clement and Clell Miller rode double on the mule—arriving back at our camp maybe five minutes after everything was pretty much over. Oll Shepherd took the buckskin. Jim Cummins had to walk, but he got to the fight before Clement and Clell.

Catching up with Jarrette and Frank about the time we cleared the little trail, I helped them turn the cattle toward the Yanks. The boys, Quantrill, and Gregg realized my plan at once and they hurried to their horses. I guess it's one thing to be shooting at people at a distance, but it's a whole lot different when you're staring at a bunch of red-eyed cattle with horns bearing down on you, driven by more than forty men screaming like banshees and fighting like demons.

The Yanks broke from the woods, cut across the field, and we followed them, letting the cattle scatter. Jarrette, Frank, and I turned our horses toward the howitzer. Frank shot down the man with the ramrod and the sergeant who kept barking orders. The others turned tail and tried to flee toward the distant woods, but they never got there. I leaped off the horse I'd liberated— never having cared much for riding bareback.

A Yank who had been playing possum, leaped out in my path. Scared the tar out of me, so I shot him in the head. When I came to the cannon, I stopped and stood there, scratching my head. By then George Todd had ridden up, swung out of the saddle, and was starting to bark orders at me: "We have no need for a cannon, Younger. We aren't artillery. We're bold dragoons."

"I'm just trying to figure out how you spike one of these things," I said.

Chapter Nine

Such was my first taste of battle. Glorious? Maybe, but not after the Yanks had fled. As George Todd and I debated how to destroy the howitzer, our boys rode around among the wounded Yankees, shooting them in the head, then dismounting to rob them. Frank James rode up and tossed a rope around the still-hot cannon barrel, and we overturned it. Todd procured a hammer and drove a spike into the touch-hole, while I shoveled mud into the barrel.

The sounds I remember far too well. The clanging of Todd's hammer. The popping of pistols at close range. The calling out for mercy that fell on deaf ears.

"Strip the dead!" Quantrill yelled as he galloped into the field.

I turned to stare, my mouth open, last night's supper roiling in my gut.

"Uniforms!" Quantrill continued to order. "I have need of those uniforms." He winked at me, and called out to our boys in the field. "Several Yanks escaped. Others will come, riding fast for retribution. Strip the dead, but hurry. We should not tarry!"

Hit and slash, Parson, and ride away to fight

another day. That's how we operated. Home base was wherever we could find shelter for a time—some abandoned farm, or with family members of our boys. All too often, we lived like rats, hiding in caves, or in the woods in makeshift shelters. We learned to sleep fully clothed, revolvers at the ready, our horses always tethered nearby, always saddled.

Soon we were wearing uniforms, and I do not mean the Yankee blue that we stole from the dead. I don't remember who was the first among our boys to put on a battle shirt, or even what it looked like. Plaid or solid, wool, flannel, or cotton? But those shirts would identify us in battle—and damn us to a firing squad or hangman's noose should we be captured wearing one. Our bushwhacker shirts had a lay-over collar with pockets and collar and a button front trimmed in a dark or bright ribbon. Some of us took to wearing over-shirts, also trimmed, featuring pockets deep and wide enough to hold pouches of leaden balls, powder horns, and tins of percussion caps. Sometimes the women who made these shirts for us would embroider the front with flowers, crosses, vines, and other designs, or create a patchwork pattern by stitching together different fabrics just like a quilt.

Mine was hunter green, with a long V-front trimmed with beige and black print—I do not recall the exact design—that matched the cuffs of my sleeves. John Thrailkill wore one with garish embroidery. Because we teased him so mercilessly about it, he would sometimes take it off when we were just sitting around or eating. It was Lizzie Brown who made my bushwhacker shirt. She sent it to me with a daisy pinned to it right where my heart was located.

"Cole," Quantrill said.

After dumping the dregs of my coffee near the stone ring of our fire pit, I tossed the empty tin cup to Frank James, and crossed our camp—in a ravine in the Sni-A-Bar—to the rocking chair where William Quantrill sat, sipping brandy from a snifter.

"Yes, sir?"

"I am promoting you to captain."

I could only blink.

"You sha'n't be in command of a specific troop," Quantrill said, "not like your brother-in-law, Jarrette." John had gotten his command a few weeks earlier. "You will be more like a captain at-large. You'll be given specific duties that require a man with your grit and spunk and, most importantly, your brains."

"Thank you, sir."

He held up the snifter toward William Gregg, who quickly refilled it with dark brown liquor. "Do not thank me yet, Cole Younger," Quantrill said. "Your first mission will likely result in our untimely deaths."

• • •

The city of Hannibal lay roughly one hundred miles northwest of St. Louis on the Mississippi River, meaning that the Yankees held it firmly. Steamboats were docked on its banks, belching plumes of black smoke, and an engine of the Hannibal and St. Joseph Railroad chugged away from the depot, hauling cars filled with Yankee soldiers and crates of supplies bound for points to the west.

When Quantrill first told me we would be riding to Hannibal, I thought he meant we would be destroying the railroad. Some Rebels had brought down the Salt River bridge, but the Yanks had rebuilt it. An Illinois bluebelly named Grant—yes, that very same Ulysses S. Grant, but before anyone knew of him—had been put in charge of protecting the rails, but at the time I didn't know if he had remained in Hannibal or not.

Bold as brass, dressed in Yankee blue, I rode on a high-stepping gray Arabian stallion down the center of the street. Behind me, George Todd flicked the lines of an empty farm wagon, and, behind him, William Clarke Quantrill drove another buckboard.

A Yankee soldier stepped out of a two-story frame house. Seeing the bars strapped on the shoulder of his navy coat and the golden leaf design, I reined up and saluted. "Major," I said in acknowledgement as I reached inside my blouse, my fingers touching the pocket Colt I had slipped inside for extra security, but I pulled out only some papers. "Requisition, sir."

The fat officer took the papers, patting his various pockets until he found his spectacles. As he read the order Quantrill had written, he looked up at me.

"What outfit are you with?"

I told him a lie.

"You boys have been consistently whupped by that Secessionist border trash, haven't you?" He grinned.

"They fight like hell," I told him, which was no lie.

"Bushwhackers. Ought to hang the whole lot."

I nodded. "If we catch them, we will."

"I could catch them"—sighing heavily, he handed the papers back to me—"if the Army would just give me the chance. Playing nurse-maid to a damned railroad . . . well, this isn't why I joined."

"No, sir." I returned the papers to the inside of my shirt next to the small revolver.

"Supply depot is at the river's edge, just past town, Lieutenant," the major told me.

"Thank you, sir." I indicated by gesture to Todd and Quantrill, and they followed me down the street. The weather had started turning warm so the town was packed. Turning toward Quantrill, I had to grin as we watched bluecoats, who had shed their tunics and rolled up their sleeves, load our wagons with kegs of powder, plenty of lead bars to mold bullets, and perhaps fifty thousand percussion caps. I spied a couple of crates labeled Springfield, so I nudged my horse over toward the sergeant overseeing the loading of our wagons.

"What's the chance of us getting a box of them rifles?" I asked.

The sergeant spit tobacco juice in the mud. "Your requisition don't say nothin' 'bout no long guns does it, bub?"

"Don't say nothin' 'bout no brandy, neither," I told him, "but you go to that smaller wagon there, and you tell the driver I was thinking we might be willing to hand over a bottle . . . well, for an equally beneficial trade."

That caused the Yank to study Quantrill, who kept his eyes trained on two lovely ladies twirling parasols and squawking like hens as they walked down the boardwalk.

"Brandy, would it be?"

"Came all the way from Gascony," I told him.

"Where's that?"

I shrugged. "Sure ain't Saint Louis."

"Sullivan!" the sergeant barked. "You and Muldoon put that top box of Springfields in that second wagon. And . . . maybe that there box of Colt's fast-shootin' revolvers, too, should they be willing to throw in a second bottle." He looked back at me.

"Sergeant," I said, "we only have one bottle of brandy." I had not even noticed the box of revolvers.

"Your choice then. But make it snappy. Revolvers or rifles?"

I answered without hesitating: "Revolvers." The sergeant quickly ordered his men to forget about the rifles, and instead load the box of revolvers. "Infantry that we are," I lied when the bluecoat looked at me again, "we don't see much in the way of 'em revolving pistols."

Hell, that's all we used.

We killed. We foraged. We did what it took to survive, hitting by surprise, wearing the federal uniforms on those occasions when we needed to lull the stupid bluecoats into that false sense of security, like they would live forever. I never popped a cap on an unarmed man—unless he deserved it.

But I think about what I did do, and what Quantrill and others—Todd, Gregg, Bill Anderson—did for boys like me. They gave us a purpose, a cause. They gave us a reason to kill. They put revolvers in our belts, and hate in our hearts. We forgot the teachings of Jesus, the Ten Commandments. We lived to butcher the men who wore the blue. And it was easy, too damned easy. You want to command an army with unquestioning loyalty? Find boys and put guns in their hands.

"You read Shakespeare?" Frank asked a Yankee officer we had captured along the Big Blue. While rooting through the man's grip, he had found a fancy book with a cover of Morocco leather, which he tossed up to me. *The Pictorial Edition of the Works of Shakespeare: Histories Vol. I: (King Henry VI, Part I; King Henry VI, Part II; King Henry VI, Part III; King Richard III; King Henry VIII).* I stuck the volume in my saddlebag.

"Listen," the bluebelly said, his voice cracking while Little Archie Clement and Bill Anderson trotted around the road, putting bullets in the brains of the wounded, or slitting throats. "I don't know anything about what's going on here. I'm from Iowa. The Army just sent me here. I'm not even a real soldier."

Frank was checking the loads in his revolver. "What did you do before they made you a lieutenant?"

"Nothing. I mean . . . I was a . . . lawyer."

I laughed, and Frank grinned at me. "Nothing. A lawyer. Makes sense to me, doesn't it?"

The Iowa lieutenant gave me a feeble smile.

"My favorite work of Shakespeare is 'Macbeth'," Frank said as he turned toward the lieutenant.

"The Scottish Play." The Iowa attorney's pale head bobbed up and down.

"Though I must admit I have a fondness for 'One Henry Four'. Yet," continued Frank, cocking the Remington, "there is a line in the tome you carried that has always utterly fascinated me. 'Henry the Sixth, Part Two'. It's . . . 'The first thing we do, let's kill all the lawyers'." He shot the Iowa attorney between the eyes.

"That's not what the Bard meant," I said as I handed Frank the reins to his horse. Holstering his .44, Frank James gave me that cold stare. I continued: "When Dick the Butcher says that line, he means only the attorneys who lacked all ethics. Shakespeare, to my way of thinking, was paying tribute to all attorneys and judges who strive for justice."

Frank climbed into the saddle. "Maybe . . . Bishop Cole . . . that there bluecoat was one of those pettifogging sons-of-bitches before he put on that uniform." He gestured at the dead lieutenant. "No ethics. No morals. Maybe he followed the ideas of that rebel, Jack Cade, who revolted against the British back in the Fifteenth Century."

"You've changed, Buck," I told him.

"Like hell I have. Yanks took my stepfather. They strung him up by the neck with a rope, leaving him dancing in the air while my mother, on her knees, screamed and begged for mercy. Oh, those bastards let him down, all right. Asked him again to tell them where I was hiding, where Quantrill was camped. . . . Then they jerked him up again to dangle and choke some more. Ma was making soap when they rode up. They pulled over the black cauldron and told her . . . 'You Jameses are dirt. You don't need any soap.' And they beat my kid brother, split his head open with one of their sabers while he was working the fields, and cut his back with a blacksnake. Jesse's not fifteen years old, and he knew less than my stepdad knew. They left my stepdad hanging from that rafter in the barn, and if Ma hadn't somehow managed to loosen the knot, well old Doc Samuel would be walking the Streets of Glory. Instead, my stepdad's in bed with his throat swollen up whilst Jesse can't even sleep on his back. And had this here little set-to turned out different . . . had it been that Iowa attorney who held court and we were his prisoners . . ."—he paused to bite off a mouthful of tobacco—"they would have done us the same as we did them. I haven't changed, Bud. It's this damned world that's changed."

I didn't believe my good friend, not then. But I soon realized that Frank James was right. Two weeks later, in the heat of a July afternoon, I rode into our camp along Lumpkins Fork, only to learn what living out your worst nightmare means.

Frank took the reins to my horse, and jerked his head toward Quantrill, who stood underneath a tree, frowning.

Dully, I walked to our commanding officer, and stopped in front of him. Quantrill cleared his throat, but, for once, words failed him, so he shot a timid glance at John Jarrette.

With a heavy sigh, John handed me a letter.

"It's," he said softly, "your father."

Chapter Ten

What kind of anarchy reined in western Missouri in July of 1862? Try to fathom this: After they murdered Pa, they left him on the side of the road that led from Westport. People passed by, saw his body, but they didn't stop, because, in those days in Missouri, people knew to mind their own business. If they made the wrong decision, tried to help the wrong people, they could very well end up dead.

You see, Parson, various business matters had often taken Pa to Kansas City, Westport, and Independence. On this trip home he had kept $500—I learned this later—in his pockets, but he had hidden $1,500 in a money belt under his shirt.

On July 20th, when Yanks met him a few miles southeast of Westport, they shot him off the buckboard he was driving, took his watch and the $500 they found in his pockets, and rolled him over, no doubt admiring the three bullet holes they had put in his chest. Laughing, they rode off, leaving his body to the ants, to swell up in the muggy heat like some stray dog or coyote that had been run over by a buckboard.

Finally, Mrs. Washington Wells, a God-fearing woman, who was traveling home to Strother with her son Samuel, stopped. They wrapped Pa's body in a blanket, loaded it on the back of their Studebaker, and took him to our home in Harrisonville.

"Your father's funeral is today, Cole, but you cannot attend," Quantrill stated after I had finished reading the letter.

Shock still rattled me. It took several seconds before I realized he had said something to me.

"Yankees will surround the cemetery," Quantrill continued. "They will follow the funeral procession like the vultures they are. Expecting you to be there . . . so they can bury you next to your father."

My hands balled into fists, even though I knew Quantrill spoke with sagacity.

"You don't want to go, Bud," John Jarrette said.

I turned toward John, whose face showed no emotion as he told me: "You'll want to kill the swine that murdered Mister Henry."

"Go on," I managed to whisper.

"They bragged about it in an Independence grog shop," Jarrette said. "The man who ramrodded the murder couldn't hold his liquor. A bluebelly general had the leader arrested. What Billy heard"—Jarrette nodded toward Bill Anderson—"is that the captain confessed as soon as they had him in the camp. Ain't that right, Bill?"

Anderson's head bobbed, but his eyes looked right through me. It was young John Thrailkill who had best described Anderson's eyes when he called them "unfathomable". In time, history would remember him as Bloody Bill when his actions during the rest of the war were equally unfathomable.

You see, Bill had grown up in Kansas, where he learned to steal horses. Most likely he would have been hanged as a mere thief had Yankees not killed his father. The killing drove Bill to Quantrill. His dark, long hair and beard were unkempt, his eyebrows prominently stretched almost across his forehead. He donned a black slouch hat, the front brim pinned up with a five-point brass star. A wiry man maybe five-foot-ten, he wore a suit of black velvet, carried four revolvers at his waist, and always rode black horses, most of which he had stolen. He even carried a silk cord in his jacket pocket, and tied a knot in the strand every time he killed a Union man. Yet what everyone remembered of Bloody Bill Anderson were those eyes, blue, gray, cold, that rarely blinked.

"They're takin' the murderers to Harrisonville," Anderson said softly, damned near pleasantly, in an accent more Mississippi than Kentucky, where he had been born. "To stand trial."

"When?"

"Day after tomorrow," Anderson said, "is what this dyin' bluebelly told me on the road to Olathe. And he wouldn't lie to me . . . not whilst I was pullin' his guts out from the hole I carved across his belly."

Still numb from the news, I turned back to John, glad to escape those eyes of Anderson.

"The bluecoat who confessed . . . ," Jarrette was saying. "The man who led the Yanks and killed Mister Henry. It was the captain from that dance last year. Walley. Irvin Walley."

In the woods along the Harrisonville pike, we waited. Twelve of us hidden in the thickets just east of East Creek. Another sixteen waited on the west side of the road. Wearing the uniforms of Yankee soldiers, Frank James, Clell Miller, and I busied ourselves replacing the left rear wheel on an Army ambulance, while our "major", George Shepherd, watched and smoked his cigar.

As the bluecoats slowed down their approach, Shepherd removed the cigar from his mouth and waved his gauntleted hand. The Army boys stopped their horses. I counted fourteen in all, but I focused on the five men whose hands were shackled in iron. I could not make out any of the faces since their kepis were pulled down low and their heads were drooping as if in shame.

Besides, I was keeping my own head down, obeying Quantrill's orders. He had not wanted me to be with the wagon in the road, because he feared the prisoners—especially Walley—would recognize me, sound the alarm, and spoil our ambuscade. However, quoting from Romans, I had told Quantrill as we made our plan: "'Vengeance is mine.'"

"'Afternoon, Lieutenant!" Shepherd called out. "Where you bound?"

"Harrisonville," the officer said. "I see you've had trouble?"

Shepherd shook his head. "No, Lieutenant. You've found trouble."

At that moment Frank shot the Yankee officer off his horse, and revolvers began booming from both sides of the road. Horses fell. Men fell. In less than one minute, it was over, except for a shot to the head of any bluebelly found to be only wounded. Filled with bloodlust, I stormed over to the dead men and dead horses at the center of the patrol, where I kicked over the first body of one of the shackled men who was lying face down. Sightless eyes stared up at me.

Quickly I glanced at another, and knew instantly that he had not been our target. Nor was the third man, who Thrailkill had just dispatched with a bullet in the temple. Not the fourth. When I jerked up the last of the prisoners by his blue blouse, I spit in his face, threw him back down against a dead horse, and palmed my Colt. The man was already dead, but I still emptied my revolver into his chest.

"He's not here!" I yelled, and slammed the empty .36 onto the blood-drenched earth. "Walley isn't here!" My head tilted back skyward, and I screamed an unholy, primeval shout, cursing God, Captain Irvin Walley, and myself.

Frank James and John Jarrette hurried over and steered me away from the carnage. I sobbed as they boosted me into the saddle, and then we fled the massacre site.

Four nights later, I sneaked my way to the farm near Strother, where Ma was staying with my sister Belle's family. The night was dark as pitch, but I made my way to the cemetery, and found the headstone over Dick's grave, and where Baby Alphae had been resting all those years. As the leaves rustled in the wind, I moved the lantern I held around until I located a fresh mound—but no marker.

"Coleman."

I whirled, dropping to a knee, drawing a Navy in my right hand. The yellow light from the lantern illuminated my mother.

"I knew you'd come tonight." A shawl covered her shoulders that shifted as she brought the tin can to her mouth and spit snuff into it. "New moon."

"It's nigh midnight, Ma," I told her, walking slowly toward her. "How long have you been waiting?"

"Since right after sundown." She gestured toward the home. "Bob's yonder, but likely sleeping, if you want to see him."

My head shook. "Let him sleep. Bob doesn't want to see me, anyway."

"The rest are in town, or back at their own homes," she said. "Jim's settling your pa's affairs. Caroline up and got hitched to George Clayton. Don't reckon you knew that, did you?"

"George is a good man," I told her.

"He's in the barn. Wants to join you and your soldier boys."

I put the lantern on the ground, and the .36 in my holster. "They're not my soldier boys, Ma."

"You'll take George with you."

It was not a question, but I nodded. I feared she would say Jim—or worse, Bob—wanted to join the cause now that Pa had been murdered.

"You know what happened on the Harrisonville pike." Again, she wasn't asking.

"I was there, Ma."

She spit before telling something that would haunt me more than anything for all my days. The men we had murdered in that ambush, the prisoners, had been bound for Harrisonville. Yes, they likely had taken part in Walley's crime, but they had merely been following the captain's orders. Walley had been held back in the Independence jail, and the soldiers we had killed were going to testify before a military tribunal *against* Walley. Now there were no witnesses. Word had reached my mother just the day before that Captain Irvin Walley had been freed from

101

the Independence jail, that charges against him had been dismissed.

And I was to blame.

"Coleman," she said, and quoted Ephesians, Chapter Four, Verse Thirty-One: " 'Let all bitterness, and wrath, and anger, and clamor, and evil speaking, be put away from you, with all malice. . . .' "

I held my breath.

" 'Judge not,' " she continued, " 'and ye shall not be judged: condemn not, and ye shall not be condemned: forgive, and ye shall be forgiven.' "

Luke, Chapter Six, Verse Thirty-Seven.

"Forgiveness is overrated," I told her.

"Don't you dare blaspheme, Thomas Coleman Younger." Her tough hand pointed past me. "Your father lies there in an unmarked grave. We figured it best so red legs wouldn't come here and desecrate it. Now you'll listen to me, Son, and you'll obey your tired old mother. You've done enough killing already, but you won't go after Irvin Walley. He shall pay for what he did to your father, and what he drove you to do. God will be his judge. You won't be his executioner."

My head fell. Tears wet my beard.

"I'm waiting, Coleman," Ma said.

"Yes, ma'am." When I raised my head, Ma wrapped me in her arms.

"It is better this way, Son," she whispered. I could smell the snuff on her breath. "And any time you feel that need for revenge in your heart, your head . . . you think about this. After what you did to those bluecoats the other day, Walley is going to spend the rest of his days living in fear, looking over his shoulder, worried sick that you might be there, ready to send him to hell. That's the kind of revenge he deserves. He won't have a life to speak of any more. He'll be scared until he's burning in the fiery pit."

I walked her back to the porch, stopped, and kissed her forehead. "Give everyone my love," I told her, and headed to the barn to find George Clayton.

"Ride with God!" Ma called after me.

That was one thing I could not do, for I rode with Quantrill.

Chapter Eleven

Manassas . . . Shiloh . . . Fredericksburg . . . Chickamauga . . . Gettysburg . . . Those are the battles you read about, even today all these years since the last cannon fell silent. Nobody outside of Missouri recollects Lone Jack, and I guess it doesn't really compare to any big to-dos back East. Yet Lone Jack was probably the only real battle in which I took part.

We fought alongside regular Confederate troops. Our brethren in gray needed new recruits after the big fight down in Arkansas at Elkhorn Tavern, where Tom Brown, my dear friend and brother to Lizzie, fell with mortal wounds. A new colonel named Jo Shelby came along, hoping to sign up as many Missouri fighters for his "Iron Brigade" as he could.

Quantrill and George Todd decided that fighting with the regular troops would be good for us, and might make the Yanks think of us as soldiers and not just cut-throats. So we rode with bonafide Confederate soldiers.

Our army, maybe eight hundred in all, had camped on the outskirts of Lone Jack, a little burg in Jackson County east of Strother. Most of us bushwhackers had a good laugh at all of the tomfoolery the boys in gray did, but secretly I admired all that discipline, the pageantry and pomp, and how they marched in order.

I wondered how they would fight. The next day, I found out. They learned how we did, too.

As we charged past soldiers in gray uniforms, pinned down by lethal grapeshot and musketry, we heard their shouts, saw their hats raise in salute.

"Hurray! Hurray for Quantrill!" they shouted.

George Todd didn't care much for that, since he was leading the charge and Quantrill was nowhere to be seen.

Yet this is what I remember to this day about that affair. We rode upon a bluebelly command, and hit those Yanks hard. Before five minutes had passed, survivors had taken cover behind their dead horses, firing single-shot rifles in our direction.

"Surrender!" George Todd yelled.

"Like hell we will," came an answer.

They fired a volley, and we answered with a charge before they could reload, wheeled our horses around, and stopped, exchanging our empty revolvers for others with six beans in the wheel.

"Surrender!" Captain Todd screamed again.

"And be butchered?" They fired again.

This time we rode the rest of them down. I swung off my horse, raised my Colt, and killed one fool who was swinging his musket at me.

Then I hurried to a bluebelly colonel, crawling toward a saber one of his officers had dropped. My boot crushed his right hand as he reached for the hilt, and he rolled over. Blood leaked from two holes in his shoulder, his nose, and a nasty cut over his left ear.

"You're my prisoner," I told him.

"Like hell," he said. "You bushwhackers take no prisoners."

I took God's name in vain and pressed my boot harder against his hand. "Is that why you got your whole command killed? You thought we'd murder you?"

I lifted the colonel up, and shoved him to my horse. "In the saddle," I ordered.

He couldn't make it. I had to boost him onto the horse, and lead him to a house I knew had been converted into a hospital by gray-coat sawbones.

As I was leaving the colonel in the house, a boy came in. He was one of ours, though I did not know his name. Aiming a pistol, he said he would turn all these prisoners into good Yankees. My fist slammed him against the wall in the foyer, and I jerked the pistol from his grip, then booted him out the door. Finding George Clayton, pale-faced but steady, I tossed him the pistol.

"Guard this house," I told Duck's husband. "If any man tries to shoot a wounded enemy, kill him."

• • •

The bluebellies retreated to Lexington, but we were gone in a day or two as more Yanks had been spotted. Leaving Jo Shelby's troops, Quantrill must have decided that we fought better alone than with other troops. Besides, Jo Shelby did not let his men rob or scalp the dead. East of Strother, I found our camp and heard a timid voice call my name.

Looking up, I spotted a man wearing a Yankee uniform. He had fled during the battle, or maybe had gotten lost, or had been captured by one of our boys who wanted a manservant until he grew tired of the novelty. You see, Parson, sometimes we did take prisoners. To barter with. Hold as hostages. Or toy with until we murdered them.

I walked to the circle of prisoners, most of them squatting, shivering despite the heat, knowing their fate. The one who had called my name stood, but his skin had turned considerably pale and his eyes were red from crying.

"Stephen," I said in a dry whisper. "Stephen Elkins."

His smile showed hope. "You remember me."

Well, you didn't forget a schoolmaster as fine as Stephen Elkins had been. He wasn't so fine on this evening, though. "Cole," he said as tears poured down his cheeks, "you have to tell Quantrill not to kill me. You have to, Cole. For God's sake, please help me."

My gut soured. "Stephen," I said truthfully, "Quantrill keeps his own counsel. He might not kill you. But, most likely, he will."

I walked away toward Frank James, who offered me a cup of coffee. I shook my head and kept walking to Quantrill, who stood over his plunder from Lone Jack—two bronze cannon—asking men if anyone knew how to work artillery. I don't think we ever fired either of those little Howitzers.

"Captain Younger," Quantrill said. His smile stretched across his face. "A glorious day for our cause." He stepped away from the shining artillery and moved to his desk, where he poured brandy into a snifter for himself and a splash into a tin cup for me. Hell, we even toasted.

Since he was in such high spirits, I decided to push my luck. "Sir, there's a prisoner over yonder that I think was taken by accident."

He took a quick sip of the brandy while studying the circle of condemned souls. "All the men I see wear Yankee blue," he commented as he swirled the liquor in his fancy crystal glass.

"Yes, sir, but one of them . . . well, his father and brother fight for the Confederacy." That was a damned lie. "He was left behind to tend to his poor, sick mother." I was stretching things mighty thin. "He was on his way to visit his girl in Cass County."

Quantrill finished his brandy, and set the empty snifter on the desk. "Who is he? Really."

"My old schoolteacher," I answered. "And I think we've put the fear of God in him, sir. He won't fight us any more."

"Hell's fire, Cole, I once taught school myself." As he started back toward the cannon, he whispered: "I put him in your custody, Captain, but, know this . . . the others want to kill him, and no death sentence shall I commute, so you had better do what you do best. Think fast."

Drawing the Colt, I approached the circle of prisoners. Nearby, Little Archie Clement honed his massive Bowie knife on a whetstone, Bill Anderson stared through me with those bone-chilling eyes, while a few others played mumblety-peg with Black Jack Chinn's jackknife. "Get up," I told Stephen Elkins, who was leaning against the trunk of a toppled tree, rubbing both eyes with his fists.

"You were right, by the way," I told Elkins. "A man in these parts can't straddle a fence."

My old schoolmaster's lips trembled when he saw the revolver aimed at his chest, yet he obeyed, stumbling weakly toward me.

Frowning, a few of the men rose, but I shoved the barrel against Elkins's spine and pushed him into the woods. Luckily no one followed me, for we had plenty of prisoners to butcher. Elkins pushed his way through vines and brush, and two hundred, long, brutal, sweaty yards later, he emerged from the thicket, standing on the high banks of a ditch. Beyond the ditch a road stretched north to south.

Mouth still trembling, Stephen Elkins turned to face me, but he showed himself to be a man. He did not fall to his knees, nor did he grovel, beg for mercy, or sob. I think he had cried himself out, and was now resolved to die as a brave man should.

"Cole . . ."

He flinched when I pulled the trigger, and toppled backward into the ditch. When I stepped forward, I holstered the Colt.

Stunned beyond comprehension, Elkins blinked. He wet his lips, pushed himself up slightly among the weeds, rotting leaves, and sticks filling the ditch, and stared up at me. "What . . ." he finally managed to say, "shall I do now?"

"See that road?" I said. "I know what I would do."

I left him there, and returned to our camp.

Frank James beckoned me over when I emerged from that dark thicket, and this time I took that cup of coffee he held out to me.

"Bud," he said, and pointed at some puny teen in duck trousers and a muslin shirt sitting next to him, "meet my kid brother."

"I ain't no kid," the boy snapped.

"You ain't fifteen," Frank said, smiling. "I told you about him," Frank reminded me. "Got whipped by bluebellies . . . but he has sand. I'll give him that much. Didn't tell the Yanks a thing." He looked back down at the blue-eyed boy. "Sand he has. But he's sure lacking in brains."

I didn't offer my hand to the teen to shake. Instead, I sipped coffee and asked Frank: "What brings him here?"

"He wants to ride with us," he said with a laugh.

The boy's hair was sandy, and he told us he had lost his hat while looking for us. He had not found us. Andy Blunt had found him and, seeing some family resemblance that I did not, pulled the boy onto the back of his horse, and brought him to our camp. Frank's brother had not met his growth potential yet, and he would shoot up over the next couple of years. I finally decided to shake his hand, admiring his grip when I did. The grip of a hard-working Missouri youth.

"Go back to Ma," Frank advised him, which made the boy pout. "With the doc still mending from that hurt the red legs put on him, she'll need you."

The kid drew back as if to punch his brother, but stopped when Quantrill stepped up.

"So this boy wishes to join our brotherhood?" Quantrill asked. "I like a boy with gumption," he added, shaking his head as he chuckled. "But I prefer one with size. I doubt you could hold a Navy Colt."

"I could hold two," the boy said. "And I will."

"When you can do that, boy, come back to find me. Now do as your brother says, return to your mother, your father . . ."

"Stepfather!" the boy sang out in anger.

"Return to your family farm." This time Quantrill spoke with finality.

"Here." Frank put a long arm around his brother's shoulders, and steered him toward the woods. "I'll get you back to the main road. You walk this whole way?"

"Had a mule," the boy said with a sniffle, "but he run off on me ten miles back."

Often I have wondered why we did not accept Jesse James right then. Boys his age rode with us. Black Jack Chinn and others were even younger. I would like to think that Frank did not wish his baby brother to become the killer Frank had . . . that we all had become.

Jesse James walked out of my life that day, but, Lord help me, he would return.

Chapter Twelve

Winter came, and many of our men drifted into Arkansas to scout with Jo Shelby's boys, or just enjoy the baths at Eureka Springs. Others found camp in Texas. Some returned home, and a few set up camps on the Sni-A-Bar or made their winter homes in caves. The latter became my fate, as John Jarrette left me in charge of taking care of our wounded.

Few campaigns came about during the winter. For one reason, we relied on our horses—like Indians—and needed good grass to keep those mounts carrying us out of harm's way. Oh, there were fights here and there—a big battle, which I missed, took place at Prairie Grove on the western edge of Arkansas, and Quantrill killed some Union men in Olathe and Shawneetown on a quick raid into Kansas.

Anyway, I found myself playing nursemaid to mayhap a dozen of our boys too incapacitated from Yankee bullets to ride south. Three times, I had to play gravedigger, swinging pickaxe and shovel till my muscles screamed in agony as I tried to claw away enough frozen dirt to bury our valiant dead.

While I was doing this, Reason Judy buried two of his boys. A resident of Cass County, Judy was one of the few men from that area to back the

Yankees. He had even fought at Lone Jack, before he got discharged with some injury he had dreamed up. His two sons, James and John, had fought alongside him. So when two bushwhackers found James Judy on a road near Paola, they killed him. A month or two later, John Judy was shot dead.

I had nothing to do with either, but no one could convince Reason—a man more misnamed I never met—that I was innocent. He swore out a complaint, and got me posted for the murder of his first son. Judy and other Yankee zealots then saw to it that a reward of $1,000 was put on my head, dead or alive. For forty years, that absurd charge haunted me. I could not ride through Cass County without looking over my shoulder, but the real pain, thanks to Reason Judy, would be inflicted on my loved ones.

Yankees hounded Ma so much in Harrisonville that she had to move the family to our farmhouse in Jackson County. There wasn't much left to protect in town by then anyway. Red legs had plundered everything out of our store and livery, and with Pa having gone to Glory, no one could resupply what had been stolen from us. Besides, my family had been reduced to starvation rations by the coming of 1863.

> . . . all persons who shall knowingly harbor, conceal, aid or abet by furnishing food, clothing, information, protection or

assistance whatsoever, to any emissary, Confederate officer or soldier, partisan ranger, bushwhacker, robber or thief, shall be promptly executed by the first commissioned officer into whose hands he or they may be delivered. . . .

Thus read the Yankees' General Orders Number Three. No trial, no jury, no mercy. The only crime my mother or sisters ever committed was being blood kin to Thomas Coleman Younger.

Little wonder then that my brother Jim made his way to our camp in February. His clothes were in shreds, and his body was covered with scratches, dirt, dried blood, and mud. Little Archie Clement, my nursemaid assistant, had found him hiding in the brush, and brought him to our makeshift hospital ward.

"Cole," Jim said after I gave him some water to reduce the swelling of his tongue, and corn liquor to warm his half-frozen body. "They done it."

For, you see, there was this other part to that order.

The houses at which these persons receive food, protection, or assistance in any way, shall be destroyed.

Growing numb, I squatted by the fire and listened to Jim's story.

February 9th, a short while after the $1,000 bounty had been posted on my head, Jim and Bob were helping Ma into our house when several scum in blue jumped Bob, not even ten years old, while Jim, just turned fifteen, was dragged to the barn where he was to be lynched, just as had been done to Doc Samuel, Frank James's stepfather.

Ma screamed. John and my sisters cried for mercy, but none was shown.

"You deny that you have assisted your son and the blackhearts who ride with him?" the bluebelly captain demanded.

"I deny nothing, young man," Ma sang out, having done enough crying and begging till gall rose in her throat. "I fed my son. I gave another poor boy fresh socks and unmentionables for his were covered with filth."

"That, you Secessionist witch, is aid and comfort."

"I am no Secessionist," Ma sang right back at him. "Ask anyone in this or any neighboring county and they will verify my statement. But aid and comfort? Gladly. Gladly I would provide those to my sons, or the lads who ride with him. And, with a kind heart, I would have done the same to you and your men. It is the duty of a Christian."

Unmoved by my mother's charity, the captain held out his hand to one of his men. A private brought a torch, which the captain snatched. With a cruel grin, he offered the fiery brand to my mother.

"If you want your sons here to live, you will burn down your house, your barn, and all the surrounding buildings."

As Jim related that dreadful tale to me, I could almost see the reflection of the burning in his eyes. Not one action of the war sickened me as much as when I pictured Bursheba Leighton Fristoe Younger, our mother, carrying that torch, burning our home, our barn, our memories. Turning our world, already a nightmare, into hell.

"They could've killed Bob and John," Jim said. "Could've killed me. Or Ma. Guess we were lucky in that regard."

Maybe. But, the way I see it, the bluebellies killed Bob, Jim, John, and Ma that night. Killed any chance I had of living in peace.

On a frosty morning two days later, I crawled out of my cave, pulled on the blue greatcoat, and made my way to the fire. Oh, it is not that I had forgotten Frank James's teachings—that a good soldier waited till some other soldier had the fire going, the coffee boiling, and the bacon frying— it's just that in this camp, I was the only one capable of such duties. Jim lay asleep, and Little Archie Clement's only skill was killing Yankees.

As I squatted by the fire, stoking the coals, a horse's whinny was answered by another. Instantly

I froze, and stared into the woods. Twigs snapped, leather creaked, but eventually a form appeared riding a brown horse with a white star crowned on its forehead.

"It's all right, Cole. We're friends," said a voice.

It was John McDowell, waving his left hand in a friendly greeting. A few months earlier, in a fight across the border near New Santa Fe, while riding with George Todd and Albert Cunningham, I had saved McDowell's life. As we had retreated to the timbers, McDowell's horse had been killed, throwing him into the grass.

Hearing McDowell's cry for help, I had wheeled my roan around, emptied one revolver into the bodies of two of the closest bluecoats, and galloped back to where McDowell was climbing to his feet. "Up here!" I had yelled, and kicked my left boot out of the stirrup. Reins held in my teeth, I holstered the empty Colt, and drew two other revolvers, one in each hand. McDowell had swung up behind me, and we galloped back toward Missouri.

So into our camp rode McDowell to repay his debt. But in a manner of speaking, he had already been rewarded with thirty pieces of silver. And no one trusts a Judas, not even the Yanks he had led to our camp, for I noticed muskets trained on him as he made it through the clearing. That's when I understood he was no friend. McDowell's voice, which faltered as he tried to smile, also gave him away.

"Cole, it's good to . . ."

I shot him dead.

Then, standing, I killed the riders on either side of him. The others, that I could not see, began shooting. The men I had been nursing or guarding came to my assistance. And we answered the bluebellies in kind. Brother Jim found a Colt revolving carbine, and fired away. Dragoon in his right hand, Navy in his left, Little Archie Clement walked boldly toward the Yanks, whose sneaky assault was faltering rapidly. Calmly Clement aimed, fired, never saying a word, so dedicated was he to his duty.

The bodies of twelve Yanks and one Judas Iscariot littered the ground, but how many others had whipped their horses into frenzy as they hurried through the dense forest no one could say for sure. But four more died somewhere in the woods at the hands of Brother Jim, Clement, and three of our walking wounded. As he walked back into camp, Clement stopped long enough to replace his revolvers with a Bowie knife, before proceeding to take McDowell's scalp.

"They'll return," I said, casting a sad glance at what had been my home that winter. "They know where we are."

"We can walk, Bud," said one of the wounded. "Or ride."

They would have to.

"All right. Saddle up. Pack what we can, leave what we can't, and take any revolvers or weapons you can find off the dead." Clement and Jim went to help the wounded who could not walk, as others brought litters to help carry them out of the woods to . . . where? That I had to figure out, but it soon struck me that the burned remains of our farm lay not far from here. I didn't think bluebellies would figure that we would camp there, but I feared such a place would fuel my hatred of the Yanks.

Before we went anywhere, I had to go to the cave where Deacon Salzer lay. Due to gangrene, his right leg below the knee had had to be amputated—with an axe—and bullets still remained in his chest and right arm. As I entered I saw he had propped himself up against the rock wall, and fired up his pipe. He smiled with relief when I came into the light.

"Good fight?" he asked.

"Fair. Sorry you missed it."

I let him smoke and hide the pain in his chest.

"We're moving out," I said. "Some of the blue-coats got away."

"I ain't goin' nowhere, Bishop Cole, and you know it."

"We'll take you with us. Got litters ready."

"The hell you will," he said angrily, which made him cough. "Think I want to watch my own pall-bearers tote me off to Glory? Hell's fire, Bud. . . ."

"Deacon," I said wearily, "I can't leave you here."

"Damn right you can't. Because I'm a sick old man." He was nineteen, but looked to be in his fifties. "And if Yanks catch me alive," he continued, "I'll tell them all I know. Won't like it, but I know I will. Been talkin' to myself already. Gone crazy, I am. So, no, Bishop Cole, you can't leave me here . . . alive." He pointed the pipe's stem at one of my revolvers.

"Deacon, I can't kill you," I said.

"You have to. On account I ain't got the guts to do it myself."

We stared at each other, long and hard. "Maybe . . ." I understood my cowardice. "Little Archie," I offered.

"Bullshit!" Deacon Salzer bellowed. "That pip-squeak runt. Be damned if he'll be the one to pop a cap on me . . . besides, Clement is crazy as a loon. He'd enjoy it. I'm a deacon, you're a bishop . . . we're men of God. God forgives."

"I'm no bishop," I whispered. "Haven't been to church in . . ."

"God forgives. Yankees don't." The pipe returned to his mouth momentarily, before Deacon Salzer pitched it aside and started whistling "Jesus, Lover of My Soul".

It was the hardest thing I ever had to do, Parson, and I don't like to speak of it all these years later. But the hell that was 1863 had only just begun.

121

Chapter Thirteen

This came from Yankee President Lincoln himself, as General Orders Number One Hundred, in April of 1863:

> All wanton violence committed against persons in the invaded country, all destruction of property not commanded by the authorized officer, all robbery, all pillage or sacking, even after taking a place by main force, all rape, wounding, maiming, or killing of such inhabitants, are prohibited under the penalty of death or such other severe punishment as may seem adequate for the gravity of the offense.

I guess no bluebelly officer in Missouri must have seen those "Laws of War".

Jim Lane and Doc Jennison continued their raids, and other Union outfits followed suit. When one of our boys died in an ambush, he was left to rot. We reciprocated.

Jim Vaughn, a red-blooded, cold-hearted bushwhacker, was captured and hanged in Leavenworth by General James Blunt's boys. So Ben Parker, one of our partisan brothers, hanged five Union prisoners.

No compromise. No quarter. No retreat. No surrender.

We hit hard, and ran harder, finding shelter in the brush. Dick Yeager led a few raids into Kansas, and George Todd and his crew shot down maybe twenty Kansas horse soldiers near Westport.

Since the Yankees had trouble finding our camps, or setting up ambushes for us, they decided to make war on our women. Ignoring Mr. Lincoln's commands, General Ewing issued Orders Number Ten, which allowed for the arrest of men and women "who willfully aid and encourage guerrillas." The order also said:

> The wives and the children of known guerrillas, and also women who are heads of families and are willfully engaged in aiding guerrillas, will be notified by such officers to move out of this district and out of the State of Missouri forthwith.

Ewing sent his bluebellies to round up our womenfolk, labeling them prisoners for aiding and comforting the enemy. Is that what the mothers and sisters did, aided and comforted their sons, brothers, and husbands? Armed soldiers rode up on horses and wagons, with no warrants, no writs, nothing but Springfield muskets and vile curses. Two of my cousins, Charity Kerr and

Nannie Harris, were arrested. Bill Anderson's young sisters, Josephine, Jenny, and Mary, were taken. Can sixteen- and ten-year-old girls—which is what Jenny and Mary were—be a threat to society, even in a time of war? Should they be arrested while walking on a public road on their way to school? Susan Vandiver, Susan Womacks, Armenia Gilvey, Mollie Cranstaff, and Sue Mundy were shoved out of their homes and into the wagons. Mollie was arrested as she came out of a mercantile. Her crime? She had a bolt of cotton, from which the Yanks said she planned to make a bushwhacker shirt.

Those wagons made their way to the last standing farmhouse built by Henry Washington Younger.

There, the Yanks stopped around suppertime, and with bayonets, forced my sisters Josie (twenty-three years of age), Duck (twenty-one), and Sally (eighteen) from the table to the wagon. I guess they considered arresting eleven-year-old Emilly and six-year-old Retta, too, and even Ma, but decided three would do the job. Besides, had they tried, Bob, not quite ten, and John, twelve, would have fought them.

These most desperate characters found them-selves hauled to Kansas City, where the bluebellies had turned a three-story building in McGee's Addition at No. 13 Metropolitan Block into a jail. They put the women on the third floor, telling them that they would be transported to St. Louis, Yankee territory, for trial. No bail would be offered, and no bond allowed.

Seventeen women prisoners, and one boy—whose name or crime I do not recall, and who was put on the second floor—sweated in the brick warehouse in sweltering Kansas City. Oh, but the guards showed mercy. Jenny Anderson, whose temper matched her older brother's, railed and clawed so much that her jailers shackled her onto a bed. Such is a fitting punishment for a girl sixteen years old.

Quantrill planned a raid to rescue those brave, young ladies, but this was never implemented because on the 14th of August, the building collapsed. Three stories of bricks crushed seventeen defenseless women. Suffocating them with dust and dirt. A hell I could never imagine.

Yeah, I have heard the lies. That the women were tunneling their way out, and that is what caused the disaster. Tell me, Parson, how do you dig a tunnel when you are thirty-six feet off the ground. Here's the truth, sir. The day before the tragedy, dust and débris fell like October rains from the ceiling above the first floor. A guard saw this, told his lieutenant, who reported this with alarm to Ewing. Ah, but our gallant general ignored any warning. Want more evidence? After treating the women prisoners, a Yankee sawbones named Thorne also complained to the deaf fools that the building was unsafe, especially after soldiers had removed columns from the first floor. George Caleb Bingham owned that building, and we knew Bingham to be a Union-loving die-hard. Yet even Bingham would damn General Ewing, writing fifteen years later in a Yankee newspaper that the death of these poor women crushed beneath the ruins of their prison was a deliberately planned murder.

Did Ewing bring our women to Kansas City to die?

Perhaps we'll never know the answer. Murder? An accident? Fate? No charges were ever filed. What we knew then, and what I know to this day, is this. Susan Vandiver, Armenia Gilvey, Josephine Anderson, and, my cousin, Charity McCorkle Kerr, lay dead. Josephine, witnesses said, kept crying out: "Please, please, somebody get this brick off my head." No one could reach her. Eventually her pleading ceased. She was fourteen years old. Chained to the bed, sweet Jennie suffered from a crushed back and broken legs. She never walked again.

Quantrill sent my brother Jim to Kansas City with John T. Noland, a Negro who scouted and spied for us. Noland had just returned from Lawrence, Kansas, and Quantrill believed that Jim could pass himself off as our younger brother John, because no man of color dare ride with bushwhackers.

You don't believe me, either, do you, Parson? I'm used to that. Two other Negroes rode with us, John Lobb and Henry Wilson, but they were slaves. Noland did things of his own accord. A freedman about my age, he rode, he spied, and he battled alongside us. He served with distinction at Lone Jack, and when he died in 1888, six white bushwhackers served as his pallbearers.

Jim and Noland were to meet us at Pardee's farm along the Blackwater River. They returned on the evening of the 18th. And after this, others, both men and boys who had never fought amongst us, began finding their way to our camp.

"Bud . . . ," Jim said as he walked toward me, but, before he could make it to me, his knees buckled and he fell, sobbing. I hurried over to him. "Bud. . . ." He sniffed, trying not to bawl, fearing what others might say about him. Hell, John McCorkle, could barely get out what had happened to his sister he was crying so hard.

"What is it?" I asked Jim as I held him close to me.

"It's Duck, Bud," he said, and began crying even harder.

My stomach knotted, and I let out a bitter curse. "Is she . . . ?"

"I never . . . never seen her cry . . . Bud . . . never . . . but . . . ." His whole body shook as he wiped his snotty nose on the sleeve of his shirt.

Thinking back, I realized that Jim was right.

I had never seen our sister Caroline cry. Caroline, who rode harder than most boys, including me.

"Sally?" I asked. "Josie?"

"They're alive. But . . . I guess . . . shock . . . is that the right word?"

"I reckon."

"It's just . . ."

"Hell," I said.

"Damn' right." Somehow, he suddenly willed his tears to disappear, and I pulled him to his feet.

Standing on a stump, Quantrill beckoned us over. I walked past Bill Anderson, and if those blue-gray eyes had been unfathomable before this night, now they had turned vacant, almost dead. I knew then that all reason, any humanity, he may once have held had slipped away. If he were not already insane, the death of one sister, the maiming of two more, had driven him mad.

Looking back on things, I believe that William Quantrill had been planning to destroy Lawrence for some time. Why else would he have sent John T. Noland to spy on that city? A few times the previous year, he had broached the subject with his captains, but we had always told him such activity would be a fool's errand. Fate, and that cold bastard Ewing, had given him another chance to lay waste to a city where he had once lived.

"Lawrence or no?" was all he said, and first he addressed his captains.

Instantly Bloody Bill Anderson spoke. "Lawrence or hell," he said. "With one proviso . . . we kill every male thing."

"Todd?" Quantrill asked.

"Lawrence, if I knew that not a man would return to Missouri alive."

Added William Gregg: "We make sure Jim Lane is butchered." Lane, the worst of the red legs, lived in Lawrence.

John Jarrette, George Shepherd, Dick Maddox all agreed. At length, Quantrill jutted his jaw at me.

"No." My head shook. "The Yanks will be on guard. We would have to ride through Yankees, in Yankee country, and then retreat through Yankees. The risk is too great. The danger is too much."

"You are a snivelin' damned coward," said Bill Anderson as he strode toward me, putting his hand on the butt of one of his revolvers.

With my right hand on one of my Colts, I challenged the crazed man. "Make your play, Bill, and show us that *you* are no coward."

Frank James stepped in front of Anderson, and Jim put his hand on my right arm.

"This I must rebuke," Quantrill said. "We are men of honor, and we must not quarrel amongst ourselves. Captain Younger has never shown yellow, and, Anderson, I would trust with my life." He drew in a deep breath, held it, and smiled sadly at me. "I understand and appreciate our bishop's sentiments, yet, Cole, I ask you this . . . will you ride with us?"

I could only nod. "By majority rule I abide."

The vote was three hundred and nine to destroy Lawrence. Two joined me in dissent, but Quantrill refused to count the votes of slaves. The slaves, John Lobb and Henry Wilson, remained on the Blackwater. I rode with Quantrill.

Chapter Fourteen

Always, it comes back to Lawrence, doesn't it? Lawrence or Northfield. In the memoir I published in 1903, I called Lawrence "a day of butchery". Oh, Parson, it was that, but much, much more horrible.

Colonel John Holt joined us on the Big Blue, with a hundred new men, and Quantrill persuaded him to "christen" his recruits in our assault on Lawrence. Hard we rode, in columns of fours, to the middle fork of the Grand, where we camped in the big woods and rested until midafternoon. By the time we reached the Kansas line, our numbers swelled to around four hundred and fifty.

In the rough country north of Gardner, Oll Shepherd kidnapped a farmer who agreed to guide us through that labyrinth. When the sodbuster got us lost, Oll Shepherd slit the befuddled fool's throat, tossed the body into a slough, and Quantrill sent John T. Noland to locate a better guide. That man got us out of the rough country, but he, too, was paid with a Bowie knife to the neck and left to sleep the eternal sleep propped up against a hackberry tree.

The moon approached its half phase, but clouds often obscured it, and as good of a scout as Noland was, it is hard for a man to know a country he has visited but a few times. We rode to another farmhouse around midnight. As fate would have it, when we barged into the home we found Joseph Stone, a renegade Missourian who had fled our state to settle in Kansas, in his nightshirt with a musket in his hand. The weapon dropped, and he ran, only to be tackled by two of our men.

"Please, George . . . ," he begged.

George Todd grinned. "Well, bless my soul, Joseph Stone. I haven't seen you since you got me arrested in Kansas City." Todd picked up the musket the farmer had dropped, but Quantrill cleared his throat.

"We are close to Lawrence, Captain," he said calmly. "Yankee patrols might be in the area, and a shot could raise the alarm."

Todd lowered the musket. "Let's hang him."

But no one had thought to bring a rope, so Todd used the musket on the poor man, crushing his skull, his dignity. On we rode, guessing our way, and when the grayness appeared behind us, we pushed our mounts into a gallop. Reaching the outskirts of Lawrence, we halted, letting our mounts breathe while checking the caps on our pistols. Yes, nerves tested our resolve, and, though few men spoke, Quantrill understood his men.

"Do as you will," he snapped. "I ride to Lawrence."

Quantrill kicked his horse into a trot, and we

watched him ride off. I glanced at Frank, who was biting off a chaw of tobacco just as my brother Jim was first to ride out after our leader. To a man, four hundred and fifty followed.

She was a pretty city, on the banks of the Kansas and Wakarusa Rivers, a home to perhaps two thousand people. Most were sleeping or just beginning their day on that fine Friday morn, August 21, 1863.

We arrived at a farm to find a man in homespun milking his cow. "That's Snyder," John Noland said, and the farmer, recognizing the black man, nodded and rose from his milking stool. Snyder's crime? He preached Abolition and had raised a militia of Negroes to fight for the North. When we rode off, Snyder lay in his barn, his blood mingling with the spilled milk.

"You have your lists," Quantrill said, standing in his stirrups, referring to the names we had been given of men who must die. "Women, Negroes, and children *must* be spared. Now give the Kansas people a taste of what every Missourian has suffered at the hands of red legs and Jayhawkers. Kill! Kill! Kill, and you will make no mistake."

Thinking of Duck, and the horrors that still disturbed her after having survived the collapse of the building in McGee's Addition—of my father—of my mother forced to burn down one of our farms, yes, I rode like some bloodthirsty

133

butcher. Down Massachusetts Street, following Quantrill. Some of the men turned onto New Hampshire Street. Or Vermont—streets named after Yankee states, which fueled our hatred even more. Gunshots exploded. Men stepped out of their businesses or homes, their expressions confused, fearful. They died like that.

"Remember our women!" came a cry from behind me.

"Osceola! Osceola! Kansas City!"

John T. Noland swung out, pointing the way to the Army camp. Several boys followed him to cut down the soldiers as they stirred from slumber. Many tried to swim across the river, only to drown, or be shot.

Now, the Kansans understood what was happening. "Secesh!" came their cry. "Secesh!" Eventually people must have realized an even greater horror had descended on their city.

"Quantrill!"

As we passed a house, a second-story window opened and a Negro woman waved her fist. "You sons-of-bitches!" she yelled, and died from a pistol shot, tumbling out of the window, rolling over the awning, and landing in the street to be trampled by dozens of horses.

Jim Cummins killed the poor woman. "I didn't see she was a woman till I pulled the trigger," he said later. Oll Shepherd forgave him. "Boy, don't go sobbin' over no uppity darky wench."

At the Eldridge House, a hotel and known gathering spot of Jim Lane and other Jayhawkers, Quantrill reined up, and swung from his horse. He motioned several of our followers to ride on, and they obeyed with murderous glee. I dismounted, as did Jim, Frank James, Little Arch Clement, George Todd, and several more.

"I'm hungry," Little Archie Clement said, and he shot a man who had stepped out the door, his hands raised.

The lobby of the Eldridge House was beautiful.

Men and women stood about nervously, most of them raising their hands without having to be ordered. Already, we could smell the smoke that would soon blacken the morning sky.

The handsome clock against the wall chimed. It was 6:15 a.m.

"Is Governor Carney in town?" Quantrill asked, looking resplendent in his gleaming black riding boots, a gray hunting shirt, a flat-crowned black hat of Spanish style with golden cord around his neck and the brim adorned with another gold cord with tassels on the front.

"No . . . sir," came a whispered reply.

"Your name, sir?"

The man, his shirt untucked and wearing only stockings on his feet, wet his lips, swallowed, and glanced at his neighbors as if asking for help with the question. Finally, receiving no assistance from any of the men and women standing about, whose faces were ashen, he replied: "Spivey. Arthur Spivey."

"Mister Spivey"—Quantrill holstered the pistol he held in his right hand—"do you know where Senator Lane lives?"

His head nodded slightly.

"Good. You will lead a detail to Lane's house. If you mislead them, you will die, but if you fulfill your obligations, I assure you that you will survive this day. Is this contract agreeable, sir?"

"Yes," Spivey answered after a long pause.

"Then do your duty. Captain Younger, I give you the honor of killing Lane. See to it that Mister Spivey survives, unless he betrays you. Now, I believe Mister Clement said something about breakfast. . . ."

Arthur Spivey walked in front of our horses as he led the way to Jim Lane's mansion. We passed burning buildings, and as I walked my black steed—the orneriest horse I would ever own, named, appropriately, Jim Lane—I recognized many of my fellow bushwhackers for what they were . . . or had become.

"Is this your son, ma'am?" a woman was asked.

"Please, spare him . . . he's fifteen years old," she cried.

"Old enough to be carryin' a gun, I see."

"Please."

"How old are you, ma'am?"

"Thirty-two."

"Well, hell, woman. You's young enough to have another son."

The pistol cracked. The woman screamed as she fell to her knees. "Maybe your next boy won't be no Jayhawker."

John Jarrette walked out of a home as smoke and flames belched behind him, the body of a man in a blood-soaked nightshirt on the porch. Jarrette, a man I had always admired, even before he married my sister, carried a pillowcase filled with plunder in one hand, and a silver candlestick in the other.

We passed crushed gardens, dead dogs, dead men in the streets, while all around us, smoke rose. It was not yet seven in the morning, but the air felt chokingly hot. Sweat poured down my forehead, and drenched my bushwhacker shirt.

I saw women clutching their young children, and I yelled at them: "Get off the street!" I pointed my Navy at a cornfield. "Hide! Get your kids and hide, women! Don't watch this. Don't let your little ones see this!"

Some obeyed, while others could not move, could not look away from the horrors we—I— kept inflicting.

Whooping, hollering, waving his hat over his head, William Gregg came galloping by, dragging the Stars and Stripes behind him. Gregg had led the butchery at one of the Army camps.

"That's it." Arthur Spivey pointed at a fine house. Behind it stood a beautiful cornfield where, at last, some of the women were taking their children to hide from the barbarity. A woman stood by the front door, arms folded, her countenance rock-hard.

After reining up, I removed my hat.

Behind me came the awful noise of cries, shouts, prayers, pistol shots, laughter, and the crackling of flames.

"We've come for Jim Lane, ma'am," I said.

"You won't find him inside." She was cool. "Go in and see."

Six boys quickly dismounted, climbed up the steps, and went through the open door behind her. One accidentally brushed her right arm, and George Shepherd stopped, removed his hat, and said: "Sorry, ma'am." Then he followed the others. Inside the house, the men shouted. Glass shattered. The woman just stared at me with cold, unblinking eyes.

Ten minutes later, George Shepherd led the boys back out. Most of them carried silver. Bud Pence even had one of Mrs. Lane's dresses wrapped around his neck, a present, he said, for his mother. Three had bottles. Whiskey or wine? I could not tell.

"He ain't here," Shepherd said, who had claimed but one spoil of war.

"I told you," the woman said, and Shepherd,

grinning, unfurled the flag he had taken from above the Lanes' mantle.

A black flag, inscribed: Presented to General James H. Lane by the ladies of Leavenworth. That was the flag he had carried to Osceola. That was the *one* black flag we saw during the war. Quantrill later mailed it to General Sterling Price with his compliments.

We had missed the craven butcher. Turned out, Jim Lane hid in that cornfield where I had sent women and children, on his belly in his nightshirt.

"You best take to that field, Missus Lane," I said, and turned to my brother Jim and best friend Frank. "Burn this damned house to the ground."

By ten that morning, little remained of Lawrence except widows and children, flames and ashes. When Noland saw Yankee troops approaching, Quantrill decided that we should ride like hell back to Missouri.

We did, leaving behind between one hundred fifty and two hundred dead. Oh, the Yanks chased us, but not too hard. Someone shot John Jarrette's horse from under him, but I wheeled my horse, kicked free of a stirrup, and popped a Navy at the bluebellies, who no longer seemed riled enough to avenge Lawrence. Jarrette lunged for the pillow-case of loot but missed it.

"Forget the plunder, John!" I roared.

"But . . ."

"Leave it, damn you, or I leave you."

A bullet whistled overhead. With a curse, Jarrette hurried to my skittish black horse, found my arm and stirrup, and leaped behind me. We galloped to disappear in the cloud of dust.

"What's got into you, Bud?" Jarrette said as we bounded across Kansas sod. "I had at least eight thousand dollars and goods in that sack."

"I came to Lawrence to avenge those dead and injured women, not make off like some petty thief."

"Eight thousand dollars is no petty amount."

"Shut up."

Chapter Fifteen

I have little else to say of that day. Except I would like to correct one myth. Jesse James was not with us. In fact, Frank's kid brother would not join the cause until the following year, when feuds had divided Quantrill and Bloody Bill and George Todd, when, as our numbers fell both to bullets and hangman's nooses, our leaders no longer turned away anyone who could fork a saddle and pull a trigger.

Some of us rode away sickened by what we had witnessed, what we had done. Many, of course, felt the elation of victory. Quite a few thought they were rich. Bloody Bill Anderson, when we slowed our horses to a walk, busied himself tying fourteen new knots in his silken cord.

Then said Jesus, Father, forgive them; for they know not what they do.

Luke, Chapter Twenty-Three, Verse Thirty-Four.

We did not know what we had done. We did not know what we had wrought.

Vengeance is mine? No, retribution belonged to Senator Lane and General Ewing.

On August 25th, while bushwhackers hid in the hills of Arkansas, General Thomas Ewing instituted the worst crime ever allowed in the history of warfare: General Orders Number Eleven.

All persons living in Jackson, Cass, and Bates Counties, Missouri, and in that part of Vernon included in this district, except those living within one mile of the limits of Independence, Hickman Mills, Pleasant Hill, and Harrisonville, and except those in that part of Kaw Township, Jackson County, north of Brush Creek and west of the Big Blue, are hereby ordered to remove from their present places of residence within fifteen days from the date thereof.

Eventually we bushwhackers went to winter in Texas, but our loved ones had nowhere to go.

Oh, the Yanks said that anyone could stay, providing they proved their loyalty to the Union, as if any Missourian could do that to a damn-yank's satisfaction. As if any Missourian with sand would dare attempt to bow to bluebelly rule.

The exodus broke our hearts. Twenty thousand families cast adrift in a war-ravaged land, many with no money, no shoes, little food, and no direction. They had no place to go, except out of this burned-over district, where they could perhaps set up a shelter to see them through the coming winter.

When we returned to western Missouri, we found empty homes, starving dogs, shattered memories. Or ashes.

Since the Yanks had forced the burning of one of

our farms, Ma had taken the young ones to our other place in Jackson County. She had lain sick in bed when bluebellies had burst through the door, demanding that she take her brood and leave.

"I have nowhere to go," Ma had said.

The captain in charge did not care, but, oh, he found his heart. With my siblings crying, servants shivering, and Ma coughing that ragged cough that would turn into consumption, that upstanding Yankee acquiesced. He gave my mother until the following day, providing, before she left, she burned the house herself.

Ma never broke her word. She asked Hardin, our loyal slave, to put a bed in the back of the one wagon the red legs had yet to steal. Mammy Suse guided the little ones outside, and Hardin returned, carrying my mother in his giant arms. She came out with a torch, which she feebly tossed inside as they moved toward the farm wagon.

We still had that house in Harrisonville, but Ma refused to go back there. Sick as she was, the memories would have killed her even sooner, and, besides, they couldn't have made a living in town. Jayhawkers had looted the store, and plundered and practically destroyed the livery. So north they went, to Independence, over to Lexington, and then following the Missouri River to the town of Waverly over in Lafayette County, where Aunt Nancy, Ma's sister, lived. Sixty, maybe seventy miles in a wagon pulled by two mules, one half-lame and the other blind—otherwise the bluebellies would have confiscated them, too. With little victuals, they survived for four or five days on the charity of church-going folk. That made Ma even sicker, and it would harden John and Bob, although my brothers did find some peace after Ma left them with kinfolk in St. Clair County.

I didn't know if Lawrence had disturbed Quantrill back then, but, upon arriving in Texas, he did take to drink much more than he had. We made our winter camp about ten miles north of Sherman, and there the bickering began. Bloody Bill wanted to ride back to Missouri immediately, and keep spilling Yankee blood. Jim Cummins backed Anderson. "I ride with the worst devil of the bunch," he told me. "That's Bloody Bill."

Frank James just sat and chewed tobacco. He didn't quote Shakespeare, and hardly spoke to anyone until Jesse showed up. This time, we did not send him away—even when the fool kid was playing around with a Colt Dragoon, and the hammer dropped on the middle finger of his left hand.

"That's the dod-dingus pistol I ever saw!" he wailed.

Now that got us to laughing, and he laughed alongside us, though he would not be laughing two days later when the infection set in and we had to cut off the top nub of his finger. From then on out, however, we called Frank's baby brother Dingus.

Yet rarely did laughter sound. What we had done at Lawrence tore at some souls, and as Quantrill brooded, drank to a state of intoxication, and consorted with his concubines, I realized that this was not the war I had wanted to fight. I had sort of liked being a soldier during that brief campaign with Jo Selby, and felt I had proved how good I could be at this, so when John Jarrette approached me with an offer, I listened.

"Jo Shelby's over in Shreveport," my brother-in-law said. "I've a mind to join him."

Maybe John's conscience tore at him, too. Maybe now he understood why I had not let him retrieve that $8,000 when we had fled Lawrence. He did not have to twist my arm.

"I'm game." Instantly I crossed camp to tell Frank James.

He sloshed the mixture of rye and coffee in his tin cup, shook his head, and, without smiling, said: "'Away, boy, from the troops, and save thyself. . . .'"

'Twas good, and warmed my heart, to hear him cite Shakespeare again.

"You'll ride with us?" I asked.

He took a drink, set the cup on a rock, but shook his head. "I got my brother to look after, Bud."

I understood, and with sadness walked away. The sadness deepened when I found my own brother, and told him my plan.

"Ride off, then," Jim snapped at me. "I'm stickin' with Colonel Quantrill."

"Jim," I pleaded, but he backed away.

"Why in hell would I want to ride off to Louisiana? I don't give a dead rat's ass about anyone there. Nor should Jo Shelby. Missouri's our home. That's where I'm fighting. That's why I'll stay with Quantrill."

"I'm going, Jim," I said.

He nodded, but, ever the loyal brother, he held out his right hand. "See you," he said, "after we've licked them."

Years later, I recalled what Jim had told me, and only then, aged by time, did it strike me that perhaps that was why we lost the war. Most Rebs, like Jim, were fighting for home, and, for Jim, home meant Missouri, western Missouri. Others fought for South Carolina or Alabama or old Virginia. We Confederates remained divided. But the North? Whether the Yanks enlisted to save the Union or free the slaves, or just for the hell of it, they remained united. They had a cause. They fought as one, and there were a lot of them.

Amongst ourselves, our rift widened. After I left, George Todd abandoned Quantrill. So did Bloody Bill Anderson. By then, even Frank and Jesse were divided, with Jesse riding off with Bloody Bill, to help in the butchery at Centralia in 1864. Having to choose between blood and loyalty, Frank stayed with Quantrill. So did my brother Jim. They would be there when Quantrill was mortally wounded and captured in Kentucky in 1865. Frank would manage to escape, but Jim would spend months in a prison in Alton, Illinois.

When I told Quantrill I was leaving with Jarrette—and maybe a dozen others who joined us—he nodded, muttered a thanks, and poured four fingers of brandy into a champagne flute. "You were a fine lieutenant," he said. I thought I had been a captain, but ranks never much mattered in our outfit, and I wasn't exactly sure when Quantrill had been promoted to colonel. "Just keep killing Yankees," he concluded.

Before I left the bushwhackers, I returned to Frank, and we embraced. He had quoted from "Othello", so I did the same. "'For the love o' God, peace!'"

As Frank pulled away, I saw sadness in his eyes. "Bishop Cole, you and I will never know peace."

Time would prove him right, but I already understood the veracity of his comment on that freezing afternoon in 1864.

Basically the war ended for me when I enlisted with Jo Shelby, who deemed my skills better suited for the spying business. I found myself dispatched to Louisiana to chase after cotton thieves. To Arkansas, to spy on General Steele. I took fifteen men to Mexico, where we made our way to California and up to British Columbia to take charge of a couple of warships to sail back to the Gulf of Mexico and help our cause.

In Canada, the numbing, though half-expected, news reached us. The war had ended. The Confederacy was no more. Our cause was lost, turning us into soldiers without a country.

So I returned to California, to find my namesake uncle, Coleman Younger, who lived in San Jose. I drank wine, ate grapes and fish. I danced at *bailes* with pretty *señoritas*. Gambled some in San Francisco. Put on some of the weight I had shed during the war. Tried to forget about the past few years. One thing I never did, though, was recite these words:

> I, Cole Younger, do solemnly swear, in the presence of Almighty God, that I will henceforth faithfully support, protect, and defend the Constitution of the United States, and the union of the States thereunder, and that I will, in like manner, abide by and faithfully support all acts of Congress . . . so help me God.

Later that fall, homesick for Ma, my brothers, my sisters, and any comrades in arms that might still be alive, I bade farewell to Uncle Coleman, and set off for home.

Only to realize, upon reaching Missouri, that I had no home.

PART II

1866–1876

Chapter Sixteen

People often asked me if there's anyone I really wished I had killed. Irvin Walley, who murdered my pa. Doc Jennison, Jim Lane, and other Kansas red legs. Maybe Jesse James. Although desire to murder no longer blackens my heart, I think Charles D. Drake would have topped that list.

One of those high-minded Radical Republicans—and worse, a St. Louis lawyer—Drake pretty much wrote the new state constitution for Missouri after the war.

By the time I got home from California, I couldn't vote, nor could I hold any office had I wanted to follow in Pa's political footsteps. By Jehovah, I couldn't even serve as a deacon in Ma's church. But I could be arrested and tried because while our "Drake" constitution allowed that no Yankee, red leg or Jayhawker could be prosecuted for crimes committed during the war, we bushwhackers could still be hanged.

The war had not ended, not for bushwhackers like me. Hell, when I finally got home, Ma, Emilly, and Retta were tending to Mammy Suse. A Kansas posse had come by the previous night, saying they were searching for me, but in reality they had strung up that fine old Negress in the barn, trying to get her to tell them where Pa's fortunes had been buried. As if my dead father had any fortune left. Emilly was thirteen and Retta only eight. The bastards had made the girls watch.

They were replacing the bandages on our loyal servant's throat when I found them. Our home was a cabin Pa had once leased to tenants who worked a farm we owned in Jackson County. The roof leaked, the walls needed chinking, and the fireplace sucked more heat out of the cabin than it put in, but the building still stood. Most of the houses I had passed had been reduced to blackened timbers, or merely crumbling brick fireplaces—gravestones in place of what once had been right prosperous farms.

"Where are the boys, Ma?" I asked.

"John and Bob took off to see if we got any rabbits in the snares," she said.

"Rabbits? I saw a deer in the woods as I rode in," I said.

"Got no shotgun or rifle to shoot a deer, Coleman," Ma said as she patted Mammy Suse's shoulder, and pushed herself off the stool placed by the straw-stuffed ticking on the floor. The war had aged Ma considerably. Bone-thin, pale, she covered her mouth as she coughed hard, then turned to the fireplace to fetch a kettle and pour us some tea.

"Where's Duck?" I asked.

I had lost track of my favorite sister's husband, George Clayton, after leaving Quantrill in Texas.

Ma did not turn from the fireplace as she filled a tin cup with tea. Mammy Suse groaned, and little Retta started to sob.

"Caroline's with Jesus, Coleman."

It took a while for those words to register, and maybe I didn't really comprehend what Ma had just told me until Retta ran to me, her sobs now full-blown bawling. My knees buckled, and, as tears welled in my own eyes, I lifted my baby sister to me to cry on my shoulder. Emilly ran to me, too, but she was trying to be brave as she told us: "It's all right, Retta. It's all right, Cole. Duck's with Jesus. She's in heaven. She ain't in pain no more."

I raised my eyes to see Ma staring at me. It seemed as though, in just a few minutes, she had aged another five years.

"Caroline never got over what happened . . . when . . . that jail in Kansas City . . . ," Ma couldn't finish, and she set the teacup down, sank into a rickety old rocking chair, and stared at the fire.

After I killed and butchered that deer I had seen and hunted down, I gave Bob my Enfield. He and John had brought home three wormy rabbits.

"You always showing me up," Bob said, dropping the rabbits on the floor and storming outside. I followed him.

Near the ramshackle corral, he whirled and

pointed at the Enfield still in my hands. "That the one you used to murder those Yankees?"

"Never murdered any Yankees," I told him. "And I rarely used a rifle during the war. This Enfield I picked up in California. You can use it. Never was much good with a long gun myself."

John had followed us outside.

"Where's Hardin?" I asked.

"Doing whatever free darkies do," Bob answered with the bitterness of an old man, not a teen-ager.

"How many pistols you got, Cole?" John asked in awe. At least he still sounded like a kid.

"Four." Quickly I changed the subject. "Don't any of our old neighbors or our friends in Strother help you out?"

"It ain't Strother no more," Bob snapped. "Yanks renamed it Lee's Summit. And it don't pay to help the Youngers. And your being here sure won't help us," Bob said in conclusion before storming back inside the house.

"You teach me to shoot?" John asked, pointing at one of my Navy Colts.

"Shoot what?" I asked.

He didn't answer.

But, yeah, I took John into the woods and, over the next few days, gave him a lesson in shooting revolvers. Bob even warmed up to me slightly, and he came out to learn from me, too. So I told my kid brothers some blood-and-thunders, showed them how to do the border shift—with empty revolvers, of course.

I had plenty of practice during the war, throwing a Navy from right hand to left, or vice versa. Retta and Emilly came out to watch, too.

"Why would you do that?" Emilly asked.

"Get shot in one arm," I said, remembering the first lessons John Jarrette had given me, "you gotta toss it to the other. Or empty one pistol, toss the empty to your other hand and draw another."

"You ever get shot, Cole?" John asked.

My head shook. "I was lucky." And I thought about Quantrill, shot in the spine and slowly dying in Kentucky. Or George Todd, felled by some Yankee snake-in-the-grass with a Sharps rifle near Independence in 1864. Or Bloody Bill who, after being killed in an ambuscade, was brought into Richmond, where his head was cut off and stuck atop a telegraph pole and his body dragged down the streets while the citizens and soldiers cheer.

"Did you pray before each fight?" Retta asked.

"Of course," I said, though I didn't tell her that once the battle had actually started, we forgot about prayers and started cursing vilely and continued blasphemy and profanity until the gunsmoke cleared and the ringing left our ears. And you've been listening to me long enough, Parson, to know that's one habit that I haven't quite figured out how to break.

155

There was no room for me in the cabin. Or, at least, that's what I told Ma. I slept in the woods, with my horse saddled nearby, knowing the new laws passed in Missouri fostered night raiders. And they did show up twice during my visit, yelling and cursing, but not harming any of my family, or Mammy Suse again.

Fearing that the Yanks might soon find me, I rode over to Howard County to visit Uncle Thomas, but I came back home to the cabin for Christmas, and again for New Year's. By then, Jim had been freed from the Illinois prison. At home, he tried to put the war behind him—as well as me, too. Jim worked to get our big farm back into shape. I rarely saw him.

It was in January that I came to regret teaching my brothers how to shoot handguns.

John and Bob had ridden into Independence with Ma to buy supplies with the money I had given to her. While my brothers were loading blankets, winter clothes and boots, and grub into the wagon, this bluebelly named Gillcreas began saying the vilest things about me. I would have let such slander pass, knowing the fiend meant only to provoke a fight. Hell, Bob probably agreed with everything the Yank said about me, but John told him to shut up.

That was exactly what Gillcreas wanted to hear. He grabbed a frozen mackerel that Ma had bought for the next day's supper, and used it to knock John to the dirt. John leaped up, the Yankee laughed, and Bob cried out to my brother: "Why don't you shoot him?"

I did not know John had brought one of my Navy Colts with him to town, but as he stood, his hand reached behind, and pulled the .36 from the back of his waistband. Gillcreas was bringing up a slingshot. To my way of thinking, the Yank had figured a slingshot was enough to use on a young boy.

The coward died with a bullet in his brain.

The marshal held John in jail overnight, but the coroner's inquest ruled that John had acted in self-defense. A slingshot once had slain a giant, and, surely, in the hands of a beast like Gillcreas, could mortally wound a boy.

My family came home, but we knew we could not stay. The Yanks now would want to avenge the death of Gillcreas. Ma went down to Cass County. My sister Martha Anne took in Emilly and Retta in Pleasant Hill. I rode with John and Bob to St. Clair County, where I left my baby brothers with Uncle Frank.

I wanted to ride over to the Wayward Rest, and surprise lovely Lizzie Brown with a visit. Instead, I made my way to Clay County, found a small town called Centerville (later to merge with another town and become Kearney), where some kindly old Rebels directed me to the farmhouse of Zerelda Samuel.

• • •

We Youngers were not the only Missourians persecuted for choosing the losing side in a war.

Frank James introduced me to his mother, who was already showing with child; his stepfather Doc Samuel, whose neck still bore the burn marks from his hanging by Yankee troops during the war; and his little siblings, Sallie, Johnnie, and Fanny. Fanny, just two years old, had been given the middle name, Quantrill. Frank didn't need to introduce me to his brother, though I almost didn't recognize Jesse, weak and pale as he was.

"Dingus took a ball through a lung last May," Frank told me, "while he was riding in to take the oath of allegiance."

"Put me in a dreadful fix," Jesse said weakly. "Liked to have died."

"You're too ornery to die, Dingus."

After Quantrill had been shot, Frank said, he stayed around Kentucky for a while, just to let things cool down. The war was over, but he figured the Yankees meant to hang anyone who had ridden with Quantrill.

I related to him my experiences after joining Shelby, and what I had seen upon my return to Missouri.

"About the same here," Frank said. "When I got home in August, I found a nice corn crop in the field. Then some bluebellies rode up in the middle of the night, trampled the crops, even crushed our cantaloupes and tomatoes."

"The bastards," Jesse said.

Mrs. Samuel brought me a plate of corn pone and bacon, and Frank produced a jug of liquor. I did not want to impose on a good Southern family, especially knowing first-hand how hard food was to come by, but I had not eaten in days. Frank's mother could not cook like Ma or Mammy Suse, but I felt much better after that meal.

After thanking her for the hospitality, I offered to pay for the food, which proved an error in judgment. Mrs. Samuel laid into me with a stream of cussing that would have shocked Oll Shepherd, and then she cursed the Yankees and the Missouri people who made life so hard on good Baptist folks like her and her family.

Frank sniggered and Jesse grinned as the hard rock of a woman walked back to care for her brood. My fingers still held a gold piece.

"Can I see that?" Jesse asked.

I flipped the coin to him.

"Newly minted," he said, and the devilment flashed in his blue eyes. "How many more you got?"

"I don't have many more," I said. "Won it playing monte in San Francisco."

"Most folks here pay their debts in apple butter," Frank said. "We figured to pay ours in corn, till the Yanks fixed our flint."

We sampled more of Frank's liquor.

"I've been thinking about Texas," I said. "Try to start over there. Or maybe Louisiana, though it's hotter than hell and folks talk funny."

"Not me," Jesse said. "Not by a damned sight."

"I don't know." Frank sighed. "I just don't know what to do any more."

"Besides," Jesse said, "it would cost money for even us to get to Texas or Louisiana. And other than this . . ."—he flipped the coin to Frank—"I don't know where you can find any cash money."

Suddenly Frank got up, and closed the door. "I do," he said in an urgent whisper. "Plenty of money. Money that belongs to damnyankees."

Chapter Seventeen

The bullet wound kept Jesse in bed, though he bitterly complained about us leaving him behind.

"Next time," I told him as we prepared to leave.

"Next time?" Frank asked.

I gave both brothers the most serious look I could summon despite my nerves. "We start this," I told them, "and there's no turning back. Are we agreed?"

"Damned right," Jesse said.

"All right," Frank added. "But we'll need help."

Finding men to join us came easy. We kept it in our family, the brotherhood of bushwhackers. My brother-in-law, John Jarrette, met us at an abandoned farm on Rush Creek.

Laughing, he shook my hand and reminded me that I had once made him leave behind $8,000 in Yankee greenbacks in Kansas. "As I recollect, you said something about not becoming a petty thief," he reminded me.

Little Archie Clement, Payne Jones, Dick Burns, Bud and Donny Pence, George and Oll Shepherd, Joab Perry. Ten of us in all, wearing gloves, mufflers, and Yankee greatcoats, for the day had turned bitterly cold, and snow flurries would begin to fall. At Blue Mills Ferry, we crossed the icy river, stopping at Captain B.S. Minter's for food, hot coffee, the warmth of a fire, fine conversation, and two sacks of meal. On the outskirts of Liberty, we dumped the meal in a ditch, and I stuck the empty sacks inside my greatcoat. A few of our colleagues pasted fake mustaches and/or beards on their faces, but such frivolities I shunned. Then we split up—the boys coming to the square from different directions, and finding their positions at various locations, leaving Frank and me to ride in alone a few minutes later.

On the southwestern corner of Liberty's town square, a fine two-story building of red bricks housed the Clay County Savings Association. A week or two earlier, the bank's owners had led a meeting of black-hearted Radical Republicans.

Just around 2:00 p.m., Frank and I swung from our horses, wrapped the reins around a hitching rail, and walked inside the bank.

It was February 13, 1866.

The cashier's name was Greenup Bird. He had been pointed out to Frank by his mother often. Bird's son, William, glanced at us briefly when we walked inside before he went back to his scribbling. As a county clerk, the banker had helped settle the estate after Frank's pa died of fever in California during the Gold Rush. The Birds, Frank assured me, wouldn't know him from Adam's house cat, and they sure did not know me.

As we warmed ourselves by the stove, I pulled a crumpled $10 note from the pocket of my trousers. My eyes locked on Frank's. The next decision would change our lives, but Frank merely shifted the quid of tobacco he chewed to the other cheek. After that, he smiled. So did I, and, clearing my throat, I moved to the counter.

"Mister"—I tried to smooth the bill on the cold countertop—"can you change this note for me?"

"Certainly." William Bird's chair legs scraped against the floor. When he reached for the banknote, I stuck my .36 in his face.

"Make one sound and I'll shoot you down," I said. "We want all the money you have, and you had better be damned quick about it."

The younger Bird blinked in utter confusion, whilst the old man rose and started to say something that he did not finish because Frank came through the opening and shoved a Remington into the banker's gut.

"What is the meaning of this?" Greenup Bird croaked after a second.

We have been credited with robbing the first trains in America, but that is not the case. The Reno boys in Indiana beat us there. Yet, unless you count the affair at St. Albans in Vermont in 1864—and that was a Confederate raid, an act of war—we were making history that snowy afternoon. No one had ever dared rob a bank in broad daylight.

"Damn you, be quick!" I spun William Bird around, pressed the Navy's barrel against his spine, forcing him toward the vault, while Frank pushed the old man to the cash drawers.

William Bird filled my cotton meal sack with gold and silver, while Greenup Bird dumped greenbacks, Union Military bonds, and three-year 7-30 notes into Frank's sack. My sack, obviously, weighed more, but I was bigger than Frank James.

"Stay here," I told the now panting William Bird, and backed out of the vault. Frank, his sack also bulging, sent Mr. Bird toward the vault.

"Where is the key to the vault?" I asked.

The old man paled. "Merciful Jesus, please, do not lock us in there. We could asphyxiate."

"Or you could die with a bullet through one of your eyeballs," Frank said, moving the barrel from the man's blinking left eye to his right.

The banker pointed feebly. "In . . . the . . . door."

I stepped aside, saying: "Don't you know, sir, that all Birds should be caged." Frank shoved him into the vault, and we closed the door. We did not, however, lock it. Cold-blooded murder was not our nature, though we would soon regret that bit of charity.

Outside, I tied the heavy sack onto the horn, and as I swung into the saddle, the window in the bank jerked up, and Greenup Bird stuck his head out, screaming: "Saint Albans! Saint Albans! Thieves! They are stealing our money!"

Panes above his head shattered as bullets rang out from the revolvers of our comrades.

Liberty was crowded that afternoon, with court in session. Men tended to flock to courthouses more than they frequented an opera house for a good show. Horses' hoofs pounded, and our boys shot and yelled: "Get off the streets or get killed!" "Stand back!" "Remember Osceola!"

A boy on the corner, however, had taken up the cashier's alarm, shouting: "Thieves! Thieves! Robbery! Murder!"

Murder. The last word Jolly Wymore ever spoke. George Shepherd shot him down, and the boy, no older than nineteen, slumped onto the boardwalk. Later, George told us that his horse had reared, and he had missed his aim.

Few of the townsfolk carried any weapons, or, if they did, none dared present one against ten rough men. I emptied one of my Colts, and, as my horse carried me away from the bank, I glanced at the boy George Shepherd had shot down. A few men had run over to him, but I could tell his soul had departed. I had seen enough death in the war.

"Ride!" Frank shouted. "Ride!"

We did. As hard as we could.

Down Franklin Street, and east, as the flurries soon blew into a blizzard. The posse quickly lost us in the storm, and turned back. After swimming across the Missouri near Sibley Crossing, we stopped at Mount Gilead Church. On our knees at the altar, we divided our spoils.

"'And they parted his raiment,'" Frank said with a sneer, "'and cast lots.'"

"Don't be sacrilegious, Buck," I told him. "Not here."

"Listen to the bishop," Oll Shepherd said, and the boys laughed. Yet the laughter died as we emptied the two meal sacks, and stared at our gain.

More than $8,600 in greenbacks. Another $3,000 in the U.M. bonds, and perhaps $40,000 in the 7-30s. Farmer Bank notes totaling $300. More than $5,000 in other bonds. And that does not even include the gold and silver coins.

We divided the loot, although I took most of the bonds. The boys figured that, considering my spying days for Shelby, I could cash those bonds without getting arrested. That agreement meant I would have to travel, but such was my nature. I went to Ohio, Louisiana, and Kentucky, with a simple defense that, if I ever got caught, I would just say that I was happy to cash bonds given to me by my friends, never thinking that I might be asked where my pals had gotten such bonds.

We rode our separate ways, agreeing to meet up at a place we dubbed "the Rubicon" after our fortunes had been spent. That didn't take long. Frank took to benders, getting roostered fairly often in Centerville or Kearney, and forcing his stern mother to bail him out of jail. Joab Perry was arrested for horse stealing in Independence, so the Shepherd and Pence brothers rode up to that fortress with a few other men and tried to get Perry freed. It didn't happen, and their gunfire killed the marshal and wounded the lawman's seven-year-old son.

In October, John Jarrette, Frank, and I took Jesse along with us to Alexander and Mitchell Company in Lexington, Missouri. After the death of that boy, Jolly Wymore, in Liberty, Frank and I had agreed that ten trigger-happy men increased our risk and decreased our take. Fewer robbers, more money—and we wanted men we could trust, which ruled out Little Archie Clement and the others.

After making a bloodless withdrawal of $2,000 and change, the four of us split our take with good old Dave Pool. Pool happened to be in town that afternoon, and joined the posse that took after us. Dave must have led those boys through every briar patch and bog along the Missouri River before they had enough and went back to soak their wounds and windpipes in the grog shops in town. Dave Pool and I had a big laugh over that when I paid him his share.

But it wasn't long before the law began to laugh. Joab Perry, of course, got sentenced to hard labor at The Walls. Little Archie Clement was gunned down on the streets of Lexington before Christmas. And after John Jarrette led some of the boys to the Hughes and Wasson Bank in Richmond, Missouri, things turned really sour. The town's mayor was shot dead during the hold-up. So were the jailer, and the jailer's son.

When Tom Little and Fred Meyers were arrested in Warrensburg, a mob took them to the livery and left them swinging. Andy McGuire danced from the end of a rope in that town a short while later. Felix Bradley was arrested in Richmond, and lynched, even though Jarrette swore to me that Felix had been in jail during the bank robbery. Dick Burns was found with his brains bashed out a few miles south of Independence. Payne Jones met his maker the same night, but with a bullet in his back, not an axe buried in his skull. George Shepherd almost got himself arrested in Nashville, Tennessee, after trying to cash one of the bonds he had kept from Liberty.

About the only ones who showed good sense were the Pence boys and John Jarrette. In fact, Bud and Donny Pence each married the daughter of a judge and found steady, honest work, in Kentucky, but I guess it was my brother-in-law who topped even the Pence brothers. After that dreadful affair in Richmond, when bushwhackers, some of them innocent, started paying for the crimes of other Missourians, John took his wife and family—along with the money he had stolen—to Arizona Territory. Raising sheep, he became respectable, and forgot all about his Younger in-laws.

During new moons, between my bond-cashing excursions, I rode in the darkness to find Ma, or Jim, and leave them enough gold coin or blue notes to get them through the hard times.

The money helped, because when I visited my family in Pleasant Hill for Christmas, Ma announced that she wanted to return to our farm around Greenwood, the one Jim had been working. Jim agreed that things had turned more peaceful in Jackson County—compared to the rest of western Missouri—and we hugged, prayed, sang, and ate. Still I knew my family would need money soon.

Almost two years had passed since we had pulled the bank robbery in Liberty—the Yankee bank had been forced to close its doors—when I met Frank and Jesse James at the Rubicon, a little bend of the Big Blue.

Jesse gave me a grin. "Bud," he said, "Missouri's become a little hot for us old bushwhackers. So we're thinking about making a trip to Kentucky. Want to come along?"

Chapter Eighteen

From Lexington, we boarded a side-wheeler and made our way along the Missouri to the Mississippi, and then up the Ohio.

"I ain't never been on a steamboat before," Jesse said, his eyes bright. "This is gonna be fun."

"Might be more fun, Dingus," I told him, "if you'd leave those pistols in our berth. Folks keep eyeing you with a great bit of suspicion."

He spit tobacco juice into the dark, churning waters of the river, and turned to me, each hand on the butt of his revolvers.

"You telling me that you aren't heeled?"

"I have a Derringer in my pocket and a Manhattan in a shoulder holster . . . just to be safe."

"All right then."

The boy was too ignorant to know what I had just told him, so Frank explained it.

"Folks can't see Bishop Cole's hardware, Dingus. Like they can't see mine. Our *business* revolvers are in our grips."

Jesse shook his head. "These guns come off when I'm dead," he said, and walked away, pushing his coattails back behind the holsters, to spite us, to show off, leaving me staring at his older brother.

" 'I am his brother,' " Frank said, " 'and I love him well.' "

"Richard III", Act I, Scene Four.

"Remember what happens to Clarence," I reminded my friend, and went to the next deck to find a friendly game of poker.

Grinning, Frank followed me. "Like I said, this is his dance, his idea."

"I don't remember voting him to the captaincy."

"Dingus has ambitions."

"So do I. Like staying alive."

"Sounds like a plum bank, Bud," Frank said. "But you and I shall check it out before we commit."

We arrived in Louisville. The next morning, after cashing one of my bonds from Liberty, we bought some fine thoroughbred horses and followed Jesse. After all, this was his idea, and he intrigued me when he said we were going to meet a couple of brothers I knew who had told him about the bank. I figured I'd soon meet up with the Pence boys.

Instead, Oll and George Shepherd were waiting for us at the Marshall Hotel in Chaplin. George had moved there after the war, and Oll had come to visit from Jackson County, Missouri, after talking to Jesse.

I pretended that seeing them made me happy, when, in fact, it soured my stomach. When

George started talking about a bank down south, however, I became more and more interested.

"Nimrod Long is just one of 'em bankers," Oll whispered. "Got hisself a pard named George N. Norton." He stressed the man's name.

I wiped my mouth with my napkin. "Am I supposed to know him?"

"You might recollect his brother, Elijah," George Shepherd said.

Indeed, the name made me frown and drop the napkin. Judge Elijah Hise Norton, of Platte City, had served as a 4th District Congressman in the Missouri House of Representatives during the first few years of the late war. He opposed Secession, and did everything he could to keep the Yanks in office, and in the field of war.

"It's a Yankee bank," Oll said, "filled with Yankee money."

The Nimrod L. Long & Company did business in Russellville in a fine two-story brick building with big fancy windows on a pretty, tree-lined Main Street.

I rode in alone, leaving the boys in a hollow on the outskirts of town. Dressed in duster and a fine frock coat of green, I climbed the steps and entered the bank, and produced one of those $500 7-30 bonds to the cashier. With a sorry frown, he walked to the office and brought back Mr. Nimrod Long himself.

I shook his flimsy hand. "Thomas Colburn, sir," I said, "of Louisville."

"You desire to cash this, young man?" he asked, squinting through his spectacles.

"On par," I told him.

"The note has matured," he said. "A six-percent premium would be in order."

"But I'm not greedy, Mister Nimrod, and desire to make it home to my ailing grandmother."

"I see." Oh, Nimrod L. Long saw all right, saw right through me. "I am sorry, Mister Colburn, but at this moment we lack the funds to cash your bond."

I didn't like it, and over the next week we scouted some other banks in the area, but nothing appealed to Jesse or the Shepherds. Not that I blamed them. So Frank, Jesse, and I rode into Russellville, and ate dinner at a café across the street, while George and Oll stopped at the livery and dickered with the owner about a mule they had no intention of buying.

We finished our dinner of ham and eggs, and I asked for more coffee.

"If you don't want to do this deal, Bud," Jesse said, "Frank and me'll do it ourselves."

Frank laughed and said: " 'Upon the heat and flame of thy distemper sprinkle cool patience.' "

"I wish to hell you'd quit spouting your damned 'Macbeth', Brother," Jesse said.

" 'Hamlet'," Frank corrected him. "You'd do well to read the Bard, Dingus."

"I read only the Bible."

"And newspapers," I reminded him.

"Penny dreadfuls, too," Frank chimed.

The waitress touched up my coffee, Frank's, too, and walked away. But I slid the cup away, and rose from my chair.

"Thought you was thirsty," Jesse said.

My thumb hooked at two men who had just walked into the café. Regular as a Tremont watch, the clerk and cashier had arrived to eat their dinner.

I walked back up those steps to the bank with a blue note worth $100 that I had borrowed from Frank. I asked Mr. Nimrod to cash it, and, just as I expected, Mr. Nimrod rudely slid the note back to me. "That is counterfeit, sir. Good day."

Counterfeit? Why, Frank James had withdrawn that note from the Clay County Savings Association in February of 1866.

"Is this good, sir?" I asked.

Mr. Nimrod gasped when he saw the Navy .36 I had pressed against his nose. "Now, empty the damned vault."

When the doors opened, bringing Frank and Jesse inside, the fool banker turned and ran, which almost proved to be his undoing, because Jesse popped three shots at the running man, one round grazing Nimrod's head, but fools get lucky, and Nimrod made it out, safe and sound.

"Hurry," I said, and we moved toward the vault that Nimrod, in his haste, had kindly left open.

Outside, the Shepherd boys opened fire with Spencer repeaters.

Glass shattered, bullets whined off metal and bricks, or thudded into wood. Women screamed, but Jesse, Frank, and I focused on filling our empty wheat sacks with money. With the cannonade continuing outside, we hurried to our task, then rushed through the front door, guns in one hand, sacks in the other.

This might have been the strangest robbery we committed, for, as I mounted my bay, an old man rounded the corner and bumped into me, dropping two buckets of water he had been struggling with. The gelding wheeled, the man fell backward, and as I struggled to get my horse under control, I aimed the Navy at the old man.

Blinking, he sat up, shook his head, and said: "Where is the fire, youngster?"

"Mister," I said, and popped a shot across the street, "we are having a fine serenade here, and I think it would be best for you to go back around the corner there. Or you might get shot."

He obeyed, leaving the buckets where they had fallen.

A pretty girl, no older than ten, ran out from the schoolhouse, stopping in the middle of the street. She had blonde pigtails and wore a calico dress. "Jennie!" the schoolmarm cried from the door. "Get back! Get back inside this instant. You might be killed!"

"No, ma'am!" Frank called out to her. "We are here to get money. Not shoot children."

Having emptied their Spencers, the Shepherd brothers filled their hands with Colts, and we put spurs to our horses and thundered out of Russellville, ducking as bullets sailed over our heads.

A few miles east of town, we stopped in the woods, half expecting to hear hoofs pounding the road behind us. Kentuckians were no quicker at forming posses than Missourians, so we had time to shed the shabby clothes and ill-fitting hats we had donned, and put on better duds, dusters, and nice hats. We trotted off like fine businessmen. The law would be searching for men in trail duds—if the law ever came.

After crossing a railroad, we made camp that evening near the Barren River, and opened the wheat sacks.

"What did I tell you?" Jesse said as he picked up a $100 bill.

"You did fine, Dingus," I said. "Just fine."

Fine? Better than fine, I had to concede, though only to myself. We had taken $9,000, although Mr. Nimrod would claim we had made off with $14,000. I wonder if that brittle skinflint stole that extra $5,000 for himself.

Before reaching Bowling Green, we rode to a

small burg called Gainesville to partake of horizontal refreshments, play monte, and drink fine Kentucky bourbon. Then we split up. George and Oll took their share of the money and rode to Scottsville. At Glasgow, Frank asked a stage-coach driver for directions to Bardstown. The one-armed ex-Reb good-naturedly told us, and we thanked him. Then we rode northwest to Owensborough, where one of Stovepipe Johnson's Tennessee partisans had tried to burglarize a bank back in 1865, and when that failed, he had captured some colored soldiers wearing the blue, shot them dead, and burned their bodies on a barge before fleeing to Tennessee. Missouri and Kansas, you see, could not lay claim to every act of barbarism during the late war.

We shook hands on the banks of yellow mud. Frank and Jesse had decided to go to New York City, catch a steamer, and sail to California, where they had kinfolk in Paso Robles.

"Maybe we'll see if we can find our pa's grave," Frank said.

"Good luck," I said.

"Want to come with us, Bud?" Jesse asked.

"I've seen California, Dingus, but you have yourselves a fine time. I want to go home, see Ma . . . maybe find some peace."

"You want to see that gal Lizzie Brown." Frank winked.

I did not argue otherwise.

Chapter Nineteen

Somewhere along the line, however, the plan we had concocted had been flawed. A Louisville detective named Yankee Bligh started to dog our trail, and Bligh became relentless. How he found out about our stay in Chaplin, I don't know, but he did.

A short while later, lawmen knocked on George Shepherd's front door as he sat down for supper with his wife. They took him to Russellville, where citizens decided he might have been one of the men shooting a Spencer repeater. Russellville's jail wasn't sound enough to Yankee Bligh's liking, so George Shepherd was jailed in Louisville until trial.

"Might have been one of the men shooting a Spencer repeater" was not the kind of testimony needed to convict a man for robbery and assault and the wounding of one of Russellville's citizens. Unfortunately for George, though, he had kept some of our horses used in the hold-up, and witnesses remember horses much better than they recall faces. He got three years in the prison in Frankfort for aiding and abetting. His lawyer, the judge, and the county solicitors begged him to name his cohorts, promising a pardon for his testimony. But George Shepherd knew the code of the bushwhacker, and he was an honorable man.

"I ain't sayin' nothing," he said. "Find 'em your ownselves."

Well, they found Oll easy enough.

Yankee Bligh had decided that if George was one bandit, it stood to reason that Oll was another. By then, Oll had returned home, working the Missouri farm with his father. Bligh telegraphed the Jackson County sheriff, who seemed real eager to deliver Oll Shepherd to justice. After all, although no warrants had been issued, folks still thought Oll had been involved in the Richmond robbery.

One night, a deputy and twenty-five riders rode up to the Shepherd farm. Oll answered their knock with a shotgun blast through the door.

After exchanging pot shots throughout the night, Oll Shepherd knew his time was up, and he wasn't going to get his pa killed for his own crimes. He bolted out of the house, running for the field he had just finished plowing.

Oll Shepherd knew another code of the bushwhacker. He died game. His father counted twenty bullet holes in his son's body.

"Come in, Cole, come in." Mr. Robert Brown stuck out a calloused hand, and held open the door.

Everyone called the Browns' home Wayside Rest, and I don't think I had ever seen a finer place in all of Missouri. Usually, when Tom Brown, his brothers, and me would come by, there would be music, for Lizzie Brown could play that piano.

Robert and Mary Jane, Lizzie's pa and ma, came to Cass County from Tennessee before we Youngers ever left Kentucky. Mr. Brown owned sawmills, gristmills, and a tannery—and forty slaves. Pa would often joke—"Robert Brown is richer than God."—though he would never speak such sacrilege in Ma's presence.

The slave quarters had been burned down during the war, and the Negroes were all gone, and the Wayside Rest didn't look so beautiful any more. Certainly not much music had been played since Tom had died at Elkhorn Tavern.

Mr. Brown and I shook hands, and as he led me inside, he called out to his wife, who sat by the fireplace in a rocking chair, a shawl pulled up over her shoulders, a black band still around her arm, though Tom had been gone some six years now. Mrs. Brown glanced at me, shivered, spit snuff into a coffee can, and went back to her rocking, staring at the fire.

"You've been travelin', I warrant."

"Yes, sir," I told him. "Been investing in cattle. It's a good business, especially now with the Texas herds trailing to Kansas."

Cattle kept me moving. I could use it as my alibi should my name ever come up in connection with some robbery. Actually, I used cattle buying as an excuse to find a bank to cash a stolen bond, or something along those lines. Since that profitable trip to Kentucky, however, I had developed a keen interest in longhorns and in the idea of becoming something legitimate. Texas was to my liking. No one cared if you rode with bushwhackers, and ex-Rebels filled the state. The only Yankees you'd find were soldiers and carpetbaggers.

Lizzie Brown came downstairs, brushing back her hair, and touched her mother's shoulder, whispering something I could not hear. I don't think her mother heard, either, for she kept rocking.

Mr. Brown smiled. "I reckon you didn't come here to talk beef with me, Cole." Clearing his throat, he walked to the stove to find the coffee pot while Lizzie opened the door, and gestured toward the swing that hung from a tree limb.

She sat, and I pushed. Birds sang in the trees.

"How's school?" I asked.

"Thomas Coleman Younger," she said, "I finished my studies shortly after the late unpleasantness." Her head turned and she pouted as I pushed her higher in the swing. When the swing came back down to me, she said: "If you spent more time calling on me than gallivanting across the countryside, you might know that."

I pushed. "Independence Female College."

She swung up, came back down, and I said: "Then some school in Fayette." I pushed. "I forget its name."

"Howard Female College," she said, swinging back down for another push.

"And finally Columbia's Christian College."

Up she went, down she returned, and when she looked at me, I saw only that smile, and the laughter in her eyes.

"You are well-informed, sir."

"You teaching school anywhere?"

"No." Sadness laced her voice, and I let the swing come to a stop slowly. "Mother . . ." She got out of the swing. "Pa can't take care of her, and . . ." She shrugged.

I took her arm, and we walked into the yard where rosebushes once bloomed. "How's your mother?" Lizzie asked.

"Spirited," I said, "but sick." I cleared my throat. "That's why I wanted to see you."

We stopped walking, and I just let it all pour out of my mouth.

Martha Anne, one of my older sisters, had married some jasper named Lycurgus A. Jones—now that's a handle no one would want to be branded with—and they had settled down in Texas. In Sceyne, just up the road from Dallas, with a wagon factory, a Masonic Lodge, a good church, and plenty of Missourians to make Ma feel at home.

"John, Jim, Bob, and me plan to take Ma down there," I told Lizzie. "See that she gets settled."

"Emilly and Retta?"

"I guess you haven't heard. Emilly married a

gent named Rose, Kitt Rose. They'll stay here. Bob . . ."—I shrugged—"I don't know what he wants to do with his life. John, neither. Jim . . . Jim's a farmer. At least that's his plan. So once Ma's all comfortable, I'm sure he'll head back up this way."

"And you, Cole?"

I shuffled my feet. "Well, Texas interests me, as you well know. And I think I could do well in the cattle business, ranching. It's a wide-open country, though I expect I would grow to miss the trees."

"Is that all you would miss?" she asked.

Instead of answering her question, I said: "Maybe you would like to visit Texas."

"Perhaps," she said. "Though I might be like Emilly. Missouri is home."

Nodding in agreement, I said: "Well, I don't know if I could ever stay completely away from . . . you."

She reached out, and I took her hand. She squeezed. I returned the gesture. I walked her back to the house, up the steps, and to the door. The windows were open, and I could hear the squeaking of Mrs. Brown's rocking chair.

A fine, proper woman, Lizzie was. We shook hands, for I figured her mother had ears like Cass County's best gossip, and eyes in the back of her head like my own ma. After closing the door behind her, I walked to my horse.

· · ·

Parson, we might as well get this matter settled once and for all. Yes, I knew Belle Starr. Hell, most men who worked, owned, or rustled cattle in Texas knew Myra Maibelle Shirley. She was married to Jim Reed when I first met her, after we moved down to Texas. Reed had ridden with Quantrill, so when he and his wife and two children knocked on my door in Dallas County, I gave them all the courtesies I would have given any other folks with Missouri ties. Let them sleep in the hay barn, fed them, even gave them some cattle. I am sure my generosity pleased Belle, because I asked for nothing in return.

Jim Reed, of course, got himself killed in a fracas with a Texas lawman in 1874, and Belle took up with several other *hombres*, including my Uncle Bruce, but never, ever Thomas Coleman Younger. I might have seen her in passing a time or two, but by the time I was actually introduced to her, she already had that daughter of hers, Pearl. I am not Pearl's daddy.

Now, I admit I am a red-blooded male, with manly desires, but the only woman I ever loved is Lizzie Brown. There was nothing between Belle Starr and me, because not only was that woman meaner than sin, she was plug-ugly to boot.

In the winter of 1869, Brother Bob brought me a newspaper from St. Louis. I always loved catching up on the news from my home state, even if the newspaper leaned Republican, but Bob pointed to an article. It was not good news.

On December 9th, two men walked into the Daviess County Savings Association on the southeastern corner of the town square in Gallatin, Missouri. The banker and another citizen had been visiting inside the office, when the banker rose to tend to his customers. One of the newcomers asked to change a $100 note. Then both men drew revolvers.

As the taller of the pair began stuffing greenbacks and coin into a sack, the other man turned to the banker and said: "Major Cox, this is for Bloody Bill." And he put a bullet into the man's chest, killing him instantly. As soon as the body hit the floor, the killer leaned over, cocked his revolver, and sent another bullet into the dead man's head.

The bandits fled, but the shots had alerted the town, and Missourians were tired of bushwhacking thieves. Gunfire exploded across the town square, causing the killer's fine bay horse to rear. The killer fell to the frozen earth, left foot caught in the stirrup, and the bay dragged its rider forty feet. The citizens charged, but the other robber wheeled his horse, firing a pistol that stopped the advance.

The killer kicked free of the stirrup, hurried to his valiant rescuer, and swung up behind the man. Spurring the steed, the rider put his horse into a gallop, and the two men, on one horse, escaped with $700.

They left behind a dead man inside the bank, a man who was not Major Samuel Cox. No, Cox, who had led the ambush that claimed Bloody Bill Anderson's life, was having his hair cut at a barbershop on the other side of the square during the murder. The dead man was Captain John Sheets, a Democrat and one of the most generous men in Daviess County. His widow would be brought to the bank, where she cradled her loving husband's bloody head in her arms and wailed with intense grief.

The robbers had also left something else behind, a fine bay mare, saddled. The posse lost the trail of the bandits, but a horse like that proved easy to identify.

I read the rest of the story.

As the Gallatin *North Missourian* recently reports, "Accompanied by two citizens of our town, the Clay County sheriff went to a home, but the killers were hiding in the barn and made off, killing the sheriff's horse and escaping as 20 or 30 shots fired at them proved ineffective. They are two brothers by the name of James."

Lowering the newspaper, I cursed.

Chapter Twenty

"Coleman," Ma said. I gripped her hand, but she had no strength, no will, to give me even the slightest squeeze. "I want to die at home."

"Ma," I told her, "you'll bury all of us."

"Take me home, Son." She turned her head and coughed that ragged cough, spitting flecks of blood onto the pillow. Tears briefly blurred my vision. Jim, John, and Bob approached while I untied my bandanna to wipe blood off my mother's lips.

God had cursed my mother with consumption. I could not grasp why He would do such a thing to such a wonderful woman who already had endured so much pain.

"Missouri," she said weakly.

I had no strength to deny my mother, though I wish I had. I let my mother go home. And that killed her.

Martha Anne, her husband, my brothers, and I agreed that we should send Ma back to Lee's Summit, but I should not go. Although no one had associated me yet with any crimes after the war, or with the James brothers, posses still mentioned my name. The war had not ended for Cole Younger.

Since Jim had served his punishment in Alton

after Quantrill's death, he decided to lead Ma back home. Retta went with him, as did Bob and John. Jim would see that they got settled, and then return to Texas and help me with my cattle kingdom. They left in April. By June, Ma was dead.

It didn't take long. Jim told me that a posse came visiting the old tenants' farm almost as soon as the Younger family had returned to Jackson County. While Jim was away, they rode up, demanding to know the whereabouts of Jim and me.

John snapped back at those dogs: "Jim Younger done his time in Illinois, and I ain't seen Cole in years."

"We'll be back, boy," the leader of the posse said, and they thundered off.

Ever the peacekeeper, Jim agreed that he should light a shuck back for Texas. When the posse realized that Jim and Cole weren't around, everyone could live in peace.

What fools we were. Those so-called lawmen returned, dragged John out of the house. Bob jumped to help, but a big cur shoved my brother down so hard, his head struck the side of the kitchen table, knocking him out cold. As Retta screamed, Ma ran to help Bob, but they shoved her down, too.

Six fine, upstanding citizens of Jackson County dragged John to the barn, threw a rope around his head, laughing as they did so. No, they did not hang John. They whipped him with a blacksnake, demanding to know my whereabouts. John was unconscious after the second stripe was laid on his back, and the men turned to Bob, who had regained some sense and pulled free from Ma, then darted outside to help John. They split Bob's lips, busted his nose, and knocked the breath out of him while Ma and Retta pleaded for mercy.

"You tell your son," the leader of the posse sang out, "that if he ever sets foot in Jackson County again, we'll bury the son-of-a-bitch."

That proved too much for Ma. She took to bed. A doctor came, treated John and Bob, but shook his head after examining my mother. She was worn out, had lost her will to live, and her lungs were pretty much gone. The deathwatch began. On June 6th, God called Ma home. The Browns and plenty of other good folks came to Ma's funeral. They buried Ma in the plot Belle and Richard had bought in Lee's Summit, and put a nice marble headstone on her grave. I thought about Pa, and how we had not even put a stone over his grave, fearing the red legs would desecrate his body.

"Pa should be lying next to Ma," I told Martha Anne after Bob returned to Texas to tell us the sad news.

"Pa's walking alongside Ma on the Streets of Gold, Cole," my sister told me. "It does not matter a whit where their bodies lay now."

• • •

Maybe Ma had held this family together. I don't know. Desperately I wanted those words Martha Anne had spoken to comfort me, but no solace came. Everything began to tumble around us.

Bob found himself a girl, took a job clerking in some dry-goods business, and planned to get married—till word started circulating around Dallas County that the Youngers were not all that respectable, that they butchered men, women, children, even babies—a bald-faced lie if ever I heard one. The girl told Bob she never wanted to see his face again.

Any time I rode into any town, cold stares bored through my back and the biddies started gossiping. It didn't seem right for me to stay in Texas, despite the cattle I ran. Having Cole Younger around made things hard for Martha Anne and her husband.

Fed up, Bob decided to return to Missouri. Jim wanted to visit Ma's grave, so he rode off with Bob. They figured they would settle in St. Clair County. After all, the only peace they had ever known since the war had been when they stayed with uncles in Appleton City and the Osage River country.

Then Brother John killed a lawman.

Tom Porter had worn a bushwhackers' shirt during the war, and had settled in Texas the way a number of us old Quantrill men had. I told John to stay clear of Porter, but he sounded like Bob.

"You ain't Dick." Laughing, he added: "You ain't Ma, either."

So John rode into Sceyne one cold January night in 1871, and took to drinking with Porter. A simpleton named Russell lived in town, and most folks treated him with kindness. But Tom Porter and John, well in their cups, plied Russell with forty-rod whiskey, made fun of him, and then decided to act out William Tell. There were no apples at that time of year, but Porter lent his pipe to Russell, backed the poor fool to the saloon's wall, and he and John began trying to shoot the pipe out of Russell's mouth.

Not as drunk as Porter, John finally holstered his gun, and when Porter started to reload his Colt, John stopped him. "Russell's had enough. Keep this up, we'll wear out our welcome. Let me buy you another drink."

That worked, but some drunken fool decided to improve the joke. After leading Russell outside, this man told him: "Those men mean to kill you. If I was you, I'd hurry down and fetch the law."

Which is what the simpleton did.

He alerted a deputy sheriff, a decent man named Charles Nichols—he had ridden with Jo Shelby during the war, and we often drank coffee together by the cattle pens. So Nichols walked into the saloon, hand on the butt of his pistol, and said: "What is going on here? You . . . John Younger. . . ."

After reloading, Porter had left his Colt on the bar as he drank. He spun, saw the badge, saw the hand on the revolver, and dropped his tumbler as he reached for the .44.

"No!" yelled Deputy Nichols as he pulled his pistol.

John, senses and sensibility clouded by rotgut, turned, too, and caught a bullet in his right arm fired by the deputy. I guess Nichols had aimed for Porter, but his first shot hit my brother, instead. Drunk, Porter missed his aim, as well, the bullet splintering the door above Nichols's head.

As John fell to the floor, Nichols put two shots into Tom Porter's chest, and the old bushwhacker slammed against the bar, rolling away from John. Nichols sent another round into the back of the man, already dead. Now, he turned the .44's barrel toward John, who had, in an act of self-defense, drawn the Navy .36 I had given him after the war.

John knew his right hand wasn't strong enough for a steady aim, but I had taught my brothers how to shoot all too well. He remembered the border shift I had shown Bob and him. The revolver flipped from right hand to left. Three bullets sent Nichols staggering out of the saloon and onto the street. Gut shot. It took the deputy four days to die.

"You've got to get 'em out of here, damn it!"

"Shut up, Lycurgus," I snapped at my brother-in-law, "and hand me that bottle."

Lycurgus A. Jones did not move. I ripped the sleeve off John's shirt, and studied the bullet wound. "Went straight through." I let out a breath. "Don't think it hit any bone."

"I didn't . . . mean . . . nothing . . . ," John stuttered as tears flowed down his pallid cheeks.

"Shut up." Whirling, I pointed a finger across the kitchen table at Lycurgus's face. "The bottle, damn you."

Fear had a strong hold on my in-law. Not fear for my brother's life, but for his business, his reputation. He still could not move. Maybe he could not even hear me.

It was Retta, who had just turned fifteen, who brought over the Kentucky bourbon.

"Can I have a drink?" John asked.

"You've had enough to drink," I snapped, and poured the good liquor over the two holes in his right arm. He screamed, and was still screaming when Martha Anne brought over the clean bandages. I began to dress the wound.

"You've done . . . this . . . before . . . ," Retta said.

I gave my baby sister a quick look, and tried to smile. "I've had some practice, honey," I said. "Don't fret. John'll be fine."

"But you . . . can't . . . stay . . . here . . . ," said Lycurgus haltingly, having found his voice again.

He was right. I knew that. Everyone in the house that horrible night understood what had happened. Briefly I closed my eyes, wishing that months ago I had lit a shuck for anywhere, and that I had taken John with me.

Retta said: "I'll saddle the two thoroughbreds."

Martha Anne said: "I'll pack you some grub."

I finished with the bandaging, and let John explain what had happened again, though he did not know why the lawman had come to the saloon—the particulars of which would be discovered in the months to come—and was too drunk to realize that, had he acted with any sense, he would probably have just been arrested until he sobered up and paid a fine the next morning.

"We'll have to ride hard," I told John, "at least till we get into the Indian Nations. You up to that?"

"Tie me to the horn if you need to, Cole."

After I helped him to his feet, and threw a great-coat over his shoulders, I led him to the door. Martha Anne handed me a sack of food, kissed my cheek, then John's, and stepped aside. The tears staining her face nearly broke my heart. I had come to Texas to get away from this kind of scene, only to bring misery and violence and blood to my sister's home. Eventually they would have to leave Texas, too.

"You take care of my cattle," I told Martha

Anne's husband, and even shook the bastard's hand. "That might ease the burden we've placed on you."

His head bobbed, and he went to his wife.

"Maybe you'll come back," Martha Anne said, sniffling as she tried to wipe away the tears. "When things settle down."

"Sure," I said, and Retta came through the door. I tousled her hair, kissed her forehead, and led John into the graying light that told us dawn would arrive shortly. "When things settle down, we'll pick things up. Don't you fret."

Oh, we all knew that would never happen. I had worn out my welcome in Texas, though I had broken no law. I was Cole Younger, which was bad enough. That dream of ranching, of living in peace, had died in a saloon in Dallas County, a saloon I had never even frequented.

I had no choice. Back to Missouri we rode.

Chapter Twenty-One

Home.

And my people shall dwell in a peaceable habitation, and in sure dwellings, and in quiet resting places. . . .

Isaiah, Chapter Thirty-Two, Verse Eighteen.

After leaving John with an uncle in Roscoe, I rode to Jackson County. I had picked some flowers in Harrisonville for Lizzie, but they had wilted a mite by the time I reached the Wayside Rest, removed my hat, wiped my boots on the mat, and knocked on the door.

Jack Brown, Lizzie's brother, opened the door, and the look he gave me caused me to step back. Stepping onto the porch, he quickly pulled the door shut.

"Bud," he said urgently, "what are you doing here?"

That struck me as a fool question, but I bit my tongue, and got down to the point. "Is Lizzie . . . ?"

He didn't let me finish, but I give Jack credit for not leaving me bleeding to death, dying real slow. No, sir, the boy killed me quick.

"Lizzie's married, Bud. Been married a couple years or so, now. Henry Clay Daniel. He's a lawyer. Got a big house in town."

I clenched the flowers behind my back. I said

something, though I don't remember exactly what. Good for her. Some idiotic comment.

"How's your mother?" I asked.

His head dropped. "She passed eighteen months ago."

"I'm sorry to hear that," I said, though death likely came as a blessing to that poor woman.

"Bud . . . Lizzie . . ."

Jack Brown stopped as I settled the hat on my head, saying: "You tell your sister that I came by . . . just to say howdy . . . and that I wish her all the happiness there is." *All the happiness that I would never know.* I even smiled, but don't know how I managed that. "Your pa doing fine?" I asked.

Jack's head nodded. "Probably at the tannery. You could drop by. He'd love . . ."

"Nah," I said before he had finished, then moved toward my horse. "Just tell him I come to say hello. Came up to see Jim and Bob, but now I'll be heading back down to Texas. Good to see you, Jack. Place looks fine. Real fine."

It looked like as rawhide of a place as I'd seen all across Cass County. Dumbly I climbed into the saddle, and rode off.

Now, I don't blame Lizzie Brown—I mean, Lizzie Daniel—at all. How long had I been in Texas? Had I ever written her? Did she know where to write me? Never had I ever asked Mr. Robert Allison Brown for his daughter's hand, or even the right to call on her. Lizzie owed me nothing. But, hell's fires could not have hurt as much as I hurt when I rode away from the Wayside Rest for the last time. I rode to my mother's grave.

It was quiet, peaceful, as I walked into the Lee's Summit cemetery. Dark at ten in the evening, but the moon peeked behind the clouds, guiding my way to Ma's grave. Kneeling, I placed the flowers by the headstone at the same time I took off my hat.

"Lizzie," I told my mother. "Picked these for her, Ma, you know, but . . . well . . ."

A bullbat disturbed the stillness, and I looked past the fence, but saw no threat, no posse, no one.

In the darkness, I smiled. "Should have just fed the flowers to Jo Shelby, I guess," I told Ma. Jo Shelby was the name I had ladled upon the thoroughbred I rode. "You rest easy, Ma. Don't you fret over me. I know what I'm doing. Know what I'm good at." I rose, put on my hat, and said in parting: "I'll be seeing you, Ma. Give Dick, and Pa, and Duck my love. Tell them I miss them all . . . badly."

When I swung into Jo Shelby's saddle, I thought about where I stood in life. No woman to love. No home. I could not visit my brother Jim without risking both of our lives should the law be watching. I didn't even feel safe visiting my mother's grave in the darkness of night. They had outlawed me, a man who wanted nothing but peace.

With nowhere to go, I rode to Kearney up in Clay County, bought a chicken from a butcher, found a Negro, and gave him directions to a farm outside of town, and a Liberty dollar. I told him to deliver the chicken to Mrs. Samuel and to tell her that Bud was waiting on the far side of the Rubicon.

"What are you doing?"

We sat at an Iowa farmhouse, waiting for the good woman to bring us breakfast after we had spent the night in her barn. I had taken pencil and paper and decided to write a letter, having disagreed with a statement some ink-slinger had posted in a St. Louis newspaper.

"Pointing out some egregious errors this scribe made in his account of the Lawrence raid," I told Jesse James.

"And they'll print it?" Jesse asked, leaning over to read my letter.

"Perhaps. It depends on the editor or publisher . . . or, I guess, whether they have space."

"Could you teach me how to write?" Jesse wondered aloud.

I set the pencil down. "Dingus, you know how to read and write better than some schoolmasters I had growing up."

Frank James and Clell Miller, who had ridden with Quantrill when very young, chortled.

"Yeah," Jesse said, "but not fancy writing. Not writing to newspapers kind of writing."

Frank pushed his cup away. "What would you write to a newspaper editor, Dingus?"

"Nothing about egregious errors," Jesse said. "But I like that guy who writes for the Kansas City *Times*."

"John Newman Edwards?" Frank asked.

Jesse's head bobbed with excitement. "He could straighten up that matter about what happened in Gallatin."

"What happened in Gallatin . . . ," Frank began, and I could tell Frank's dander was up, so I interjected: "Dingus, I'd be delighted to show you how to correspond with a newspaper editor."

"Really?"

" 'I am not the poet of goodness only . . . I do not decline to be the poet of wickedness, also.' "

He blinked. "Shakespeare?"

I smiled. "Walt Whitman."

"I knew it wasn't from the Bible," Jesse said, and, with that, he bowed his head—we followed the example—as the farmer's wife brought our supper. Jesse led us in prayer, we ate, and left the woman a $5 note. Frank gave her son a silk bandanna that the boy had fancied. Then we rode to Corydon.

• • •

Hard to believe, but it seemed as though half the county had converged into the Methodist church grounds that Saturday afternoon.

Every window on the church had been raised, and people stood ten deep behind each window, listening to the goings-on inside.

"Weddin'?" Clell Miller asked as we walked our horses toward the town square.

"Must be the prettiest girl in the state," I said.

"No wedding," Frank said. "Man's preaching too much fire and brimstone for a wedding." He pointed to the sign hanging in the bunting that stretched across the façade of a hotel.

Corydon Welcomes
HENRY CLAY DEAN
Bring On The Railroad

"By Jacks," Frank said as he shifted the tobacco in his mouth, "I always wanted to hear that fellow orate."

Who didn't? After all, Henry Clay Allen was said to be one of the fanciest speakers, best politicians, and master of words that the nation had ever known. Sure, he hailed from Pennsylvania, but he had the gumption to speak up against the war Mr. Lincoln had started, and, even if he did not hold with slavery, he didn't think we needed to kill each other over that.

Lawyer, preacher, stonemason, teacher, he was a fine Democrat—Yanks called him a Copperhead—who had gotten wise and moved across the border into Missouri, at Rebel Cove, earlier that year.

Frank and I swung off our horses near the northeast corner of the square and walked inside the Wayne County Treasurer's Office.

"Mister," I said, "I was hoping that you could change this note for me." I started to show him a $100 note.

"We're closed," he said as he pulled on his coat. The man was in such a hurry, I feared he might have recognized us and had a mind to fetch the law. "Vault's locked. Treasurer's at the church, and that's where I'm going, as much as I would love to oblige your request." Basically he shooed us out of the office onto the boardwalk. "Much obliged," he said as he locked the door, and started running toward the church. I blinked away astonishment, but the man turned as he ran, and pointed. "Bank's there. Maybe they can accommodate you gents."

We stared down the boardwalk toward the northwest corner. Frank motioned to Clell and Jesse, who, still holding the reins to our horses, started walking down the street.

Wasn't much to look at. A long, skinny frame building, a door between two windows, and a wooden façade hiding the slanted roof. Painted on the wood was: Obocock Brothers Bank of Corydon, Estb. 1870.

"Well?" Frank asked.

With a shrug, I tried the doorknob. To my surprise, the door opened.

"How about you let me go in this time, Buck?" Jesse called out to his brother.

"You'd do well to stay out of banks, Dingus," Frank answered.

His brother straightened with indignity. "Ain't my fault that son-of-a-bitch in Gallatin was the spitting image of a murdering bastard."

Letting Jesse pout, we stepped inside.

Parson, I know what you're thinking. Why would I return to "the owlhoot trail"? Well, perhaps I called it back when we started planning that deal in Liberty, Missouri, in 1866. Remember what I told Frank and Jesse? *We start this, and there's no turning back.* I had tried, tried hard, to forget those words, to remember my upbringing before the war turned Missouri crazy. However, fate, the law, the Yankees just wouldn't leave me be. Or maybe I lacked the willpower to follow the straight and narrow. Perhaps I was everything Kansans and Republicans were calling Cole Younger.

Ma's words from so long ago echoed in my head.

The devil gets ahold of you, Coleman.

Pulling out the bill, I asked one of the Obocock

boys, the only man inside the bank, for change.

"Be happy to oblige you, sir." He sure was a friendly cashier, but I decided he must be a Radical Republican. Otherwise, he would have been in the churchyard, ear craned toward an open window, trying to catch every word from Mr. Dean, the great debater.

"In that case . . ."—I pulled out the Navy—"maybe you can oblige us even further."

As Frank stuffed cash into our wheat sack, I tied up the cashier, stuck a gag in his mouth. When we were through, we walked out of the bank just as calm as could be. Hell, outside of the Methodist church, the town was pretty much deserted. After Frank handed Jesse the bag, we mounted the horses, backed them away from the hitching rail, and headed out of town.

Jesse led the way, so when he stopped in front of the picket fence, we reined up, too. I guess he couldn't help himself. Apparently Dean's speech was over, for crowds were filing out of the church. It wasn't long before I got my first look at Henry Clay Dean.

A small man, but with a big belly, black hair, thick mustache and beard, and dressed as sloppily as a town drunk. Plaid sack coat and striped britches, a bowler hat, green ascot with polka dots, a vest missing at least two buttons, and one pants leg tucked partly in a boot.

"Hey!" Jesse yelled. "I got something to say."

"Shut up!" a man in a gray suit yelled.

But Henry Clay Dean smiled, and, pointing, called out: "I yield to the man on horseback!"

"Well," Jesse said, standing in the stirrups now, and bowing toward Corydon's guest of honor, "you've been having your fun, whilst we've been having ours. You needn't go into hysterics when I tell you that we've just been down to the bank and robbed it of every dollar in the till. If you'll go there now, you'll find the cashier tied up. So, if you want any of us, why, just come down and take us. Thank you for your attention."

"Get out of here, you lying dog!" yelled a farmer.

Since everyone in town had been so obliging that day, we obliged him, spurring our horses, and hightailing hard for the Missouri state line.

Chapter Twenty-Two

The $10,000 we split lasted a while. It even got Clell Miller a pretty good lawyer after his arrest by deputy marshals. I'm not sure Clell needed a lawyer, for we sent plenty of friends—former bushwhackers—who swore on the Good Book that Clell had been with them, and nowhere near Corydon on June 3, 1871. Acquitted, Clell rode back to Missouri, and we had a few good laughs over several bottles of fine rye whiskey.

The law also sent out notices for Jesse James—the boy never should have tried to show up Henry Clay Dean, because people could describe him to a T after that grandstanding—but Jesse got his wish. He wrote a letter to John Newman Edwards, and the Kansas City *Times* printed it.

> As to Frank and I robbing a bank in Iowa or anywhere else, it is as base a falsehood as ever was uttered from human lips. I can prove, by some of the best citizens in Missouri, my whereabouts on the Third day of June, the day the bank was robbed, but it is useless for me to prove an alibi.

Of course, a man has to eat, keep his horses fed, and his guns loaded. Twenty-five hundred bucks doesn't last as long as you would think it might, not when you're on the run, helping your starving kinfolk, and paying a lot of money to be forgotten. A little less than a year later, the James boys, Clell Miller, and I met again at the Rubicon, where Jesse talked us into returning to Kentucky to visit a rich bank in Columbia. This time, we brought along my brother John.

I didn't care much for it, but John said, since he was already outlawed for killing a deputy sheriff in Texas, he might as well keep on that trail. If he didn't go with us, he swore that he would go it alone. Being the damned fool that I was, I thought maybe, if I kept my eye on John, I could keep him from getting killed.

This is how we did things. Once we had a bank in mind—in this case, the Deposit Bank in Columbia, Kentucky—we rode into the area, but never together. Since I knew cattle and horses, I would usually pretend to be a livestock buyer, and just chat up some folks. We stopped at farms, always polite, always courteous, and we tipped well. When it came time to do our business, we would ride into town. At least two of the boys went inside the bank, another stood at the door near the horses to make sure no legitimate customer went inside, while maybe two other boys stayed a distance from the bank, keeping watch. If something went wrong, those two men would cut loose, yell, scream, cuss, shoot, and make sure none of our "inside men" or "second squad" got hurt.

This particular bank stood on the edge of the square. Jesse, Clell Miller, and John rode into town from the Burksville Pike, dismounted, and led their horses into the alley. Clell and Jesse went inside, while John busied himself by the front door tamping tobacco into a pipe bowl.

At the square, Frank swung down off his sorrel, busied himself tightening his cinch. Folks figure that was some ploy, to keep citizens from suspicioning what strangers were up to, but it was more than that. No bank robber wanted to get caught, captured, and killed because of a loose cinch.

"You think this is a good idea?" I asked. I remained in the saddle, scanning the windows of businesses, the roof tops, looking for any sign of an ambush or nosy Kentuckians.

Frank brought his stirrup down from the saddle. " 'I have given Him my faith, and sworn my allegiance to Him; how, then, can I go back from this, and not be hanged as a traitor?' "

The night before at a boarding house at Russell Springs, Frank had whiled away the hours reading *Pilgrim's Progress*. It had been his father's favorite book.

I tried to think of some suitable retort, but I was not familiar with Mr. John Bunyan's work.

Besides, a gunshot boomed from inside the bank, and I cursed as I filled my hands with a pair of Navy Colts.

Since we started the ball in Liberty, bank robberies had become fairly regular events across the West. Folks, not wanting to lose their money, were charging onto the streets. Reins in my teeth, I pulled triggers, controlling the fine thoroughbred with knees and thighs. Riding with Quantrill had taught us the need for mounts that would not flinch at gunfire, would not scare, but would run like hell when given rein. We damned sure never rode into town on green or skittish horses.

"Time to skedaddle, gents!" Frank called out, spinning his horse, breaking panes of glass from the courthouse with well-aimed shots from his Remington.

One thing I remember about that job in Columbia. Some old gent sat on a rocking chair on the other side of the street. He rocked back and forth, and leaned over, trying to get a good look at us, it appeared. Other folks ran this way or that, diving behind water troughs or cracker barrels, or darting into the open doors of businesses. Women screamed for the town marshal, but he never showed his head. While men pointed at us, none dared draw a revolver or shoulder a rifle. But this jasper? He just rocked. Turned out that he was blind. At least that's what the Louisville *Journal* reported, but I know one thing for sure. As much noise as we were making with all of the shooting, that fellow must have been deaf, too.

John had already mounted, and was holding the reins to the horses for Jesse and Clell. Both men crashed through the door, with Clell firing two shots into the bank before leaping into his saddle. Jesse was the last to mount, for he held the wheat sack. Once his feet found the stirrups, he shouted: "Off the street, you damned fools! We're Lowry's gang! Lowry's gang!" He shot twice, spurred the mare, and took off for Burksville. We followed.

"The Lowry gang?" Frank asked after we turned off the pike. We were following a logging trail and had begun to circle back toward Columbia—Frank and I had figured that no posse would expect us to do that. Coming to a creek, we stopped to let our horses drink, shed our homespun and duck, and put on our businessmen clothes.

Jesse grinned. "Let the law go after the Lowry boys . . . instead of Jesse James."

"They'll have to go to Hades to catch the Lowry gang, Dingus," Clell said. "Last I heard about them . . . the last living one blowed his own head off with a shotgun."

"We're a mite pale in color to be confused for them boys, too," Frank said.

I cursed, for I did not care about a bunch of freedmen who had caused a stir in North Carolina and, as far as I knew, had never set foot in Kentucky. Besides, as Clell Miller had just mentioned, they were all dead and buried. Something bad had happened inside the bank, for Brother John remained as pale as a freshly laundered sheet.

I asked: "So what happened inside?"

"Damned fool cashier wouldn't open the vault," Jesse answered, tossing the wheat sack to his brother.

"Did he look like Major Cox, too?" I said.

That knocked the smirk right off Jesse's face.

Clell Miller cleared his throat. "The fool went for a pistol. Dingus had no choice."

I let out a heavy sigh, not able to look again at my younger brother. He had killed a lawman in Texas in self-defense, although we doubted any jury or judge would see things that way. Now he was an accessory to a murder committed during a bank robbery.

"Damnation." Frank looked up from the sack, and sprayed a sweet-gum tree with tobacco juice. "I don't think there's six hundred bucks in here."

Which barely left enough to get us back home. So, yeah, Parson, I went with Frank and Jesse to the Kansas City Fair in September. It was a pretty good idea, as brazen as a shavetail Yankee lieutenant chasing glory, and I hand all the credit to Jesse.

"We ride straight up to the ticket gates," Jesse explained. "Ten, fifteen, maybe twenty thousand people." He tapped the headline in the *Times*. "That's how many will be there, according to this here newspaper. All buying tickets."

"Ten, fifteen, twenty thousand eyewitnesses," Frank warned him.

"Uhn-huh." Jesse grinned. Damn, he could charm a fire-breathing Baptist out of his Bible when he smiled like that. "And they'll think we're just part of the show."

It netted us only $1,000 for, damn our luck, the cashiers had just emptied the tills and sent most of the loot to the bank right before we rode up to the ticket gates. As I held the reins to Jesse's horse, and Frank held his Remington, Jesse went right up to the cashier.

"What would you do if I told you I am Jesse James and I am robbing you?" he stated.

The man looked up from the tin box, snarled, and said: "I'd tell you to go to hell."

"Funny"—Jesse placed a long-barreled Colt under the man's nose—"because I am Jesse, I am robbing you, and if you don't do as I say, you'll be the one going to hell."

He snatched the box, pushed the cashier down, and ran to the bay mare, tossing the tin to me. Yet as Jesse tried to put a foot in the stirrup, the fool cashier came at him in a running dive, knocking Jesse to the ground. His horse, of course, did not bolt, even when Frank fired a shot at the cashier. The bullet whined off the gravel, the cashier screamed like a catamount, and then I saw a girl—nine, maybe ten, years old—yell as she clutched her leg, and fell. Her mother and father raced to her, shielding her body with their own. Frank swore, punched the sky with two more shots, and I aimed my Navy at the cashier, who had quit playing hero. Jesse leaped into the saddle.

We rode out of the fairgrounds at a high lope, and did not stop until we had crossed the Rubicon.

"The idea," I said as I divided up our bounty, "is not to announce ourselves."

"I figured it was just like the Lowry gang in Kentucky," Jesse explained, wadding up a stack of bills and stuffing them inside his coat pocket. "Someone points a finger at us, we can say what you just said. Lowry gang didn't rob the bank in Columbia. Jesse James wasn't anywhere near the Kansas City fairgrounds."

The next time we met, Jesse showed us a copy of the Kansas City *Times*.

There is a dash of tiger blood in the veins of all men, the prose began, a latent disposition, even in the bosom that is a stranger to nerve and daring, to admire those qualities in other men.

I pushed my hat back and listened as Jesse read: "'. . . But a feat of stupendous nerve and fearlessness that makes one's hair rise to think of it with a condiment of crime to season it, become chivalric; poetic; superb.'"

We had robbed a fair in broad daylight. We had wounded a little girl. Yet this newspaper account made us out to be Robin Hood or Lancelot, and not the "thieves and pickpockets and burglars and garrotters in Kansas City."

"'. . . What they did,'" Jesse continued to read, "'we condemn. But the way they did it we cannot help admiring. . . .'"

He folded the newspaper, leaned back, and sipped rye. "What do you think?"

Frank simply nodded, but I had to shake my head, whistling. "Well," I conceded, "that John Newman Edwards can turn a phrase every once in a while."

"You like it?" Jesse couldn't hide his excitement or astonishment that I was pleased.

"I like it," I said.

But what Jesse wrote a short while later brought out the wrath of Thomas Coleman Younger.

Chapter Twenty-Three

It is generally talked about in Liberty, Clay County, that Mr. James Chiles, of Independence, said that it was me and Cole and John Younger that robbed the gate, for he saw us and talked to us on the road to Kansas City the day of September 26th. I know very well that Mr. Chiles did not say so, for he has not seen me for three months, and I will be under many obligations to him if he will drop a few lines to the public, and let it know that he never said such a thing.

Jesse James
Clay County

I balled up the *Times* and threw it at Jesse.

"You damned fool. You mention my name. You mention John's . . . when John was not anywhere near Kansas City when we robbed the fair. What the hell were you thinking?"

Maybe there had been some rumors, some gossip tossed out in the back pews of churches or at the bars in saloons, but no one had ever put in print that Cole Younger, or John, had been riding with Frank and Jesse James. Hell, yeah, I was mad. Putting my name out there was one thing, but John had not been part of our deal at the fairgrounds.

"Jim Chiles saw me and Buck," Jesse explained. "Buck wanted to go see that gal he's sweet on in Independence."

"Leave Annie out of this, Dingus," Frank said.

"Well, anyhow, we were riding with Clell Miller to meet up with you. Jim must have mistook Clell for John, and Buck for you."

I shook my head, took the bottle Frank offered me, and had a long pull, but liquor cured nothing.

"I'm sure," Frank said, "that this Jim Chiles will do as you wish . . . say we were not involved."

An eerie darkness clouded Jesse's face. He could be a charmer when he wanted to be, but when one of those moods struck him, you saw death in his eyes.

"Oh, yeah. Chiles will do exactly as I say. We've already had a little chat about his mouth."

Be not deceived; God is not mocked: for whatsoever a man soweth, that shall he also reap.

Galatians, Chapter Six, Verse Seven.

I had no one to blame for this, except myself. I had led my brother astray, and I had chosen to ride with Frank and Jesse. Oh, sure, I wrote a letter myself. Jesse had his pressman in John Newman Edwards, but I had some connections myself. My sister Martha Anne had moved back to Missouri, and her husband worked for the Pleasant Hill *Review*, so I met with him, gave him my own letter, which he published. Sure, I denied being there, which was a lie. I wrote that John was not there, which was the truth. But maybe the most truthful thing I put in the letter was this: We were not on good terms at that time, I said of Jesse and me, nor have we been for several years.

Looking back, I should have kept my trap shut. All that did was keep the Younger boys in the news. Word got down to Texas, where Jim had returned, and landed a job—if you can believe this—with the Dallas Police Department. And when another peace officer was arrested for a robbery, he said Jim was with him. Hell, why should that man be any different? Half the crimes being committed in the country were now being laid at our door. The Youngers, like the James boys, had become ubiquitous.

Facing an indictment, Jim fled Texas, and met us at the Rubicon. This time, Bob came with him, as did John. Officially, we were now the James-Younger Gang.

Others rode with us from time to time. Arthur McCoy, the old "Wild Irishman" who had ridden with Jo Shelby. Bushwhacking comrades Clell Miller, Jim Cummins, Ed Miller, Bill Ryan, Tom Webb, Charlie Pitts.

Yes, Parson, I lost my way. The St. Genevieve Savings Bank in Missouri netted us $4,000 during the spring of 1873. Sure, I was there, and not, as I've always claimed, nursing some sick neighbor down Roscoe way. The sad part about this was the fun we began to have. Drinking, racing horses, gambling, consorting with lewd women. We laughed a lot, and it felt good to be with John, Jim, and Bob, or whoever rode with us. We were family. From time to time, by Jehovah, I didn't even mind Jesse. It was his idea to rob that train in Iowa.

Well in his cups, The Wild Irishman, Arthur McCoy, tied a knot around the rail on the other side of a curve, dallied the rope over his saddle horn, and put the spurs to his roan, which strained and struggled while Clell Miller and Charlie Pitts pounded on the iron with a hammer and spike bar we had stolen from a hand-car house near Adair.

"What are we doing this for, Dingus?" Frank asked.

Jesse pointed at McCoy. "That's the way the boys did it in Kentucky during the war. Ain't that right, McCoy?"

"Right as rain," McCoy said.

Eventually the rail came loose and tumbled down the incline. We left it there, mounted our horses, and rode up a bank to hide in some woods and wait for the Chicago, Rock Island & Pacific to bring us a fortune in bullion. Long around seven o'clock that evening, we saw the black smoke from the engine, heard the wheels clicking, and watched the train round the curve.

It was a hell of a thing to see. Sparks flew as the

engineer hit the brakes, but he had no chance. The locomotive slammed off the rail and toppled over in the ditch, steam hissing, as the tender, express and baggage cars followed, toppling down the embankment and landing on their sides. The three passenger cars somehow managed to stay on the rails, but the last one slammed into the middle car, crushing perhaps the back third, while the caboose popped loose and rolled backward maybe fifty rods.

People were shrieking and moaning, and I thought for sure that the boiler would blow, but the brakeman must have shut off the valve. Anyway, we saw the brakeman first, bleeding, burned, and banged up considerably, but somehow dragging the engineer from the engine's cab. Even from the woods, I knew, from the way the engineer's head rolled about, that the man was dead as he ever would be.

"Golly," Jesse said.

Frank spurred his bay forward, and, with masks covering our faces, we rode out of the woods, firing pistols in the air. Most of the boys headed for the express car, but I led my brothers to the passenger cars still on the tracks. Men and women were dropping from the windows, staggering away from the wreckage.

"Stay where you are!" I yelled, and sent a bullet into the night sky. "Stay where you are and you won't be hurt."

Gun drawn, John swung from his sorrel and made a beeline for a drummer with a satchel, money belt, and bowler, but I stopped him. He spun around, staring at me.

"We don't rob citizens," I said.

We didn't. Not then, at least. I kept telling myself that we took money from banks, not people, and railroads, which robbed our people blind. If such is your ambition, you can convince yourself of anything.

"Watch them," I said, turning my horse. "Let them out, but keep them by the cars. And don't steal as much as a kiss from a pretty girl." I crossed the tracks, and eased my way to the express car. Charlie Pitts and Clell Miller waited on the ground, while Frank and McCoy stood on the side of the overturned car, having pulled the door open. Inside, I could hear Jesse's voice.

"Damn you, we are grangers. We rob the rich and give to the poor. Where is the bullion? The bullion? Where is it?"

He poked his head out of the door. The white mask hiding his face had been removed. Sometimes, I think Jesse wanted everyone to recognize him. "I need help," he was saying. "Help. Such a set of robbers as you are . . . get in here and help me."

McCoy jumped in, with Pitts and Clell following, while Frank shook his head, climbed down, and took his horse's reins.

Once again, Jesse's head appeared. "Damnation, we need a wagon."

As he bit off a chaw of tobacco, Frank turned, working the tobacco with his teeth. "Why don't you ride back to Adair and rent us one?"

For the son of a Baptist preacher, Jesse replied with an oath that would have gotten his hide flayed and his mouth washed out with soap had he used such language in front of his mother.

"Get what you can," I told him, "and let's ride."

McCoy came up with heavy sacks. He had followed Jesse's example and removed his mask.

Some old man had climbed out of one of the cars and assaulted us with boisterous talk. "You scoundrels can go to hell! Who's with me? Come on. Come out, follow me, and let us go for these villains!" No one joined him, of course, but he went right on yelling. He was still yelling when we rode off. As his voice trailed off, we dashed for the state line.

"This is all y'all got?" Frank said, looking up from the sack.

Dawn had found us among the hickory, oak, and razor ridges of the Loess Hills east of the Missouri River.

"How much is there?" Brother John asked.

With a shrug, Frank said: "Two thousand . . . maybe."

That prompted a loud whistle from Arthur

McCoy. "That'll make me a favorite with the ladies in Saint Louey . . . and keep me drunker than Hooter's goat for a coon's age."

Ignoring the loud-mouth, Frank stared harder at his brother. "Where the hell's the bullion, Dingus? That train was supposed to be hauling seventy-five thousand in gold and silver."

"Wasn't no bullion," Jesse said defensively. "Must've been on another train."

Frank spit.

"He's right, Bud," Charlie Pitts said. "Dingus asked for the bullion, and that damned express-man, he just pointed at some bars scattered amidst all the other truck and garbage. That was some wreck."

"Bars?" I asked.

"Yeah," Jesse said. "Like lead bars. No use to us."

Well, it had been mighty dark inside that express car. Frank stared at me, and finally I started grinning, then laughing.

Yes, this was the great James-Younger Gang, robbing from the rich to give to the poor, men who schemed robberies like Robert E. Lee planned battles. Strategists we were. Players of chess. Men who did not know what bullion looked like. On the other hand, Jesse had been right. We needed a wagon for that job, and $2,000 seemed better than a hangman's noose.

"I suppose you could have done better,

Bud," Jesse hissed, finding no humor that morning.

All laughter stopped. "I don't suppose, Dingus."

"All right. You try leading this outfit," he said.

Frank and I exchanged glances, then turned back toward Jesse. Before I could open my mouth, Frank had started.

"The way I remember things, Dingus, is that you were working the farm with Ma and the doc when Cole and I were riding with Quantrill. That Cole and I were at Lawrence, and that you didn't get your nose bloodied till you up and joined with Bloody Bill."

"I got more than my nose bloodied, Buck." Jesse was dead right about that.

"Yep. But I don't recall you being elected captain of this outfit."

Truth is, none of us had. Ours was a loose-fitting group. You rode with us if you were invited, and if you had a like mind. We divided evenly, and our captains changed with the wind. Jesse had led us at Adair, Columbia, Russellville. I guess Frank and I had planned Liberty. I'm not sure anyone organized the Corydon robbery. And that little spree we went on in 1874? Well, we all had a hand in those jobs.

Chapter Twenty-Four

During the fall of 1873, Jesse, Frank—and even Arthur McCoy—had their say in a supplement to the St. Louis *Dispatch*. John Newman Edwards had left the *Times* and moved east, taking a job in St. Louis, and we met with him outside of town near Daniel Boone's old haunts. Jesse wanted to meet the journalist in person, and, as a storied newspaperman, Edwards felt delighted at the opportunity to interview Jesse James, and other outlaws. I was there for that meeting, too.

He titled his article "A Terrible Quintette", Edwards's sanitized essay about five Missouri boys, unable to live in peace after the war, now pursued by lawmen. Frank, McCoy, John, and I made out all right, I guess, but you could tell just by reading that Edwards loved Jesse, or who he thought Jesse was, maybe even who he had turned Jesse into. I didn't care that much for the article, as most of it quoted Jesse denying that he or Frank had been involved in any robbery. He never denied any Younger presence, though. Jesse became a saint. Maybe he became the leader of our gang.

On a cold December night that year, Frank, Jesse, Clell Miller, John, and I met at the Rubicon.

"Where's McCoy?" John asked.

"He talked too damned much," Jesse said.

Talked? Past tense. John shot me a look, but we asked no questions. Hell, none of us had cared much for the Wild Irishman, anyhow. "Forget about him. Let's ride."

Most farmers we met showed kindness to us. We would stop at some home, ask for food or shelter, and we always left one of our men outside with the horses. We chopped wood for the farmers, and we paid for our meals in gold, silver, or greenbacks, and we paid very well.

With posses increasing in Missouri, we decided to spend some time down south in Louisiana. Knowing that we would likely find some work to do wherever we went, I wanted the best horses I could find—in case a posse came after us. I knew exactly where to find one for myself.

Everyone in Clay County claimed that Maise Walker raised the best horses in the state. So I rode to the farm on the other side of Liberty late one evening, dismounted, and climbed to the top pole of a round pen. Maybe a dozen horses moved around in the corral, and the worst of the lot would have sold for prime.

The one catching my eye, however, did not rank among the worst. A chestnut, she stood fifteen hands, short-backed, deep-girthed, and carrying her tail in a high arch, full of vim and vigor. Her shoulders were long and sloping, and her eyes brimmed with a fiery confidence whenever she studied me. A horse like that would carry a man far.

"Howdy, Cole."

Turning, I gave Maise Walker a nod and smile, and stuck my thumb out toward the chestnut. "Admiring your horses, Mister Walker," I said. "I'd like that mare yonder."

Maise Walker had forty pounds over me, and I was not a small man. His muscles strained at the threads of his muslin shirt, and his hands looked like hams. Neighbors said he had little use for firearms, but, before I could jump, he had reached behind his back and pulled an old Colt Dragoon.

He waved the big .44 at my face. "You'll pay gold, Cole," he demanded.

"Such was my intention, sir." My left hand came out of my vest pocket with a leather pouch that jingled. Maise Walker's Dragoon disappeared, though how a man could carry a massive horse pistol stuck in his waistband at the small of his back intrigued me.

I rode out with a bill of sale in my pocket.

So we drifted down to Louisiana, gambling in Shreveport, where Jesse wrote a letter to the St. Louis *Dispatch* denying any involvement in the Adair train robbery. He said he was in Deer Lodge, Montana, and thought that to be a fine, fine joke. By January, the weather turned bitterly cold, so, donning heavy Yankee greatcoats, we drifted back home. That's when Jesse got the idea to rob the eastbound Shreveport-Monroe stagecoach.

While Frank, Jesse, Clell, John, and I began retrieving valuables from passengers, the westbound stagecoach rode up—so we robbed that one, too. The eastbound netted us $800, or so. The westbound, on the other hand, carried no passengers, and no mail, so we paid the driver $5 for his trouble, and sent him on his way. That made us laugh, and we decided to refund the eastbound folks $5 or $10 for their troubles. We also stole newspapers to read on the ride north and to help us start campfires. About an hour later, we galloped toward the Arkansas border.

Well, Jesse felt quite satisfied with our haul, which chafed Frank. So Frank came up with the idea to rob the Malvern-Hot Springs stage as we left Hot Springs after enjoying the nepenthe and relief of those warm, healing waters.

That one wasn't really well planned, either. Spotting the stagecoach, we got out of the road, and let it pass. Then Frank pulled a double-barrel shotgun from the scabbard, brought a bandanna up over his mouth and nose, turned his sorrel, and put the spurs to her. Laughing, we followed his example.

"Stop this coach," Frank told the driver, pointing the shotgun in the stunned man's face. "Or I'll blow your damned head off."

The driver stopped, and back to work we went.

When I jerked the door open, the first gent I saw was an old man with a wooden leg. "You stay put, old-timer," I said. "But the rest of you . . ." Feeling like a gentleman, I held the door open, and chatted with the invalid while John, Clell, and the James boys went to work.

Hot Springs drew all sorts, including plenty of Yankees. Jesse collected a fine gold watch, plenty of cash, and a diamond pin from a guy from Dakota Territory. Frank relieved a Massachusetts Yankee of more than $650. While the others deposited valuables into the grain sack Clell held, something came over me of a sudden.

"Did any of you wear the gray during the late war?" I asked.

An old man nodded. With the barrel of Navy Colt, I motioned him over.

"What's your name, sir?"

"Crump," he said, staring at his feet.

"Collect what we took from you, Mister Crump," I said. "We do not rob former Confederate soldiers."

Of course, Jesse had to get the last word in. "We do not rob our comrades with the Confederacy," he said, sounding a lot like John Newman Edwards. "It is Northern men that we seek. For men of the North drove us into outlawry, and we shall make them pay for such unjust treatment."

Our haul was right around $2,000, including

the watches and like. Frank explained to Jesse: "A stagecoach bringing folks to Hot Springs should be more promising than two stagecoaches bound for Shreveport or Monroe, Dingus."

Jesse chuckled at the mock rebuke. "Well, all this proves is that we James boys have better ideas than our Younger minions."

Ah, but I was already thinking of a plan. One of the Arkansas newspapers we had taken off the Shreveport coach had printed a train schedule and a small article about a railroad.

"Boys," I announced as we followed a road that ran alongside the Cairo and Fullerton Railroad line. "I have a plan for a job myself." Mine would net us more money than any stagecoach job, I figured, and give me an opportunity to show how I could hornswoggle the press, too.

As we drifted northeast, toward Cairo, Illinois, I turned to Frank and asked: "How would Gads Hill strike you, Buck?"

Frank laughed, and quoted from "Henry IV", Part I: "'. . . at Gad's Hill! There are pilgrims going to Canterbury with rich offerings, and traders riding to London with fat purses.'"

Shaking his head, Jesse spit in the cold. Frank thought of another line: "'If you will go, I will stuff our purses full of crowns.'"

Grinning at my pal, I said: "I figured you'd like the symbolism, Buck."

"What are you two talking about?" Jesse asked.

" 'Henry the Fourth', Part One," Frank explained.

"If it ain't in the Bible," Jesse said, "I don't care about it."

"It's not about the Bible or the Bard," I said. "It's about a train. And a little faraway place that actually got its name from Charles Dickens. It's about money, Dingus. Does that interest you?"

Gads Hill lay in the rough country in the southeastern corner of the state, right on the tracks of the St. Louis, Iron Mountain, and Southern Railway. Turning north, we followed the Black River into southeastern Missouri. We spent the night in the barn on a widow's farm outside of Piedmont, and rode into Gads Hill around 3:00 p.m. the next day.

Three houses, a station platform, a mercantile, and a sawmill that no longer had any saws and probably had not seen a speck of sawdust in ten years. The place wasn't anything more than a flag station for the railroad.

"This?" Jesse shook his head and let out a mirthless chuckle.

"Gather the citizens, John," I said. "Tell them it's a camp meeting."

The only gun we found was at the mercantile, and the owner gave it up a lot quicker than he did the money in his till.

When we had corralled the citizens, poor folks

with their young 'uns, we built up a good fire to keep them warm while we sat around, smoking and waiting. About an hour later, after checking the schedule I had liberated, I snapped shut my gold watch. "About that time," I said, and directed Frank to set the red flag on the side of the tracks. Five minutes later, the Number Seven came into view, chugging hard on the grade. The engineer stuck his head out the cab, saw the flag, and hit the brakes.

Slowly, but perfectly the train pulled to a stop at the station.

"That, Dingus," I whispered, "is how you stop a train."

As the engineer and conductor ran to me, I drew my Navy, and thus began our fun.

Jesse took the express car, liberating bills, coin, and the Adams agent's revolver, and even signed the receipt book: Robbed at Gads Hill.

John stayed by the station, chatting with the engineer, fireman, brakeman, and conductor, while keeping an eye on the citizens still hovering by the bonfire. Clell, Frank, and I visited the other cars—a smoker, a ladies car, and a Pullman sleeper.

"We robbing citizens now?" Clell whispered.

"Depends on the citizens," I said, and fired a shot into the ceiling of the first car. I had determined that more Yankees would ride this train. "Show us your hands!"

Frank picked up on my intention. "For we do not wish to rob ladies or working men."

I stopped to study a pair of weasels in blue suits and brown hats. "What do you plug-hats do?" I asked.

The older one ground his teeth. His fool underling said: "We're bankers."

"Bankers?" I laughed, and stepped aside as Clell leaned over with his wheat sack.

"Why don't y'all make a deposit?" Clell suggested.

A spindly gent sat alone at the rear of the car, long-nosed, big-eared, bald, and pale. He put a coin purse, a ring, and a billfold into Clell's bag.

"What do you do?" Clell asked.

"I preach the Word of God," he said softly.

"Take back your money, Reverend," I said. "And pray for us."

I'm not altogether certain that he prayed on our behalf, but he did get his valuables back.

Now, this was not the greatest crime we had or would ever pull off, but it had to be the most fun. On our way out of the cars, we stopped again to torment the two plug-hats, and forced them outside. They thought we would kill them, but all we did was make them strip down to their unmentionables, and take a stroll into the woods.

Frank gave back a watch when the baggage master said it had been a present, and I made faces at a pretty little baby that made both her and her ma smile. The daddy didn't care much for it, though.

When we were done, we walked back toward the engine, where Jesse and John had already mounted.

"Mister Wetton"—Frank stuck his hand out toward the engineer—"it has been our pleasure. Should you see any other red flags down the line, I think you would do well to stop."

The rest of us shook hands, too, those already mounted leaning down and extending their hands. We thanked the conductor, the brakeman, gave them our best, and tipped our hats to the citizens of Gads Hill still warming themselves by the bonfire.

Frank gave them one more bit of Shakespeare. " 'And I have heard it said, unbidden guests are often welcomest when they are gone.' "

"Henry VI", Part I, Act II, Scene Two.

Before I climbed aboard my Arab mare, I pulled a piece of paper from my coat pocket, and gave it to the conductor.

"Would you see that this is telegraphed to the *Dispatch* in Saint Louis, sir?"

The conductor blinked, swallowed, and said: "Certainly, Mister . . . James?"

That got Jesse to howling so hard, I thought he would taste gravel.

"Have a good day," was all I could think to say. I mounted the mare, and we rode out of the sleepy settlement.

The conductor proved a man of his word, and the St. Louis *Dispatch* published the article, which I have kept all these years and now paste below.

THE MOST DARING ROBBERY ON RECORD!

The southbound train on the Iron Mountain railroad was robbed here this morning by five heavily armed men, and robbed of _____ dollars. The robbers arrived at the station a few minutes before the arrival of the train, and arrested the agent, put him under guard, and then threw the train on the switch. The robbers are all large men, none of them under six feet tall. They were all masked, and stared in a southerly direction after they had robbed the train, all mounted on fine-blooded horses. There is a hell of excitement in this part of the country.

We rode northwest, of course, and not all of us stood six feet tall. I was just shy of that height myself.

Turned out, though, that everyone in the world thought the article had been written by one Jesse James. I guess he got the last laugh, though we made off with $3,000.

Chapter Twenty-Five

Ah, but what we—what I—failed to understand was that robbing trains changed things for the James-Younger Gang. We had robbed an express car, in Adair and at Gads Hill, and express companies frowned upon such actions. They sought out the Pinkerton Detective Agency, and that slippery Scottish spy, Allan Pinkerton, and his stealthy agents made it their personal ambition to catch or kill us.

Of course, we didn't think too much about Pinkertons as 1874 rolled along. Jesse married his cousin, Zee, in the parlor of her sister's home in Kansas City. Annie Ralston and Frank eloped. Jim kept playing patty-cake with Cora McNeill. Which got me brooding, drinking, and moaning, though never in front of the boys. I did ride by the Daniel house in Harrisonville one night. I guess Lizzie had brought the piano from the old Wayside Rest with her, because music hummed out of the window, and I saw her shadow through the curtains while she sat, fingers tickling ivories and ebonies. Her voice remained so lovely as she sang "In the Sweet By and By".

"She sounds heavenly, doesn't she?" said a voice in the dark.

My head turned, while my right hand reached

for a rim-fire Smith & Wesson in my coat pocket just before I saw the badge gleaming from the street lamp. The constable grinned up at me, and I relaxed, returning my hands to rest on the saddle horn.

"She does indeed," I said.

His head cocked and he wet his lips. "Do I know you, sir?"

"No, sir." I studied his pockmarked, boyish face. I doubted if he was twenty years old. "I don't recognize you, Officer, and unless you come from Sherman, Texas, I doubt if we have met."

"Texas . . . by thunder. You are far from home."

Tears probably welled in my eyes. The girl I loved, who I had known pretty much all my life, played piano in a fine wooden house. Strangers lived in the house we had owned, two blocks east and west. The livery Dick had owned had been torn down, and a wagon yard put up in its place. My father's mercantile was now a grocery.

"Yes," I managed to say. "I am far from home. Heading to Kansas City."

"It's a long way to be riding, sir, at night."

"I like the night," I said. Reaching down, I shook the lawman's hand. "I am Captain J.C. King." I would use that alias a few more times over my career. I hooked my thumb toward the Daniel home. Lizzie had moved on to play "The Ship That Never Returned".

"Who is that angel?" I asked.

"That's Missus Elizabeth Daniel, Captain King. Her husband is an attorney here in Harrisonville . . . for now. I dare say he'll be a judge before long, maybe even congressman or mayor."

I nodded. "I might have need of a good judge, or lawyer. Not so certain about a politician, though."

The policeman laughed. Picking up the reins I had dropped over Jo Shelby's neck, I smiled: "Mister Daniel is a lucky man. Nice chatting with you, sir."

"Safe journey, Captain King." I kicked the Arabian into a walk, and rode out of town, the melody of Lizzie's fast-beat tune, and her voice, following me into the darkness.

"Only one more trip," said a gallant seaman,
As he kissed his weeping wife,
"Only one more bag of the golden treasure
"And 'twill last us all through life.
"Then I'll spend my days in my cozy cottage
"And enjoy the rest I've earned."
But alas! poor man! For he sail'd commander
Of the ship that never returned.

I rode back to St. Clair County to visit my brothers. Bob kept talking about starting a farm, and Jim swore that he was through with robbing and stealing. I didn't blame them. Of course, you could not talk John out of following the trail I had blazed for him.

"There's some good land at Hot Springs," I told

Jim and Bob. We sat on the porch of our uncle's house, rocking in the cool but pleasant March air. About that time, we heard the clopping of hoofs, and immediately we filled our hands with revolvers, waiting, watching, breathing slowly. One horse. The rider appeared at the edge of the woods, reining in immediately, and bringing up both of his hands.

"Bud?" he called out. "John?"

"Clell Miller," I said softly, keeping my hand on my revolver butt as I raised my voice and said: "Come along, Clell."

Lather coated his buckskin mare, and Clell looked worn out himself. "Buck sent me," Clell said. "Some trouble down at their farm."

"They all right?" John asked.

Clell Miller grinned. "Yeah. They're fine. But a damned Pinkerton detective sure ain't."

The Pinkerton man's name was Joseph W. Whicher, and if every detective were as stupid as this fool, Pinkerton would have gone out of business well before 1874. The way Clell Miller told us the story, Whicher came up to the James farm pretending to be a laborer looking for work. Farm workers usually have calloused hands. Whicher didn't.

Later, we learned that Whicher had chatted with two lawmen in Liberty after arriving from Chicago. The lawmen warned him not to try anything, but Whicher must have considered himself immortal. Which he was not.

From Liberty, he caught the train to Kearney, and put his plan into motion. The next morning, a peddler found his body along the Lexington-Liberty fork, with a note pinned to his chest: THIS TO ALL DETECTIVES.

Well, Clell didn't say who murdered the spy, and I didn't ask. Jesse would be my guess, but like Sheriff Alexander Doniphan warned Whicher back in Liberty: "Son, Missus James herself will murder you quick as Frank or Jesse would."

Having the Pinkertons in our midst did put a caution in my bones. Jim pushed us, so I agreed to take John and Bob with me to Arkansas, maybe find some good bottom land and get Bob set up farming. John, though, reared his mule head.

"I ain't running from no Yankee spy," he said. "There's a dance next week in La Cynge, and I aim to hear some fiddle music."

Jim shook his head. "If it's fiddling you want to hear, I'll oblige you." Jim reached for his fiddle.

"You saw real good, Jim, but there ain't no gals here to cut the rug with. And they's plenty in La Cynge. There's plenty of *la sin* in La Cynge." He laughed at his joke.

We argued, but John could be a hard rock when he felt ornery. Eventually we reached a compromise. Jim would ride with John to La Cynge, a fun little town with a handful of saloons just across the Kansas line. They'd spend the night with Uncle John and Aunt Hannah in their cabin a few miles outside of Monegaw.

I took Bob with me, but we found no farmland. A few days later, Jim and John rode to La Cynge, did their share of dancing, returned to Monegaw, danced some more in the hotel—Jim playing the fiddle—and stopped at Theodrick Snuffer's place on the Old Timber Road north of Roscoe. That's where they were when the Pinkerton man and a deputy sheriff showed up.

When they heard the horses, my brothers climbed into the attic and crawled toward the porch where they could spy on the strangers through a small crack. Old Man Snuffer walked to the door.

" 'Morning," Deputy Ed Daniels said.

"Howdy," said Old Man Snuffer.

"We kind of lost our way," said the other man, and he pushed back his linen duster. "I'm looking for cattle to buy, and the preacher in Monegaw suggested that I find the Widow Sims."

"You ridin' along, Sheriff, to make sure the widow don't cheat this stranger?" Old Man Snuffer grinned.

So did Ed Daniels, but it wasn't a fun grin. Sweat beaded his forehead, and it was only March.

"Well, I don't get this way much," the deputy said. "Ran into this gent, and thought I could find my way. But . . ." He shrugged.

"Sure." Theodrick Snuffer gave directions, watched them mount their horses, and ride through the gate. By the time the strangers and the deputy were out of sight, Jim and John had climbed out of the attic.

"They're packing a lot of guns for cattle buyers," John said. "The Widow Sims ain't that dangerous."

"No wonder they got lost," Old Man Snuffer said. "Can't follow directions worth spit. Told 'em to ride to the Old Road and turn east. They're goin' northwest, up toward Monegaw."

"They're detectives!" John shouted.

"Let them be," Jim said. "They're gone."

"You can't let detectives alone."

"Maybe Ed Daniels doesn't have the brains of a turnip," Jim said, and filled his cup with coffee.

"Maybe you're yellow," John said.

Now, I wish Jim had done what I would have, and just laid John out with a right to that hard noggin of his. But Jim relented because John had a point. The stranger didn't act like cattlemen, the sheriff's deputy couldn't follow directions, and both men packed a lot of iron for cattlemen.

John said he was going after those two no matter what Jim did, leaving Jim with no choice. My brothers got their horses out of the barn, and rode after the strangers.

They caught up with them just before Old Timber Road and Chalk Road intersect. Only now, there were three men. I guess one of the sneaks hid in the timber while Daniels and the make-believe cattle buyer checked out the Snuffer farm. That convinced my brothers that, indeed, these boys were lawdogs. Seeing my brothers, or, rather, their guns, the newcomer put the spurs to his mount and took off across a cornfield.

"Stop!" The coward didn't listen to Jim's cry, so Jim fired at him, but missed. That yellow-backed Pinkerton man did not slow his horse down even when he leaped the ditch and entered the woods. By then, though, John had trained both barrels of the shotgun he had borrowed from Old Man Snuffer at the other two men.

"Drop the hardware, gents."

Cocking his .44, Jim eased his horse closer to the deputy and the stranger.

"The widow lives down that way." Jim swung down from the saddle and picked up the gun belt the stranger had dropped.

"Oh," said Ed Daniels. "Thanks."

"What is this?" Jim held up the revolver he had pulled from the stranger's holster.

"It's a Trantor," the man said nervously, while he kept glancing at the fields and the woods, as if praying his colleague would ride back to the rescue, leading a whole regiment of bluebelly cavalry.

"A Trantor?"

"Made in England."

Jim shoved the big .43-caliber pistol in his waistband. "You buy cattle in England, do you?"

"They're damned detectives!" John snapped.

"No . . . ," the deputy said, swallowing and nodding at the stranger. "He's from Osceola."

"I've been to Osceola," John said, "and I never seen this . . . Pinkerton man."

"I tell you, John . . . this is . . . ," began Daniels.

"You know me?" John trained the shotgun on the deputy.

Jim was looking at the lawman, too, and the pretend cattle buyer took advantage, drew a No. 2 Smith & Wesson, and put a bullet through John's neck.

John almost fell from his horse, but, tougher than a cob, he squeezed the first trigger of the shotgun. Buckshot tore into the Pinkerton man's arm and shoulder. The man screamed, dropped his hideaway pistol, yet somehow managed to stay on his frightened horse as it galloped east toward the Widow Sims's place. Jim fired, too, but missed. John, who by all rights should have been dead, spurred his horse and chased after the fleeing Pinkerton man. While this was happening—faster than I can tell the story—the deputy spurred his horse, forcing Jim to dive out of the path. Coming up to his knees, Jim cocked his revolver, steadied his arm, squeezed the trigger, and Ed Daniels let out a gasp and crashed to the ground.

"John!" Jim screamed, but my brother was pursuing his killer.

Quickly Jim glanced at the deputy, realized he was dead, mounted his horse, and rode after John and the Pinkerton man.

A branch knocked the wounded detective from his saddle, and he landed on the Old Road near the farms of two colored men. Sitting up, the Pinkerton man tried to stand, but John pulled the shotgun's second trigger. The blast slammed the detective against a tree.

Turning his horse, John tried to ride back to Jim, blood pulsing from his neck. The horse stopped, and John lacked the strength to kick it into a walk. The shotgun slipped from his hand. He tried to speak as Jim leaped from his horse. All that came out of my brother's mouth, though, were gurgles. Before Jim could reach my dying brother, John slid from the saddle, fell against the rails to one of the Negroes' hog pen, flipped over, and landed in the muck.

Jim climbed over the rails, looked down, and cursed. Our hot-headed brother, poor John, stared up at him, but no longer saw anything in this world. Dropping into the pen, Jim collected John's revolvers, his billfold, and a pocket watch.

A Negro had come to the edge of the pen. Jim glanced up at him, and tossed the farmer one of John's pistols.

"See that my brother gets a decent burial," Jim said.

Chapter Twenty-Six

They buried John under a fine cedar tree at the Snuffer place. The detective John had shot lived long enough to be carted down to Roscoe, where he gave a statement. He died a few days later.

The war had killed my father, and it wound up killing my mother, my sister Duck, and now poor John. And I did not get to see any of them buried.

Jim had seen enough. He left his blood, left sweet Cora, even left his fiddle, and took a train bound for California. Bob turned bitter, and befriended Jesse James—which grieved my stomach, but . . . well . . . my kid brother turned twenty-one years old in 1874. And I'd never been able to rein him in.

And me? I slept with a revolver under my pillow, hiding in the woods, in barns, in cornfields, or in the worst gambling dens and most miserable saloons. If I slept at all. I brooded, I gambled, but I did not return to the Rubicon.

The James-Younger Gang, if you read all the newspapers, went on a tear. We robbed a stagecoach down in Texas at a time when Frank and I were fishing down in the lake country near the Arkansas border. We held up two omnibuses outside of Lexington, Missouri—twenty-five miles apart. We even robbed the Tishomingo Savings

Bank in Corinth, Mississippi, and the next day held up the Kansas Pacific Railroad near Muncie, Kansas. Hardly a crime committed in the United States and her territories those days did not wind up on our record. You won't believe the truth, Parson, but while all those robberies were going on, I found myself working cattle away down in Florida for $20 a month and found.

Yet during this time, many good citizens of Missouri came to our defense. Hard-working farmers had little love for railroads, and the Pinkerton men favored railroads, so Missouri folk began to take a strong dislike to detectives— especially after what happened one evening in January, 1875.

Those Chicago dogs and traitorous neighbors sneaked like petty thieves to the James farm. Yes, I know, what Allan Pinkerton claimed, but I will go to my grave believing that those agents of Satan arrived at that farm with murder in their hearts. It was not some torch that they tossed through an open window, not a smoking device, but a grenade. A bomb, which blew the room to hell, sending shards of metal into the belly of Frank and Jesse's stepbrother, a boy all of eight years old. It destroyed so much of Mrs. Samuel's right arm that much of it had to be amputated.

An addle-brained boy who had never done anyone any harm had died an agonizing death. The widow of a Baptist preacher had been invalided—though I don't think anything could have crippled Mrs. James at all, hard as she could be. People began to think that Frank and Jesse and Jim, Bob, and me should be given amnesty.

Amnesty. A full pardon. The chance to live like free men.

Not just Missouri folks. In Jacksonville, I saw an editorial in the Chicago *Tribune* declaring that amnesty would end the terror in Missouri. I read a copy of an amnesty bill introduced into the Missouri House of Representatives by Jefferson Jones of Callaway County. Callaway County was not in western Missouri, but over in the eastern central, Yankee, part of the state.

Whereas, Under the outlawry pronounced against Jesse W. James, Frank James, Coleman Younger, James Younger, and others, who gallantly periled their lives and their all in defense of their principles, they are of necessity made desperate, driven as they are from the fields of honest industry, from their friends, their families, their homes, and their country, they can know no law but the law of self-preservation, nor can have no respect for and feel no allegiance to a government which forces them to the very acts it professes to deprecate, and then offers a bounty for their apprehension, and arms foreign mercenaries with power to capture and kill them. . . .

Whereas, Believing these men too brave to be mean, too generous to be revengeful, and too gallant and honorable to betray a friend or break a promise . . . amnesty should be extended to all alike of both parties for all acts done or charged to have been done during the war. . . .

"Jefferson Jones?" I said.

"Of Callaway County," Frank told me.

"He sounds a lot like John Newman Edwards," I said.

"He's no John Edwards," Jesse sang out, as he pulled a white mask from his saddlebag, and began fitting it over his head.

"You think it stands a chance of passing?" I asked while tightening the cinch on my saddle.

"Wouldn't that be something?" Frank said, snapping shut the loading gate on his Remington.

I swung into the saddle, drew my Smith & Wesson, and we rode into Huntington, West Virginia.

The Amnesty Bill died, of course. It might have died long before I even saw that newspaper Frank showed me when I met them in Nashville, before we rode to rob a bank in West Virginia. It might have ended when Jesse rode up to the house of his neighbor, walked to the door, and waited for Daniel Askew to answer it. As soon as he did, Jesse shot him in the chest, and when the man fell dead onto the floor, he put two more bullets in the back of Askew's head.

"The sorry son-of-a-bitch helped the Pinkertons kill Archie," Jesse explained, "and maim my ma. You ask me, if I deserve amnesty for anything I've done in my life, it's for ridding the world of that Judas."

Maybe it wasn't that good of a bill anyhow. It pardoned us of anything we might have done during the war, but stated that we would have to stand trial for anything we had been charged with since the surrender. And the way things kept being laid at our front door, we would have spent a thousand years in courthouses from the Atlantic to the Pacific.

We took $10,000 from the bank in Huntington. But Bud McDaniels caught a mortal bullet as we tried to get out of West Virginia. Tom Webb was arrested shortly afterward, and the judge sentenced him to twelve years at hard labor.

Finding men to ride with us had never proved difficult. Finding good men, however . . .

Jim Cummins had gotten fed up with Jesse. My brother Jim had settled down in California. John Jarrette had found a peaceful life on an Arizona sheep ranch. The Pence boys had quit their wild ways. Oll Shepherd was lying in his grave while his brother George, fresh out of the Kentucky prison, wanted to stay clear of any man named James or Younger.

By the summer of 1876, I was back in Missouri, back at the Rubicon. Clell Miller brought a solid hand named Charlie Pitts. I brought my brother Bob. Frank was already there, alone. And Jesse introduced us to a Yankee who called himself Bill Chadwell and the brown-eyed son of a schoolteacher named Hobbs Kerry.

The plan belonged to Frank.

"The Missouri Pacific is building a new bridge over the Lamine River. When the train comes to Rocky Cut, it'll have to slow. We'll wave the red lantern, and that'll get the engineer to stop. Express cars should be carrying a nice little pay day . . . for us."

"Good," said Hobbs Kerry. He wasn't much to look at—average height, no older than twenty-five. Too young to have fought in the war. He said his father had worked in the lead mines down in Granby, but I could tell when I shook the boy's hand that he had never worked in a mine. I'm not sure he had ever worked anywhere. "I need a grubstake for a good poker game."

"Bishop Cole," Clell Miller said, "you sure you want to join us? You and Bob, I mean. That amnesty deal . . ."

"I think Dingus took care of that amnesty," I said.

"Lay off Jesse!" my brother barked.

I did. I pointed at Frank and said: "If this is Buck's idea, you can deal me in."

Once we stopped the train, Frank, Clell, and I went to the express car while Jesse led his boys to fleece the passengers. We left Hobbs Kerry with the horses. A minister, fearing that we would murder everyone on the train, began leading his congregation of frightened passengers in singing hymns. Their singing sounded more like Rebel yells.

I took a pickaxe to the Adams Express Company safe, and punched out some of the metal, but my hands were too big to get much out of the safe. Clell Miller stepped forward, though, laughing as he said: "My hands will fit where those big paws of yours won't."

If only we had more soldiers like Clell Miller. And fewer like Hobbs Kerry.

Frank went through the letterbox, and while Clell filled the wheat sack with plunder from the safe, I discovered the newsboy's chest, and broke it open, too. This was what we needed. Not gold. Not bullion. Not silver and thousands of banknotes. Little pies, chocolate candy, peppermint sticks, lemon cookies, cakes, apples, oranges.

It had been a long time since we had eaten that well.

"Should we save some for the other boys?" Clell asked as I tossed him a pie and an apple.

"Hell, no," Frank said, and we laughed.

Not counting the food we plundered, or the bellyaches we had the next day, we left Rocky Cut with $15,000.

"Tell Allan Pinkerton!" Jesse yelled before putting spurs to his mount, "and all his detectives to look for us in hell."

Chapter Twenty-Seven

Gray hair is a crown of splendor; it is attained in the way of righteousness.

Proverbs, Chapter Sixteen, Verse Thirty-One.

I was thirty-two years old, and I envied men with gray hair. Or any hair. Mine began thinning out at a right fast clip, which I jokingly blamed on my brothers. I blamed Jesse, too, but that really was no joke. After the robbery at Rocky Cut, I lost a great deal more of that fine sandy head of hair, but I kept a mustache and goatee to make up for my loss on top.

Some of our boys—Bud McDaniels, George Shepherd, Tom Webb—had been sent to hard time. Each convicted felon had been promised a pardon if he would name his accomplices. Men like those boys do not betray their comrades. But Hobbs Kerry, who was arrested first, did. He talked. Hell, he wouldn't shut up.

It was definite. We would find no amnesty after Hobbs Kerry confessed. And I did not want to risk a trial with a traitor like Kerry testifying against me as the state's star witness. Missouri no longer felt like such a good place to be in at that time, and I thought about returning to Florida. Frank kept mentioning Virginia. And Jesse had been living for a spell in Nashville, Tennessee. Then

Bill Chadwell brought up Minnesota. He hailed from those parts, bragged about the banks being filled with greenbacks for the taking. He said he could guide us out of the state after we robbed a rich bank, and told us there would be nothing to worry about. Only hayseeds and Swedes lived in Minnesota.

Bob, my brother, was all for it. He acted like a puppy dog the way he followed Jesse around.

"Bob," I argued, "Jesse James is not Mephistopheles."

"And," my kid brother barked right back at me, "you ain't Dick."

That I had heard enough since my older brother had died, but Bob's words never hurt so much. Sometimes I wished I'd been an only child. Is that a sin, Parson? So I curbed my tongue, unclenched my fist. Maybe I shouldn't have done that. Perhaps I should have given Bob the whipping he deserved. I needed help. Thought I did, anyhow, so I sent a telegraph to Jim in California.

Come home. Bob needs you.

Once he arrived, even Jim could not talk sense into Bob.

"We take our war to the Yankees," Jesse said. "Like we did in Iowa and West Virginia."

Frank let out a mirthless laugh. "Dingus, this is not a war. It hasn't been a war for a long time.

It's just because you and Bud and me are too lazy to work for a living. . . ."

Jesse shot back: "Because we can't get a job, can't go to church without being persecuted. . . ."

Frank went right on. "And we don't have the guts to turn ourselves in and stand trial."

"You siding with Bud?" Jesse's eyes had that mean look.

Frank spit tobacco juice and shook his head. "I've been sick of what we're doing for some time now. I have to sneak in to see my wife, Dingus, or pretend to be someone, some *thing,* I'm not."

"You won't go with me?" Jesse backed up in shock.

Frank had a look in his eyes, too, but not of death, not of defiance. It was that deep pain, a sadness. His head shook.

"You're my brother, Jesse." He called him by his real name, not Dingus. " 'Let brotherly love continue.' "

Hebrews, Chapter Thirteen, Verse One.

Now, the boys turned to me. Frank had done it. *Brotherly love.* That bond that tied us together. John was dead. Bob was going to Minnesota with Jesse, who, in a rare instance of placation, said softly: "Hell, Bud, we might not even find a bank worth robbing up there. Could just be a vacation, till this Hobbs Kerry news dies down. And Colonel Chinn's in Saint Paul. He could get us some fine horses, and he runs a gambling parlor in town."

Yes, the same Black Jack Chinn who had ridden with Quantrill, but I'm not altogether certain who had promoted him to colonel. But he did know horses. Chinn had stolen plenty during the war and, the last I had heard, was raising thoroughbreds.

I could find great horses at Maise Walker's place, but I only had two brothers living, and when Jim shook his head and said—"I'll ride with you, Bob, but I don't like this one damned bit."—I knew I could not ride away. Not from Bob and Jim. Hell, not from Clell or Frank. Maybe not even from Jesse.

Besides, after ten years, what was I good at? Robbing banks. Robbing trains. I knew I could not go back to Florida where the mosquitoes grew larger than crows, and alligators and snakes preyed on cattle.

"Deal me in," I said.

We were going to Minnesota. I was making a bad mistake. I knew it. In the back of my mind, I heard Lizzie Daniel's voice. That lively song I had heard her sing had become a dirge. I was sailing on "the ship that never returned".

As the train rocked its way north, Frank and I buried our noses in books. Frank frowned, nodded, and remained intent as he devoured *Shakespeare: A Critical Study of His Mind and Art* by some Irishman named Edward Dowden.

I kept grinning as I read a book I had bought from a newsboy in the smoking car.

"How can you read that . . . on a train?" asked a feminine voice.

I closed the book, keeping a finger on the page so as not to lose my place, and looked up at the woman on the aisle seat just ahead of me. She was a handsome lady in her sixties, in a peach calico dress and blue bonnet, holding a basket on her lap that contained sandwiches and sardines and apples she had brought to eat.

"Ma'am?" I said.

Glancing up from his book, Frank grinned.

"I could not read a book such as that," the woman said. "Every time the train stopped for water or wood, I would jump out of my skin, fearing those cut-throats would be here to rob and ravage."

I nodded. "They do seem like desperate characters, ma'am, but we are out of Missouri. I think we should be safe."

"I pray so." She smiled, reached in her basket, and offered me an apple.

I accepted, thanked her kindly as she turned around to face the front. She took out a sandwich for herself, and began eating.

"You ever *rode* a train before, Bud?" Frank asked, closing his book, reaching over, and taking my apple for himself.

With a laugh, I found my place in the book, and

continued to read *The Guerrillas of the West; or the Life, Character, and Daring Exploits of the Younger Brothers* by Augustus C. Appler, a Yank by birth, who claimed to have settled in Osceola. Though parts of it read fairly truthful, a bunch proved to be as accurate as penny dreadfuls and Yankee newspapers. Hell, this book even told that lie about me lining up ten bluecoats to see how many bodies an Enfield bullet would go through.

Reading Appler's account made me feel . . . well . . . famous, but that's not why I was reading it on that train. Jesse sat a few rows behind me. It burned the bitter hell out of him, because no books had been published about him, though soon they would flood the market.

We took in the sights in Minnesota. Had us a regular vacation.

Never had I seen so many folks crowd into a place to cheer and curse a bunch of grown men dressed in what looked like jodhpurs held up with belts, wearing funny caps with brims on their heads, trying to hit a ball with a stick.

"They're *seats* all over this park, so why is everyone standing?" I yelled at Bob—and I had to yell so my brother could hear me, even though he stood right next to where I was sitting. I had paid 75¢ for this seat. Damned if I was going to stand up for hours.

Jim and Clell Miller had joined us at Red Cap Park in St. Paul to watch the Red Caps play a bunch of "ballists" who called themselves the Clippers of Winona. There must have been a thousand people there that afternoon, crowding into the amphitheater in a park maybe five hundred by three hundred sixty feet surrounded by a ten-foot wooden wall. We had seats, not that anyone used them.

"Come on, Bud," Bob said back to me. "You're missing a good game."

I lighted my cigar. That was one good thing about this baseball contest. The concession stand sold cigars, and fruit, and drinks—but no liquor.

"Yeah!" Even Clell seemed impressed.

Shaking out the match, I sighed. The cheering had stopped, and now the crowd was groaning, so I knew something bad must have happened . . . though damned if I could see it. "I don't see much sense in trying to hit a ball with a stick," I said.

Someone punched my shoulder. I figured it might be a woman who found the stench of a nickel cigar offensive, but when I turned, I stared into the wide brown eyes of a boy.

"Mister," the tyke said as his ma and pa smiled, "that's Dory Dean coming to the plate."

If you should be in Rome . . . I stood.

Dory Dean, who had played for the National League's Cincinnati Red Stockings in '75 and had been doing the "hurling" for St. Paul's ballists, came to the plate. He scratched his groin, spit into his hands, and hefted a big round stick before giving the fellow holding the ball the mean eye and sending out another waterfall of brown juice.

The hurler for the Clippers struck Dory Dean out on three pitches. The kid behind me burst out crying at the same time as just about every adult in the crowd moaned or cursed. Out on the dirt and grass, all the gents in the white caps started jumping and pointing fingers as they laughed at the boys in the red caps. Folks started filing out of Red Cap Park, and, finally, Jim, Bob, and Clell sat down beside me.

"That's a shame," Bob said.

"Pretty excitin', though," Clell said.

"I'll have to take your word for it," I said, sucking on the cheap cigar.

This was our vacation from the Missouri law and the Pinkerton scoundrels. I never cottoned to baseball. Nor did Jim. Clell wouldn't see another game, for he would soon be lying dead in Northfield. The sport won Bob over, though. And Dory Dean? He quit baseball, but I hear he found a lot more success swinging a tennis racket. You ask me, that's just as silly as hitting balls with sticks on a perfectly fine summer afternoon.

Oh, we found other excursions. We got some fine horses from Colonel Chinn in St. Paul, and raced them up and down the streets, winning a right smart of greenbacks. We lost most of that money at the poker tables and faro layouts in some of Chinn's saloons, and at Mollie Ellsworth's brothel. We read newspapers, clipping out a few articles about certain banks and vaults, and studying the advertisements in those newspapers.

You want to know how rich a town is? You look at what is being advertised in that burg's newspaper, or how many ads are being bought and published in that paper. Our coffers kept decreasing—thanks to Chinn's cardsharpers—but we might have forgotten all about Chadwell's promises of fat Yankee banks when we stepped out of the Nicolette House one evening.

"Hey, Chadwell!" a voice called out.

We turned, and froze as our eyes set on a city policeman tapping his nightstick in a beefy hand and scowling at our Minnesota guide.

"Pat Kenny," Chadwell said, and shoved his hands in his pants pockets.

"How are you, Chadwell?" the copper spoke in an Irish brogue.

"Dandy, Pat. And you?"

The policeman did not answer, did not even look at Chadwell, but studied our faces. "What are you doing in town?"

"Planning to strike out for the Black Hills," Chadwell said. "Make myself a pile in some gold mine." He grinned. "Wanna grubstake me?"

"Enjoy Dakota Territory, Chadwell. You and your . . . pals."

Still slapping that club, the policeman walked away.

"Friend of yours?" Jesse asked.

Chadwell did not detect the sarcasm. "Not hardly. Bastard arrested me last time I was here."

Figuring that to be a sign that we should move on, Jesse came up with a plan. We would split up, check out the banks, find a likely candidate from which we would make a handsome withdrawal, and ride out.

Jim, Clell, Frank, and Jesse rode out for Red Wing. Chadwell and Bob headed for St. Peter. Charlie Pitts and I went to Madelia. We agreed to meet in Mankato by the 1st of September.

Mankato looked like a fine town, but the farmland along the Minnesota River was something straight out of the Old Testament. Frank and I rode past a tent revival meeting, and we stopped, took our hats off, sang a few hymns, before chatting with a couple of sodbusters. We learned from them that locusts had been stripping the fields the past few years. We left a few greenbacks when the preacher passed the hat, and returned to town.

"Fat bank," Jesse said. "What do y'all think?"

I cleared my throat, but it was Frank who

spoke. Likely he knew Jesse—and Bob—would veto anything I had to say, on the principle of the matter. Frank, though, pulled some weight.

"Bank's fine," Frank said, "but these people have suffered enough."

"They're Yankees, Buck," Jesse said.

"They're also farmers. Like our neighbors back home. Grasshoppers have given them plenty of misery, same as they've ruined some of our friends' crops in Missouri. We don't need to add to their troubles."

"Yeah." Bob, who always wanted to be a farmer, nodded sadly. Bill Chadwell only sighed, for he liked the layout and the loot in Mankato. Jesse knew he had no hope of bucking Frank—and me—when Bob agreed with us.

"All right," Jesse said. "Let's check out Northfield."

Chapter Twenty-Eight

You'll want to know about Northfield, of course.

Like everyone else.

Who murdered Heywood, the cashier inside the First National Bank? Who shot down that Swede in the streets?

I've kept silent for many a year, never answering questions from any newspaperman. Never did I admit that the James brothers rode with us. I've named our accomplices, Woods and Howard, but I guess everyone in the world, along with the Good Lord, knows the truth. Already I've told you enough about who I'd trust inside a bank. But things didn't work out. You see . . . the boys had been drinking.

When Clell and I crossed the bridge and saw the streets and boardwalks crowded, I thought for sure our "inside men" would get back into their saddles and ride right out of town. Mankato certainly seemed like a better place for us to be than this pretty little town on the Cannon River. At least it did on that particular Thursday afternoon.

Clell was smoking his pipe. You see, he had bragged that he would smoke it right through the whole robbery. When our three inside men rose from the boxes they had been sitting on and walked into the bank, Clell was struck dumb, and he removed the pipe from his mouth. "They're goin' in," he managed to say, dismounting.

"If they do . . ."—my throat turned dry and my hands suddenly felt clammy—"the alarm will be given as sure as there's a hell."

Cursing, Clell emptied the bowl and stuck the pipe in the pocket of his duster.

Hell, the boys had been drinking so much, they didn't even think to close the damned door to the bank. Clell quickly took care of that himself, while I swung down onto the street to tighten my saddle's cinch.

The next thing I heard was Clell screaming at one of those damned hayseeds, as Chadwell like to call them. "Get out of here, you son-of-a-bitch!"

Clell's shout was followed, as I knew it would be, by a call to arms by one of the locals. "Get your guns, boys! They are robbing the bank!"

It only took seven minutes. Chadwell and poor old Clell were dead. A bullet had shattered Bob's right elbow, but, I have to give him credit, he did that border shift I had taught him, emptying his pistol as I rode up.

"Get up behind me!" I yelled.

We galloped out of town—six men on five horses—shot to pieces. Terribly wounded, Bob gripped me hard around my stomach as we were chased out of Northfield, whipped by men who damned sure were no hayseeds.

All for $26.70.

Honestly I can't say who killed the Swede. It might have been me. It could have been a towns-man. Could have been anybody. They say he couldn't understand English, which is why he got killed. Ask me, though, and I'd say he was a drunk or a fool. English? The language of bullets and gunsmoke is universal, don't you think?

Who shot that brave man in the bank and left him dead? Remember, I was not in the bank. Anything I say would be ruled in a court of law as hearsay. God knows the truth. And, Parson, I think you do, too. You're smart enough to figure out who did what, who we might pick as our inside men. That's all I really have to say about Northfield. Don't look glum, Parson. I even refused to tell Retta when she asked, and I love my sister. And I can die knowing that I never betrayed a friend.

We bathed our wounds in the Dundas River, stole horses, stole chickens when we could, or bought bread, rode hard or walked what seemed like forever. Jim had been hit in the shoulder; I had a bullet in my thigh; Frank had one through the leg. Charlie Pitts had escaped unscathed. So had Jesse, but, you ask me, he should have been one of those killed. Bob was hurt the worst, though, his right elbow shattered and bleeding like a stuck pig, already becoming feverish.

"Leave me!" he wailed. "Leave me! I'll just slow you down."

Grimacing from the pain in my leg, and the thought of what probably awaited us, I somehow said: "We rode here together. We ride away together. Or we die together." I said that more to Jesse, because I could tell he thought that we should leave Bob.

The next day, as we hid in the Big Woods, full of swamps, ticks, and mosquitoes, it started to rain. And it rarely stopped.

Folks say the state of Minnesota sent a thousand men after us, and I say not a damned one of them was worth spit. How else could we, as badly shot up as we were, strangers in a strange land, have managed to hold out for so long?

Let me make one thing straight. It is my belief that Jesse was all for leaving us as soon as we rode past the Dundas, but he stuck with us. Perhaps because Frank would not abandon us. It was after we had crossed the Blue Earth River, with rains still drenching us, and Bob growing weaker and worse, that I waved Frank and Jesse over.

"Take the horses," I said, which was not as honorable as it sounds. The horses we had managed to steal would not get anyone far. "Leave us. Save yourselves."

We parted friends, Frank and me. Jesse and me? We parted friendly. Honorable. Those stories that Jesse wanted to kill Bob, or Jim, are bald-faced lies. Oh, after our capture at Hanska Slough and while we waited in Faribault for our trial and sentencing, lawmen would come in, telling us that Jesse voted to shoot us down like dogs, but those lawmen weren't there, and they just wanted us to forget the code of the bushwhacker. Die game. Never betray your friends.

Frank and Jesse rode out, vowing to lead any posse away for us. Charlie Pitts could have gone, too, but he stuck with us to the end, though I wish he had not.

It was September 21st and we were limping and stumbling through the vines, eating off plums. That's when the posse finally caught up with us at Hanska Slough. That's when Charlie Pitts told me: "We're surrounded. We had better surrender."

I told him: "Charlie, this is where Cole Younger dies."

Only, I didn't die, though I took a lot of lead, lead that still weighs me down. It was Charlie Pitts who died, and that's what I truly regret.

Buckshot tore into my shoulder, a bullet went into my jaw, another through my arm, and one in my armpit. Jim caught buckshot in his thigh, but his worst wound was the bullet that smashed part of his jaw and lodged in the roof of his mouth. Bob got hit in a lung.

No one thought we would survive, but we were

268

Youngers. I remember pulling myself to my feet, bloodied as I was, hurting as I did. By Jehovah, I was so waterlogged from all the rain that when they pulled off my rotting boots, the toenails came off with what was left of my socks. Yet I tipped my hat to the ladies as they took us to the Flanders Hotel in Madelia.

Feelings ran hot in most of Minnesota after our capture. Plenty of folks wanted to see us swing, and I heard that a few lynch mobs had gathered here and there. Yet, for the most part, we were treated with kindness and charity. We did not look like cold-blooded killers. We looked like the miserable men we were—shot to hell, rained on for two weeks, sick, pale, half dead.

Ladies were praying for us. They brought us cookies and tea and hand-me-down clothes to wear. They treated our injuries. They read Scripture with us, serenaded us with hymns.

By the time we arrived in Faribault for our trial, Retta and Aunt Fanny had traveled north from Missouri. It hurt worse than my feet or jaw or leg, seeing those fine women pained so at our conditions, and our probable future. We had been indicted with accessory to the murder of Joseph Heywood; assault with a deadly weapon—for Charlie Pitts had shot Alonzo Bunker inside the bank when the banker bolted for the door—; murder and accessory to the murder of the

Swede, Nicholas Gustavson; finally, of course, robbing the First National Bank of Northfield.

A Yank named George W. Batchelder agreed to defend us. When I first saw him, he asked how my wounds were healing.

"I don't mind being shot," I told him. "It's the hanging that I dread."

"I might know a way for you, Jim, and Bob to keep your necks out of a noose," he said.

I stiffened. "I've told every Pinkerton man, every sheriff, every preacher, and every jailer the same thing, Mister Batchelder. The names of the two gents who got away were Howard and Woods. They joined us late in the game, and neither me nor my brothers know anything about them."

The lawyer grinned slyly. "I never thought you would betray your friends, Cole. That's not my intention. My intention is this . . ."

That's when he told us about the Minnesota law. Back in 1868, the state had passed a law that allowed hanging only if a jury found a defendant guilty. "Plead guilty," Batchelder said, "and the worst they can give you is life in prison."

"Ain't much of a life, is it?" I said.

"But it's life," he said.

On the 20th of November, our deputies brought us in shackles to the crowded courthouse. One by one, we went up to the judge and pleaded guilty to the charges. Well, Parson, I thought, lawyers being lawyers, that they would find some way to hang us, anyway. So when the judge asked if any of us had something to say, I managed to stand.

"I feel responsible for leading my brothers into the deplorable situation in which we find ourselves." That was no lie. "I would willingly suffer death in any form . . . if by doing so . . . my brothers could go free." Which was God-honest truthful, too.

The judge bowed his head, cleared his throat, and looked up.

"I have no word of comfort to offer you, and no desire to speak harshly of the deeds, which have brought you into your present position. The sentence of the law leaves you life, but robbed of all its pleasures, hopes, and ambition."

Life in prison at hard labor.

Retta broke into tears, and Jim turned to hug her. Aunt Fanny scowled at us, but she had always been a hard woman. She came north not for our sakes, but to chaperone Retta. Yet, to our amazement, women in the gallery broke into tears, and I heard some rustling of skirts, then a woman's voice as she ran down the center aisle.

Sobbing, she cried out: "Oh, Lord, let me kiss those poor boys!"

PART III

1877–1903

Chapter Twenty-Nine

The air he inhaled was no longer pure, but thick and mephitic—he was in prison.

Yes, I had read Alexandre Dumas's *The Count of Monte Cristo*, and so naïve was I that I thought I knew everything about prisons. Yet nothing could prepare me for what I would have to endure, and Chateau d'If was a long, long way from Stillwater, Minnesota.

Sheriff Ara Barton and three deputies escorted us by train and wagon from Faribault to Stillwater. When we stepped out and stared at those dismal stone walls, Bob joked: "Well, I've finally found myself a real home."

A lot of folks had come to see our arrival, but no one cheered. If they spoke, they used only whispers. Most pointed at us. We tried not to look at them. Our "come-along" manacles jingling, we walked toward the heavy iron gate, which a couple of uniformed men opened.

They called the room "Between The Gates". I shivered, for it was November, and the room felt deathly cold. Coats and hats hung on the walls. The floor was cold, there being no rug on it. Men rose from desks. Plenty of hard wooden chairs lined the walls, but prisoners were not allowed to sit down. The deputy warden pushed back his chair, closed a big ledger book, and walked toward us, motioning some big guards in woolen coats to follow him. Sheriff Barton unlocked our cuffs, but before Bob, Jim, or I could rub the circulation back into our wrists and hands, some of these Stillwater boys began prodding us and patting us in some of our most personal places. His shattered arm still hurting fiercely, Bob cried out in pain.

"Easy with him!" I snapped, and down I went to my knees, seeing circles and geometrical shapes of orange and purple and red flashing before my eyes.

"Shut up, fish!" a big man barked behind me, and I got jerked back to my feet while another man, grinning black teeth, put his hand on my manhood and squeezed.

"They're clean," he said as he stepped away, and the deputy warden nodded, then turned to Sheriff Barton.

"You have their paperwork?" he asked.

Barton pulled some papers from his coat, and they went over to a desk. I guess everything seemed in order, because the deputy warden handed Barton a receipt.

Receipt. Like we were three horses being sold at an auction.

We each got a receipt, too, for our bundles of personal belongings, which Barton gave one of the guards. We watched as each of our tied-up bundles was handed to some prisoner—what they called a trustee—a black man dressed in a gray suit with a cap. The man said something in a whisper that we could not hear, and hurried out of Between The Gates.

"Good luck, boys," Sheriff Barton said, but we knew better than to say good bye. The gate opened and closed, and I suddenly felt the cold of November more intensely. Although my brothers stood beside me, I never felt so alone.

"All right, fresh fish." One of the guards prodded me with a billy club, pushing me toward the next gate. Jim and Bob followed, and I let a burly guard with a crooked nose lead us to the bathhouse.

It was not anything like any bath I had ever taken.

And the clothes they handed us were not the fine duds we often wore, but coarse, scratchy woolen suits of black and white stripes. Next, we were sent into the tonsorial parlor to get our hair practically shaved off—not that I had much left any more.

"Leave my mustache and goatee," I told him.

He did not listen, and the biggest of our guards pressed his club on my shoulder to make sure I didn't complain. I started to learn something right then and there.

All my life as an outlaw, and even whilst I rode with Quantrill, I had enjoyed a luxurious life.

Many folks who were neither Yankees nor Kansans treated me and men of my ilk as heroes. Riding with Frank and Jesse, we paid our hosts quite well, and they usually gave us a welcome befitting a king. Even in Madelia and Faribault, the ladies and a few men showered us with sympathy, kindness, and Christian charity—due, perhaps, to our grievous wounds and poor health.

In Stillwater, we were nothing special. We were dirt. Fresh fish as we would be called. Outlaws. Convicts. Prisoners sentenced to life at hard labor.

Our fingers were first pressed onto an ink pad, then onto a sheet of paper. They gave us a grimy handkerchief to wipe off the ink from our fingers. They marched us to the warden's office.

"My name is John A. Reed." Rising behind his desk, Warden Reed did not offer to shake our hands. "You are third-grade prisoners. That means you have no privileges. None. No tobacco. No writing or receiving of letters. No visitors. Your meals will be taken in your cells. You may have found yourselves all high and mighty outside these walls, but let me make one thing perfectly clear. This is what you are to me." He came around from behind his desk and pointed a long finger under my nose. "Number Eight Hundred and Ninety-Nine."

To Jim: "Number Nine Hundred."

And Bob: "Number Nine-Oh-One."

The warden walked back to his desk seat.

"I hear the James boys plan to break you out of prison."

Out of the corner of my eyes, I saw Bob's face brighten, but I snorted and said: "I haven't seen Frank in more than a year, and Jesse and I aren't on good . . ."

A club caught me on the back of my head, which seemed to make every bullet as well as any buckshot still in my body rattle. I dropped to my knees, shook the pain out of my head, and felt rough hands jerk me back to my feet.

"You talk," Warden Reed said, "when you have permission. Do you understand? You have permission to answer."

Another club jabbed my kidneys. "Answer the warden, fish!"

"Yes, sir," I cried.

"Griggs, get these men out of my sight and put them to work. Tubs and buckets."

Griggs? I looked at the burly guard. He wasn't my old schoolmaster, Bob Griggs, but he seemed just as mean.

"Turn to the right," Griggs growled after we had left the warden's office. Twenty feet later, he ordered: "Turn to the left." And we entered the cell house.

Iron and stone, walls three feet thick, cold, damp. I felt like Jean Valjean in *Les Misérables*, and Griggs, I feared, would be Inspector Javert.

Six-hundred and sixty-four cells over six

inhospitable floors. They put us on the ground floor. I supposed they figured we would be easier to guard that way, in case Jesse James decided to break us out. Wasn't that a joke!

"Cayou," Griggs said, "they're yours. If they give you any grief, bash their brains out. It'll give the next fresh fish that swims in here something to clean up with whitewash."

Griggs's boots gave off echoes as he marched out of the cell house and into the gray November light.

Ben Cayou, our personal guard, rattled a ring of keys as he unlocked what was to be my home for, as the judge in Faribault had decreed, the rest of my natural life. Like anything was natural about this.

I was given two cups, a tiny mirror, and a rough bar of lye soap. They gave me a comb, not that I needed one as closely as they had shorn my hair. Also one spoon, useless for digging my way out of that deathtrap. A mattress was placed on a tiny cot in the corner, before they handed me two towels,—one for my dishes and another for my face—blankets, sheets, and a pillowcase. They gave me a Bible, too. Then they closed and locked the door.

I could not turn around to see Ben Cayou march Bob and Jim down to their cells. I stared at the dark wall, and found my "window"— a six-inch ventilation hole that let in cold air.

I heard the doors open and close, the keys turn the locks, as my two brothers were also introduced to their new homes. Alone, I buried my face in my hands, and wept bitter tears.

When they fetched us an hour later, we followed Ben Cayou to a factory, with three guards marching behind us to make sure we did not revolt. Or maybe they were afraid that Jesse and Frank James were going to show up to free us.

"Most of the fish are making threshing machines," Cayou told us as we went down damp stairs into a dark basement that smelled of mold and dead animals, probably rats. "You boys get to make buckets and tubs." He handed Bob a paintbrush. "This is for you. That arm, I don't think you'd be good for nothing else."

Bob stared at the brush as if he had never seen one before.

"It's not a Colt, is it, Brother?" It was a mean thing for Jim to say, though probably only I understood the slurred words.

"Shut up, fish!" Cayou waved the club underneath Jim's shattered jaw.

"Here's how this will work," Cayou explained. "As soon as you enter this . . . ahem . . . factory, you will remove your coat, put on an apron, and commence to work. You will not talk to any other prisoner without receiving special permission from the officer in charge. Today, that officer is me." He nodded at a man who stepped out of the dark. It was the trustee we had seen when we first entered the prison.

"This is the shop foreman," Cayou said. "Erskine Green. Anything you say to him will be for work purposes only. If you need anything else, you may approach the officer in charge, salute him, show proper respect, and, upon receiving permission to speak, express your wants in a concise matter. Do your job to the best of your ability, and do it right. Failure to comply could revoke what few privileges you fish have, or send you to solitary. Now, get to work. Green, I'm going to the privy. When I return, I expect to find buckets being made. Otherwise, I'll bring Griggs in here and ask him to serve as the officer in charge."

The door closed behind Cayou. I wet my lips, but could not bring myself to speak.

Erskine Green grinned. "You boys know how to make buckets?" the Negro asked.

Our heads shook.

"Time you learned." He moved toward a bench, and looked back. "What's the matter, fresh fish? The great Younger brothers be scared?"

"Just not . . . ," Bob started, but quickly stopped, glancing frightfully at the closed door.

I finished Bob's thought in a whisper: "Just not used to all these rules."

Erskine Green slapped his pants legs and cackled. "That right, white boys?" he said mockingly. "Y'all ain't used to be bein' tol' where you can go, what you can do, what you can say?" The face hardened. "Well, Younger boys, now I reckon you's 'bout to learn how I felt the first fifteen years of my miserable life as a slave down in Alabama."

Chapter Thirty

That night I dreamed.

I stood on the white sands of a beach in Cuba, tasting the salt on the air as waves crashed against giant boulders and sprayed my face with a tangy mist. The sun felt warm and I leaned low in the saddle, guiding my blood bay stallion into the surf, letting his hoofs splash the water. Ahead of me rode Jesse James on his fine racer, Stonewall, but I gained, and laughed as I passed him, knowing my stallion's hoofs were now kicking up wet sand into Jesse's face.

Bob, Jim, John, Duck—even Dick—and old Maise Walker cheered as the stallion and I crossed the finish line. Frank James slapped his knee and pointed a mocking finger as his brother and that great steed of Jesse's limped into a second-place finish. As I swung out of the saddle, I handed the reins to Clell Miller, who, pipe clenched between his teeth, spoke.

"Now, Bishop Cole, ain't this a fine way to spend all that Yankee money?"

Before I could answer, another voice

called my name, and I turned and felt my heart increase its pace. Lizzie Brown grinned as she walked to me, wearing a fine blue-and-white striped bathing outfit, her hair pinned up in a bonnet. Wet sand coated her rosy cheeks.

"That was amazing, Cole," she said, and I could smell the oils on her body. Pineapple. Coconut. Banana. Whatever the hell they grew in Cuba.

Lizzie put a hand on my shoulder. "Cole," she murmured, and I closed my eyes.

When they opened, a dread enveloped me. Coughing, I pulled up my blanket. Something was crawling over my hand, and I flinched, sat up with a curse as pain tore through my head, my shoulder, my hip—reminders of the bank robbery that had failed. I had no match to strike, and no light shone in the five-by-seven-foot cell that was far, far away from any Cuban beach.

The bug that had crawled over my hand had dropped to the floor. I could hear the cockroach's legs pattering as it made its way across the damp floor. But not just one cockroach. Ten, maybe twenty. Grabbing the end of my blanket and biting back the pain, I flipped the thin piece of wool up and down a few times to send any other roaches off my cot.

I could not fall back asleep that night.

Worse, I would never again dream of Cuban beaches or of Lizzie Brown.

After an hour of work, Ben Cayou left us in the basement with Erskine Green to visit the privy.

"That's Cayou's way," Erskine Greene whispered as we tarred a tub. "You wants to talk, do it now, but do it quietly and quickly. Cayou ain't a bad gent. An' his wife be a bona-fide God-fearin' lady."

"This . . . is . . . hell." Just hearing Jim try to speak, each word a struggle and hard to understand, gnawed at my gut, my conscience. He had lost most of his upper teeth and part of his jaw. While Bob and I ate boiled corned beef and mashed potatoes for supper, Jim sucked up gruel through a straw.

"It's all my fault." Tears welled in Bob's eyes. "I'm sorry. . . ."

"Hush," I said. "If anybody's to blame, it's me."

"No . . . ," Bob cried. "It's me. It's all my fault. I never should have listened to . . ."

"Hush, damn it." I would not even let Bob mention Jesse's name, not in front of Erskine Green. Not in front of anyone.

Jim swallowed painfully. "We . . . got to . . . get . . . out of . . . here."

Covering his mouth as he coughed, Bob glanced

at Erskine Green, and then me. "Escape," he mouthed.

"No," I said. "Folks in this state are already ticked that they couldn't hang us. They're trying to get that law revoked. We do anything to show they can't trust us, and they'll kill us."

"That's right," Erskine Green said. "You smart for a dumb-ass white boy."

"We played a hard game," I said, "and we lost. This is our come-uppance and we'll take it like Youngers. We get out of here . . . we won't be looking over our shoulders the rest of our lives. We'll get out of here by pardon or parole."

"Or . . ."—Jim swallowed—"death."

Chilled, I made myself nod. "Or death."

So we made buckets every day.

"Mister Cole," Erskine Green told me one afternoon, "why you's becomin' crackerjack at paintin' 'em pails."

I glanced at my fingers, coated with so much tar I knew I would be tearing off skin when I tried to clean then once my shift ended.

"Up in heaven," I told the black man, "my ma is telling my pa . . . 'You see, Henry, I always said Coleman would amount to something.'"

At night, I grew accustomed to the cockroaches—but the bedbugs proved to be a much worse nuisance. They ate my legs and arms raw, or so it seemed, and I found myself spending more time in bed than in the basement. They even had to haul me to the prison hospital ward from time to time.

News came one day. A friendly guard, who had begun bringing my supper to my cell about a week into our imprisonment, motioned me over as he slid a tin plate and tin cup underneath the iron bars.

"Read yesterday's evening paper," he said softly. "The James boys made it back to Missouri. Don't know where they are now."

All I did was shrug, but my heart felt lighter. Frank was alive. Hell, so were Bob, Jim, and me. Alive. But far from living.

"You are an intelligent man, Cole Younger."

Marching out of the chapel one Sunday, in step to the music being sung and played on an organ, I felt a hand on my arm that pulled me out of line. The guard named Griggs shove me toward Warden Reed.

What, by Jacks, had I done now? I thought.

For there were rules about Sunday services, too. You rose and sat when the deputy warden hit the gavel. You sat ramrod straight, arms folded. You looked straight ahead at the preacher, or the guard in charge. You didn't have to pray. You didn't have to sing. But you had to be there.

"No demerits." Warden Reed looked at some papers in his hand, then studied my face. "You can read and write. How much schooling did you have in Missouri?"

I kept quiet, till Griggs ran that club of his up and down my backbone. "Answer the warden, you God . . ."

"Griggs," Warden Reed said, "that will be all." The club fell away from my person, Griggs muttered something, and I heard his footsteps as he sought out some other prisoner to torment.

"You may speak," Reed said.

"My mother and father saw to it that I received the best education I could get," I said.

"Yet you turned to outlawry."

I held my tongue.

"Speak freely," the warden said.

"Sir, I didn't have much of a choice."

The warden gave that sad, condescending shake of his head. "I daresay everyone housed behind these stone walls would say the same thing. I'd like to meet one guilty person in prison."

"I did not proclaim my innocence, sir," I told him. "I just said I had no choice. Nor did my brothers."

"Everyone here had a choice."

"But only Bob, Jim, and I came from Missouri, I would guess. Missouri during the war."

The warden thought about that, lowering the papers in his hand and saying: "Starting tomorrow, you and your brothers will be upgraded to second-class status. You will report to Between

The Gates to be issued new uniforms, and new privileges." He rolled the papers as he spoke, the waved them in my face like a billy club. "But know this, Number Eight Hundred Ninety-Nine. One demerit. One mistake. And you're back to third-class, and will remain so for at least a year."

The usual rule, Erskine Green told us, was two demerits in one month would send you back to third-class. But we were Youngers, and different rules applied to men of our stature.

We exchanged our striped uniforms and caps for black-and-gray checks. The roaches and bedbugs didn't seem to notice any difference. Once a fortnight, we were allowed to write a letter, and every week we could draw a four-ounce ration of tobacco: cigarette, pipe, or chewing. They brought a wooden chair to my cell, another reward for a second-class convict.

Now we got to eat with other prisoners of second-class rank. That took some getting used to.

They even gave us rules on how to eat. Griggs read the instructions to us once, but remembering everything seemed to be impossible. There were many times in the first month or two that we went hungry. Finally we figured it all out. It's amazing how hunger can improve your memory.

You did not eat, or drink, until a guard or trustee sounded the gong.

No food could be left on a plate, not even

crumbs or a crust of bread. We had to learn to eat pickled beets with beef, bread, and vegetable soup for dinner every Monday. If you wanted any extra food or drink, it went like this.

Hold up your right hand for extra bread.

Hold up your cup for coffee or water.

Hold up your fork for more meat.

Hold up your spoon for more soup.

Hold up your knife for extra vegetables.

No talking. No laughing. This appeared to be the number one rule no matter where you were in Stillwater, not that we often found any reason to laugh.

We were also transferred from the basement and the tubs and buckets to the thresher factory.

A company called Seymour & Sabin had started production on the Minnesota Chief, and I am happy to say that Bob, Jim, and I helped many a hayseed with his wheat crops over the next several years. We did not work together, of course. Warden Reed and Griggs feared that we would plot the greatest prison break in the history of prisons should we be allowed to communicate more than once a month. I made sieves. Jim helped with the belts. Again, they stuck a paint-brush in Bob's hand, since he never recovered the full use of or the strength in his hand which limited almost anything he could do. His job was whitewashing the factory's walls.

Every Friday morning, after breakfast, we got

marched to the bathhouse, twenty-eight prisoners at a time. Now, as desperate as we Younger brothers were—with Jim still taking every meal through a straw, and Bob's cough getting worse and worse—never were we put in the same group.

I'd stand in line in front of a shower, and the water would begin to spray, but I did not step naked under those blasts of stinking water until the officer in charge tapped his cane twice on the floor. When the guard tapped again, the water stopped spraying, we dried ourselves off with towels that felt like sandpaper, and went to get our fresh clothes out from a pigeonhole downstairs. They also gave us a clean handkerchief and a clean pair of socks. Fifteen minutes later, we were back in the shop, back at work, producing more Minnesota Chiefs to make Seymour & Sabin richer and richer.

Such is how we lived—if you could call that living—the next seven years.

Chapter Thirty-One

"Dreamin'," Erskine Green once told me, "will just drive you mad, Mister Cole."

Not since that first night in that cold, damp cell had I dreamed. Or if I had, I had willed myself to forget the nightmare—for all dreams are haunted when you are in prison for life—immediately upon awakening.

Shortly before midnight on the night of January 25, 1884, I awoke to the scream of a whistle. The cell-block remained pitch dark as the whistle blared outside. A faint scent of smoke reached my nostrils, yet I felt unconcerned. Then came the pounding of shoes, the clanging of iron keys, and shouts up and down the cells.

"Up! Up! Up!"

Prisoners answered with the vilest of curses.

The yellow light of waving lanterns flashed down the hallway. Doors to cells creaked open, guards barked, and prisoners moaned.

Ben Cayou appeared at my door and rammed a key into the lock. "Get up, Cole!"

Sighing, I warned the roaches. "Move along, boys. It's time."

The door opened. "*Now,* Cole!" He jerked the door open.

With the nonchalance of a lifer, I tossed aside

the blanket. "What's this ruction all about, Ben?"

A man somewhere on the upper tiers started to scream.

"Damn it, Cole!" Ben Cayou bellowed. "Do you want to burn to death? It's a fire. A damned fire. And a big one!"

I came to my feet, started to pull on my shoes.

"There's no time!" Cayou shouted.

I blinked, still befuddled by sleep. I could not quite grasp anything Ben Cayou said. His words seemed to be slurred like Jim's speech had been before he finally got that bullet out of his mouth back in '79.

"The cell house is on fire!"

At last, I understood and so grabbed the worsted wristlets that Mrs. Cayou had given me for Christmas. Once I had slipped those on, I reached for my two books: *Wit and Humor* and *God's Book of Nature*.

"No, no, no! Leave everything. Just get out."

Cayou had no more time to deal with a sleepy-headed fool. He moved down to the next cell, and, leaving the books General Henry Sibley had given me on a recent visit, I walked to the open cell door. I glanced out and swallowed down the bile as I saw the flames from hell.

"Out!" Cayou was shoving Terry Logan toward me as I looked away from the flames. Other prisoners moved down the stone-walled corridor.

"To the yard!" Ben Cayou ordered as he went to unlock the next cell.

Another guard waited down the hallway, putting iron manacles on the prisoners waiting patiently in line, then sending them into the frigid yard. By the time I reached this guard—an ashen-faced Griggs—smoke had filled the chamber, and I had to cover my nose and mouth with the crook of my arm.

Griggs looked up, his eyes filled with terror. He focused on the flames, the thick, choking smoke, coughed once himself, and glanced at me.

"Don't bother with the iron, Griggs," I said. "You have my word I shall not try to escape."

"Get out!" he yelled, and I obeyed. Yet Griggs did not wait for me, or any of the prisoners coming behind me. He left the keys and the manacles, and ran, pushing past me, knocking a man convicted of rape to the floor, and dropping below the thick smoke.

I did not blame him. I wanted to run myself.

Flames had been sucked under the cell house's roof, and suddenly the roof exploded, sending sparks and coals showering to the stone floor below.

By that time, I had fallen to my hands and knees and I was groping blindly, desperately trying to find the door. At first, I tried to avoid the hot embers that were burning my palms and knees. But within seconds, I no longer cared and couldn't really feel any pain. Reaching the exit, feeling the freshness of the bitterly cold air, I crawled through the doorway, leaned against the wall, and then reached back inside the door. It wasn't long until a hand locked on my wrist. My fingers clinched the wool of a coat, and I pulled Terry Logan out.

"Over there," I said, coughing and watching a vicious prisoner, who had killed his own brother, scramble toward the foundry. I cared little for Terry Logan. Again I reached back into the smoke-filled building, feeling the heat of flames, until my hands locked on someone else.

Erskine Green came out, coughing, spitting, trying not to breathe in the hot, scorching air.

Jim came out, and I thanked God. Then another robber . . . Bob Younger. Then Ben Cayou, his clothes smoking from the intense heat.

"Where's Lempke?" I yelled above the roaring furnace that had been a cell-block.

"I don't . . . know." Cayou's eyes were filled with fright. He blinked, turned back, and started inside, but I grabbed his waistband and pulled him back into the yard, away from the inferno. "If Lempke's not here by now," I told the guard, "he's dead." We later learned I had been right. We all ran farther out into the yard as the roof caved in.

Snow covered the yard, numbing my bare feet.

All around us was bedlam. The city's fire engine, hose cart, and hook-and-ladder had arrived, and firemen ran with axes and shovels. Jim worked alongside a city fireman, trying to connect a hose to a hydrant. But water came out only in a trickle, perhaps because of the cold, or because there was not enough pressure.

"Dodd! Dodd!"

I turned to find Warden Reed calling out, standing in his nightshirt and hood as the head guard, George Dodd, slipped on ice as he raced over to his boss.

"You've got to get the women prisoners," Reed ordered. "Put them in that room." He pointed.

"Warden," I heard Dodd say, "we've got some of the worst men alive out here . . . and not all of them are shackled. . . ."

"I know that, Dodd." Reed started toward a man in a helmet that I could only guess was the fire chief.

Outside the burning cell house, Griggs was his normal self again. "Come on, boys." Pointing at the walls, he laughed. "Try to escape, you damned fish! That fire has lit up this yard like high noon. We'll cut you sons-of-bitches down real easy. Try it. Try it, damn you!"

Ignoring Griggs, I went to George Dodd, who had stopped and was staring as though he was unable to make any decisions under the circumstances.

"Can I be of service, Mister Dodd?" I asked.

He spun, hand darting for his holstered revolver,

but then he stopped, stockstill. For some unknown reason every bit of doubt disappeared from his face. Having spent seven years in Stillwater, I had become almost as trusted as Erskine Green. He drew the heavy Schofield .45 from his holster, tossed it up, caught it by the barrel, and handed it to me, butt forward.

"Cole, will you . . . ?" Then he noticed Bob and Jim standing beside me. "Will you and your brothers guard the women prisoners?"

"Yes, sir, Mister Dodd," I assured him as I took the revolver, and led my brothers over to the storeroom where they had gathered the women.

Somehow, Jim grabbed an axe handle off the fire engine, and Bob found some little pinch bar. The women prisoners had been housed in a storeroom. Six of them—two Negresses, a Celestial, and three white women—along with the prison's matron, who looked as if she wished she were back in St. Peter. Bob had left his cell with a blanket, and, upon opening the storeroom door, he handed the blanket to the first shivering girl he saw, and advised her we were there to protect her and the others.

There was nothing to keep us warm but the massive flames coming from the cell house. Yet we stood in front of that door. Erskine Green had found the other convicts of color and he began leading them in spirituals. Before long, Jim tried to join them. His words still came out incoherent, but I smiled. My mouth moved along to the words, but I did not sing.

Then L.M. Sage and J.B. Coney walked toward us.

Coney's face had been blackened by soot, and Sage wore no shirt despite the January freeze. Both men grinned.

"Why don't you boys take a walk," Sage said, "whilst J.B. and me visit 'em women."

The Schofield came up, and I eared back that thumb-busting hammer.

"I got a better idea," I told the vile man. "Why don't you and your pal sit on that box? Otherwise, I'll give this Schofield to one of the ladies in that storeroom . . . and remember . . . three of them women are in here for murder. I bet any one of them would just love to blow your damned head off."

"That gun . . . ," J.B. Coney grinned excitedly. "Boys, you can get us all out of here. Think about it. You can get us all out of this pigsty."

"Or," I said, "I can blow your damned head off, too, and my aim's probably a wee bit better than any one of those women in there." I motioned the big .45's barrel toward the pile of boxes. They sat down and behaved themselves until Cobb returned around sunrise and ordered Griggs and another guard to shackle the two fiends together. Slowly George Cobb walked toward me, holding out his right hand.

"I'll take my revolver now, Cole," Cobb said.

"Shoot the damned bastard," Coney said.

The Schofield felt heavy in my hand as I lifted it. I grinned. "Want to see a bushwhacker's border shift, George?"

"Sure, Cole."

So I tossed the heavy .45 in the air, stuck my right hand inside my waistband to warm my fingers, caught the Schofield in my left hand, slipped my finger into the trigger guard, spun the pistol, till the butt was facing toward Cobb.

With a dry laugh, he took the .45, holstered it, and walked away. Only he stopped a few feet away, his boots crunching in the snow, and faced me again.

"Thanks, Cole," he said. "Thanks to you and your brothers."

Not everyone, of course, thought to thank us.

By midmorning, Griggs had found us and slapped manacles on our ankles, while we looked with a strange numbness at the blackened stone walls of the cell house. The fires had consumed other buildings, including our prison library. The state pen no longer could house the prisoners, or even the guards. And although the sun had broken free of the clouds, the cold remained. Erskine Green brought me socks and shoes, and I rubbed circulation back into my feet before slipping on the borrowed warmth.

Warden Reed came by, shook my hand, and

reached into his pocket, withdrawing a few sheets of telegraph paper. He held one out.

"'Keep close watch on the Youngers,'" he read.

Dropping it, he read the next one: "'Was fire plot to free Youngers?'" And a third: "'Did Youngers escape?'"

Those sheets of paper now wadded into balls, fell onto the snow, as Warden Reed walked across the icy grounds.

The governor showed up a few hours later, while we walked around, shackled, in the snow to stay warm. Most of the prisoners crowded by the gate, but I figured soldiers, and deputies, and marshals, and hayseeds stood beyond those walls.

By nightfall, the prisoners of Stillwater were being carted off. Guards would lead them to county jails across the state: Winona, Hastings, Minneapolis, and St. Paul. The women were put up in Warden Reed's house before they boarded the Winona train. But Jim, Bob, and I got special treatment.

A judge named Butts and a gent named Abe Hall came to take us to the Washington County Courthouse.

"Brothers," I said with pure delight, "this is the best start to a new year that I've ever had."

I meant it, too. All my life I had longed to take a sleigh ride.

Chapter Thirty-Two

In 1885, the news arrived. Frank James was a free man. Jesse had been betrayed by a gang member, shot in the back of the head at his home—with his wife and two kids in a nearby room—by a gutless wonder named Robert Ford back in 1882. Mark my words, I cared little for Frank's brother, but I despise the way he died. Murdered. A murder sanctioned by the cowardly governor of Missouri.

After Jesse's death in St. Joseph, Frank gave himself up. He spent a year or better in the Independence jail before a jury acquitted him of two murders and a train robbery in Winston after he and Jesse reformed the gang. A short while later, Frank was tried in Alabama for yet another crime, and, once again, a jury set him free. Finally, in 1885, he walked out of jail after the state's prosecutors in Missouri dropped its last indictment against him.

In 1886, Mr. Cobb and Mr. Cayou escorted me into Warden Reed's office, and left me there as the warden motioned to a fancy chair. I tried to settle into it, but could not find a comfortable spot so I fidgeted around like a boy forced to wear a tie for Sunday school.

"What's the matter?" Warden Reed asked.

I stopped squirming. "I don't know, sir. Guess I'm not used to all these cushions."

He laughed, looked at the papers before him, and paused before he said: "You have been a first-class prisoner for several years now, Cole." That I was, now wearing the nice gray suit and cap that befitted a convict of my status. "I see just two demerits against you."

"Yes, sir." I grinned. "Some ladies were brought into the cell-block, sir, and I just lost my head. Like most of the other boys, I removed my hat and whistled and winked."

Reed pushed back, grinning like the proverbial cat's run-in with a certain canary. "Were they pretty?"

"They were women, sir, and not wearing stripes or checks."

Again he laughed, but the lightness faded from his face quickly as he slid a newspaper across the table. "You are prison librarian, Cole. Have you seen this?"

It was the St. Paul *Pioneer Press*, and the story of the day said William Marshall, formerly the governor of Minnesota, and others thought that Jim, Bob, and I should be paroled if not outright pardoned. I stared at the headline, and read the first few paragraphs of the story, before I leaned back into the cushy chair.

For once, I could think of nothing to say.

"Don't hold out much hope, Cole," Warden

Reed said. "You have been here ten years, but many politicians and newspaper editors think you should rot behind these walls."

"Yes, sir." Nobody in Northfield would favor turning us loose.

"I don't know if I think you should be paroled, either," Reed said.

"I understand, Warden."

"Yet, I do believe you and your brothers have been reformed."

"Thank you, sir."

He pointed to some envelopes and telegrams, glancing at a few without sharing their contents with me, until he found the letter he must have been looking for. He pulled a dainty piece of paper from the well-traveled brown envelope, and slid it across the table.

With trembling hands, I lifted the letter, fearing the worst—some Radical Republican saying they should hang me and my brothers, draw and quarter us, behead us, and weight our bodies with stones before sinking us to the bottom of the St. Croix River.

Instead, my mouth fell open as I read.

I have known the true character of Cole Younger for many years. At a critical time, while he wore the gray, he did brave and unselfish things for those who were dear to me, now dead and gone. I have learned from the lips of the just dead of the true nobility of his inward character.

Sincerely,

Mrs. Elizabeth Daniel

Harrisonville, Missouri

Sweet Lizzie Brown, the girl I had so long admired, still married to another man, yet still championing an old, worn-out warhorse like Thomas Coleman Younger. Tears rolled down my cheeks.

"Cole," Warden Reed said softly. "Don't get your hopes up. Not in here. Not ever. Remember Erskine Green."

How could I forget Erskine Green? Less than a year earlier, in July of 1885, as I walked to my cell, I heard a loud commotion from the upper tiers. With Griggs walking alongside me, we stopped, turned, and looked up.

"Green! Green! Don't be a damned fool, boy!" Cobb screamed as I watched Erskine, looking so small from where I stood five floors below, shaking his head, waving a finger at the guard a few rods away.

"No, sir. No, sir. No, sir."

"Boy!" Cobb shouted. "You're a free man. Your sentence is over. You're walking out of here . . . free."

"No, sir." His voice cracked. "What the hell can I do out yonder?"

And he jumped.

I turned my head, but could not close my ears. The sound sent me to my knees, and I reached forward, gripped the bars of the nearby cell, and vomited.

Griggs spit out his disgust, and ordered me: "Get a mop, Younger. And a paint brush. You'll be cleaning up the mess you just made . . . and the mess Green made, too."

Others began working on our parole—from Missouri, from Washington City, even in Minnesota. Stephen B. Elkins, who had taught me at The Academy and whose life I had saved from Quantrill after the battle at Lone Jack, wrote on my behalf, and Elkins was now a senator from West Virginia. W.C. Bronaugh, who had fought with us at Lone Jack, visited with me, and began campaigning for our cause at every Board of Pardons meeting.

As a first-class prisoner, I could write a letter— once a week—and I did so. Not so much for me, but for my brothers. I had meant what I told that judge ten years earlier in Faribault. If Bob and Jim could go free, gladly would I die in prison.

But I was too late for Bob.

By 1887, his hacking cough left flecks of blood on his handkerchief, and we knew what that meant. Ma had caught the lung disease, which had killed her. Bob's consumption worsened in the rot and dampness of the new cell house, and he began to wither away. He had been sentenced to death.

"Warden," I told Reed in 1889, "if you can get Bob pardoned or paroled, so he can go home to die in Lee's Summit, I'll swear on a stack of Bibles that Jim and I will never write another letter, never ask for any leniency."

I don't know if Reed tried or not, but too many people were still speaking out against us. Yet Reed did allow our sister Retta to come up to see us. That was no blessing. We sat around. We waited for Bob to die.

Retta got to Stillwater on September 2, 1889. The deputy warden, a good man named Westby, allowed a photographer named Kuhn to come in with his big box of a camera and take some portraits of my brothers, Retta, and me. He even let us pose for some individual portraits. Best of all, he let us exchange our gray suits and caps that distinguished us as first-class prisoners for fine suits, ties, and fancy shirts for the photographs.

Two weeks later, Bob couldn't swallow, could hardly breathe, and his words came out in ragged breaths, staining his lips with blood.

"Cole," he managed to say, "lift me up so I can see the sky."

I did, holding him close, amazed at how light he felt in my arms, understanding then that the disease had worn him down to little more than skin and bones.

We could hear mockingbirds begin to sing, sounding sweeter than a church choir.

"Remember the birds back in Missouri, Cole?" Bob asked.

Maybe I answered. My mind was going kind of foggy by that time as I laid Bob's head back down on the pillow.

The deathwatch went on.

"Don't leave me here all shot," he sang out in a surprisingly strong voice. "Don't leave me, Cole."

Crying, I remembered those words from Northfield, after Bob's horse had been shot dead, after a bullet had shattered his elbow. "I'm not leaving you, Bob," I said, or thought I said. Perhaps he could not understand me, choking on the words, the pain.

"Cole . . ." I had to lean close to Bob's lips just to hear him. "You ain't Dick." He coughed out a faint laugh. "You're . . . better. . . ."

Four hours later, as Jim and I held Bob's hands and Retta, who had extended her stay, stroked his hair, a merciful God freed Bob Younger, not yet thirty-five years old, from the life sentence he had been given in Faribault roughly thirteen years earlier.

I told the reporters for the Stillwater newspapers—the *Gazette* and the *Democrat*—that Bob Younger had never committed any crime until I lured him to Northfield. It wasn't the truth, though maybe, grieved as I was at that moment, I believed it.

The prison chaplain, a good man named Albert, preached the funeral, gave Bob the last rites. The prisoners had draped the chapel's walls in black, and an undertaker had donated a fancy casket. Every prisoner, every guard came to Bob's funeral.

And Retta took him home.

Chapter Thirty-Three

We thought—though I did not want to admit it—
that Bob's death would change the mood of
Minnesotans. That sympathy would take over
and we would be freed. Maybe the loss of our
brother finally did it, but, sometimes, sympathy
can be a long time coming.

The year 1889 passed. So did another ten years
and more.

Christmas pageants. Plays. Lectures. Meetings
with the Board of Pardons, at which, time after
time, they demanded that Jim or I admit that
Frank James killed Joseph Heywood inside that
Northfield bank, which I never did. Visitors. I
saw them all. Henry Wolfer became the new
warden in the late spring of 1892. Jim took over
my job at the library, and I went to work in the
laundry until a new hospital was completed,
where they put me to work there because they
had heard what a fine nurse I had been down in
the Sni-A-Bar when I rode with Quantrill.

On July 10, 1901, I was bringing peaches to
some sick prisoners in the hospital, laughing at the
joke the doc had just told me. A young prisoner
named Smith hurried up to me, and told me I was
wanted in the library. That's where Jim worked,
and I feared the worst, could even picture Jim

lying on the floor, dead of an apoplexy. I handed the sack of peaches to the fresh fish, and hurried across the yard, letting out a heavy sigh of relief when I saw Jim scratching his bald head.

Warden Wolfer stood beside him, grinning as I entered the room.

Wolfer waved his hand, and his son came over, holding two telescope grips. The warden's wife followed, with suits on hangers in either hand.

"Put these clothes on," the warden said, "and you won't have to go back."

Jim blinked and stared at me. Neither of us understood a thing.

"You've been paroled," Wolfer said.

Well, there's nothing like walking away from the walls of a prison after twenty-five years. But parole . . . it's not exactly free, Parson. I was still Jean Valjean, and Inspector Javert kept chasing me, wanting me dead, or back behind bars. And the world Jim and I stepped into was not the one we had left back in 1876. Telephones and horseless carriages, though rare, could be seen. People wore different styles of clothes and hats. They walked fast. They did not stop to talk to strangers. They buried their heads in newspapers. Some on new-fangled velocipedes damned near ran us over.

We got jobs that befitted men of our stature and expertise. We sold tombstones. They paid us

$60 a month—each. When I had been ranching in Texas, I had paid my hired hands $25 a month and found. I had made less than that working cattle in Florida, but, mostly, I had never earned an honest dollar.

The conditions of the parole said we could not leave Minnesota. We could not marry, not that anyone would want to tie the knot with a reprobate like me. We remained outcasts in a land still populated by many men and women who did not want us to be alive, let alone outside of Stillwater prison's walls.

The grippe, rheumatism, and all the lead I still carried inside my body plagued me, and I wasn't very good at selling tombstones. Think about it. A tombstone. That's a hard product to move. Nobody wants to buy death. Oh, folks loved asking me inside their homes, and chatting with me, feeding me cake and cookies, and lubricating me with coffee or buttermilk. But when I asked if they wanted to pick out a headstone, they laughed, shook my hand so they could brag that they had shaken the hand of Cole Younger, and sent me on my way to see one of their neighbors.

I could handle that. Jim couldn't.

My brother just never could find that level place. He'd be up, and up high, or he would sink into the depths of depression. As the months dragged on, he got lower, lower, lower. He quit selling tombstones around Stillwater, and found work selling cigars in St. Paul. He wasn't good at that, either. I could talk, you see. That mouth wound still plagued Jim's speech. I'd go to plays—theaters gave me free tickets, for I was Cole Younger—but Jim? No church. No theaters. Not even saloons. He peddled cigars from this shabby stand, then he went to his hotel with his newspapers. He brooded. He visited Warden Wolfer more than he saw me. He went insane.

Jim was living in the Reardon Hotel. On that day, the violin player at the corner said he had looked happy when he stopped by on the way to the hotel. He had dropped a coin in the fiddler's hat, smiled, and said: "So long, Atreus. You sound great today." He had shaken hands with the bellman at the hotel, told him he would be indisposed, and walked up the stairs to his room.

There he retrieved the revolver, stretched out on his bed, put the barrel to the side of his head, and pulled the trigger.

It was October 19, 1902.

We put him in a casket, though this one was not as fine as the one the undertaker had given Brother Bob, and we sent him home to Lee's Summit, to be buried alongside Bob.

When the train pulled out of the station, I walked the long walk back to my own lodging, too numb to cry, too shocked to feel any pain.

You ask me how many men I killed. I can't rightly say, but I can think of three right off the bat.

John Younger.

Bob Younger.

Jim Younger.

Maybe Jim's death changed the way people thought. Maybe God showed them the light. But, no, probably the people of Minnesota just got sick of having a Younger in their fine state. Anyway, early in 1903, the Board of Pardons decided to end my parole. They turned it into a full pardon. They sent me home, back to Missouri, and as the train headed south, I stared out the window, watching the land change, but staring mostly at my own reflection. A fat, bald, old man with pain-filled blue eyes looked back at me. He looked lost. Alone.

It made me wonder. All those years, riding with Quantrill, with Frank and Jesse, with my brothers. All those years in prison. Hell, maybe I had always been alone. And lost.

When I reached the hotel at Lee's Summit, I signed the register as T.C. Younger. Couldn't think of anything else.

The fellow behind the counter was mighty good at reading upside down. Immediately he asked: "Are you Cole Younger?"

"Yeah." My voice sounded weary. I took my grip and went to my room, closed the door, and waited. It took a damned long while, longer than I had expected, but I was used to being alone. Fully dressed, I fell asleep.

I woke up at dawn, didn't go down for breakfast, just waited some more. Finally, footsteps sounded, stopping outside my door. I kept waiting until there came a tentative knock. I rolled off the bed, walked to the door, knowing I'd be answering a hundred more questions from some ink-slinging newspaper bub.

But it wasn't . . . not a boy, not a newspaper reporter. It was a woman, a woman with gray hair, but slight of figure, a woman with wonderful eyes that I would have recognized anywhere.

"Hello, Cole," Lizzie Brown Daniel told me. "It has been a long time."

My lips parted, yet no words came out.

"Come on," she said, and held out her hand. "I have rented a buggy. Let's go for a ride."

Well, Parson, we went from place to place, all the way to where the Wayside Rest had once stood, to the two-story farmhouse where I had grown up, to Harrisonville, and back to Lee's Summit, which had been called Strother when I was a boy.

"Everything's changed," I said in a frail voice.

Lizzie reached over, put her hand atop mine, and squeezed.

"Everything," I said. Tears flowed and memories . . . good, bad, indifferent, but memories nonetheless . . . came flooding back. "Everything was so different then."

Epilogue

1913

What else is there to say, Parson?

I did that brief little tour with Frank James, you might recall. The Great Cole Younger & Frank James Historical Wild West. As Wild West shows went, Buffalo Bill, Pawnee Bill, the 101 Ranch . . . they didn't have to fear much competition from us.

One thing I recollect from many years earlier. Frank and I had passed a tent revival meeting in some Iowa town. It got us started on religion. We could talk on that subject just about all day back then, unless someone else in our gang brought up Shakespeare just to get us to change the subject. That was all before Northfield. Before Bob Ford murdered Jesse in St. Joseph.

"You think about God, Frank?" I asked him years later.

"No."

I laughed. "A cousin of mine once asked me if we prayed before going into battle with Quantrill. I told him . . . 'Sure. We prayed. But when the shooting started, we forgot all about those prayers and cursed like bullwhackers. Cursed so much it became hard to stop.'"

"Ain't that the son-of-a-bitching truth," Frank said, and spit out tobacco juice.

"Your father was a Baptist preacher, Buck," I said. "Walking the Streets of Gold. I wonder if Jim, John, and Bob walk with him. Or even Dingus. Our time's coming. You ever thought about making peace with God?"

Frank James sighed, shook his head, and turned to me. "Why Bishop Cole," he said, "who the hell would want to go to heaven if it's filled with outlaws and murderers like us?"

I started to laugh, only to find in his eyes that he meant it. "There's no God, Bud," Frank said. "No heaven. You die, you rot, and the worms get your body."

"There has to be more than that," I said.

"There ain't."

Well, I don't see Frank so much these days. He's up at his farm, talking to tourists, charging them money to see his home. I don't see many folks . . . hell, Parson, ain't many of them around any more. But I got a sweet little niece, named Nora, and it was her who brought me to this here revival. Where I first heard you. And I come back. Got sick, but made myself come back once more. Today. You know what happened fifty years ago, Parson? The folks over in Lawrence, Kansas, certainly remember. Bet you plenty of folks are cursing Cole Younger's name right now.

But here I am, Parson. An old man, a murderer,

a thief, a liar, a scoundrel. I've walked up here alone. To turn my soul over into the hands of the Almighty. Missus Lizzie Daniel sure looks relieved that I'm doing this, but I want to ask you something before you lead me out of this tent and to the river, before you dunk my head beneath the cleansing waters, the Blood of the Lamb.

Do you want an outlaw and murderer like me in heaven?

Parson, have you ever read John Milton's *Paradise Lost*?

> Long is the way
> And hard, that out of Hell leads up to light.

It has been a hard way for me. But I am ready now, if you are. Am I supposed to feel different? I guess I do. It's like I told Lizzie ten years ago.

Everything was so different then.

Author's Note

On March 21, 1916, a little more than a year after the passing of his faithful friend, Frank James, Cole Younger died at his home in Lee's Summit, Missouri. He was seventy-two.

"He was a dignified old gentleman," Jack Lait wrote in the Chicago *Herald*, "respected by his community, wrapped up in religious work, a devout communicant and a valiant exhorter."

The sons of Jesse and Frank James attended the funeral, after which, as rain fell, the body of the old Confederate bushwhacker and outlaw was brought to the Lee's Summit Cemetery. Today, Cole Younger still rests alongside his mother and brothers Bob and Jim.

Although grounded in fact, *Hard Way Out of Hell* is a novel. For the purpose of narrative, I have taken liberties with dates and chronology, but much of what I have written is based on the truth, or, perhaps, how Cole Younger might have interpreted his own truth. Anyway, as I often say: "Don't quote me in your term paper. I make things up."

I'm not sure the definitive biography of Cole Younger has ever been written, but Marley Brandt's *The Outlaw Youngers: A Confederate Brotherhood* is the best to date, and Homer

Croy's *Cole Younger: Last of the Great Outlaws* remains a fun read. I also relied on *The Story of Cole Younger by Himself* (keeping in mind that Cole Younger was given to exaggerations, embellish-ments, and lies while remaining loyal to friends he did not wish to see in prison). Todd M. George's *Twelve Years with Cole Younger* and *The Conversion of Cole Younger* proved helpful. I also turned to *Ride the Razor's Edge: The Younger Brothers Story* by Carl W. Breihan, who had access to relatives and documents but never documented his work and sometimes appears to have stretched the truth as much as Cole Younger had.

Sorting through the myriad crimes attributed to the James-Younger Gang is a challenge in itself, especially since Frank James was acquitted in two trials. Cole Younger never implicated the James brothers. He even claimed that the only crime Bob, Jim, and he ever committed came in Northfield, when, as he wrote in his autobiography, "we decided to make one haul, and with our share of the proceeds start life anew in Cuba, South America, or Australia." Jesse, on the other hand, never even got his day in court, thanks to Robert Ford. It's hard to figure out which banks, trains, and stagecoaches the Jameses and Youngers actually robbed, and which were committed by copycats or another "gang of old bushwhacking desperadoes," as the Liberty *Tribune* called them.

Historians disagree on who was where. The James-Younger Gang might not have even committed the first robbery attributed to them (Liberty, Missouri, 1866). Even if they were there, Jesse's bullet wound would likely have prevented him from participating, but we will probably never know for certain.

In any event, I just made my best guesses for the various robberies, or chose my bandits for the purpose of narrative.

Primary sources for Younger's Civil War years included Donald L. Gilmore's *Civil War on the Missouri–Kansas Border*; Edward E. Leslie's *The Devil Knows How to Ride: The True Story of William Clarke Quantrill and His Confederate Raiders*; Thomas Goodrich's *Bloody Dawn: The Story of the Lawrence Massacre*; John McCorkle's *Three Years with Quantrill*; *Jim Cummins' Book, Written by Himself*; and John N. Edwards's *Noted Guerrillas, Or, the Warfare of the Border.*

Much of the James-Younger Gang research came from T.J. Stiles's *Jesse James: Last Rebel of the Civil War*; Ted P. Yeatman's *Frank and Jesse James: The Story Behind the Legend*; James D. Horan's *Desperate Men*; Homer Croy's *Jesse James was My Neighbor*; Robertus Love's *The Rise and Fall of Jesse James*; Mark Lee Gardner's *Shot All to Hell: Jesse James, the Northfield Raid, and the Wild West's Greatest Escape*; Dallas Cantrell's *Youngers' Fatal Blunder: Northfield,*

Minnesota; Robert Barr Smith's *The Last Hurrah of the James–Younger Gang*; Sean McLachlan's *The Last Ride of the James–Younger Gang: Jesse James and the Northfield Raid 1876*; William A. Settle Jr.'s *Jesse James was His Name, Or Fact and Fiction Concerning the Careers of the Notorious James Brothers of Missouri*; Robert J. Wybrow's *"Horrid Murder & Heavy Robbery": The Liberty Bank Robbery, 13 February 1866*; Wilbur A. Zink's *The Roscoe Gun Battle: The Younger Brothers Vs. Pinkerton Detectives*; Ronald Beights's *Jesse James and the First Missouri Train Robbery*; Frank Triplett's *The Life, Times, and Treacherous Death of Jesse James*; John Newman Edwards's *A Terrible Quintette*; Augustus C. Appler's *The Younger Brothers: Their Life, Character, and Daring Exploits of the Youngers, the Notorious Bandits Who Rode with Jesse James and William Clarke Quantrell*; J.W. Buel's *Border Bandits: The Authentic and Thrilling History of the Noted Outlaws, Jesse and Frank James, and Their Bands of Highwaymen*; and *Jesse James: The Best Writings on the Notorious Outlaw and His Gang*, edited by Harold Dellinger.

The Stillwater prison days came from *Convict Life at the Minnesota State Prison, Stillwater, Minnesota* by William Heilbron; *The Youngers' Fight for Freedom* by W.C. Bronaugh; and *When the Heavens Fell: The Youngers in Stillwater Prison* by John J. Koblas.

I would be remiss if I did not pay tribute to Koblas's other fine books: *Bushwhacker! Cole Younger & The Kansas-Missouri Border War*; *Faithful Unto Death: The James–Younger Raid on the First National Bank, September 7, 1876, Northfield, Minnesota*; *Jesse James in Iowa*; and *The Cole Younger & Frank James Historical Wild West Show*. Jack Koblas wrote several other books, but these listed above were the ones I used for this novel. He was a fine historian, with a singular wit, and I enjoyed our road trips to various James-Younger Gang speaking gigs over the years. I didn't even mind sleeping on his couch, because although he could be incredibly ornery, he had one amazing library, would often break out in songs, and he made me laugh— a lot. Jack died in 2013.

The Maise Walker story, by the way, came from Walker's great-grandson, Billy Walker, so I must thank Mr. Walker. And special thanks to the downtown Kansas City Public Library's excellent Missouri Valley Special Collections. The wonderful Guidon Books of Scottsdale, Arizona, and the James Country Mercantile of Liberty, Missouri, directed me to some rare books.

Other research assistance came from the Society of American Baseball Research; The Bushwhacker Museum in Nevada, Missouri; Missouri State Archives; the Jesse James Bank Museum in Liberty, Missouri; Jesse James Farm

& Museum in Kearney, Missouri; Prairie Trails Museum of Wayne County in Corydon, Iowa; Kentucky Historical Society; State Historical Museum of Iowa in Des Moines; and the Watkins Museum of History; and the Convention and Visitors Bureau in Lawrence, Kansas.

A final tip of my hat to Hayes Scriven at the Northfield (Minnesota) Historical Society; and all my cronies in the National James-Younger Gang and with the Friends of the James Farm. Not to mention L.C.'s for the burnt ends in Kansas City, and my son, Jack, for stopping with me at the Adair, Iowa, train-robbery site before making our way to Des Moines during our annual summer baseball trip. And, finally, to Jack Smith and Minta Sue Jack, for the loan of their guest bedroom, dining-room table, and sofa in Orange, California, where I finished a draft of this novel over Thanksgiving weekend.

This work could never have been finished without their help.

Johnny D. Boggs
Santa Fe, New Mexico

About the Author

Johnny D. Boggs has worked cattle, shot rapids in a canoe, hiked across mountains and deserts, traipsed around ghost towns, and spent hours poring over microfilm in library archives—all in the name of finding a good story. He's also one of the few Western writers to have won six Spur Awards from Western Writers of America (for his novels, *Camp Ford*, in 2006, *Doubtful Cañon*, in 2008, and *Hard Winter* in 2010, *Legacy of a Lawman*, *West Texas Kill*, both in 2012, and his short story, "A Piano at Dead Man's Crossing", in 2002) as well as the Western Heritage Wrangler Award from the National Cowboy and Western Heritage Museum (for his novel, *Spark on the Prairie: The Trial of the Kiowa Chiefs*, in 2004). A native of South Carolina, Boggs spent almost fifteen years in Texas as a journalist at the Dallas *Times Herald* and Fort Worth *Star-Telegram* before moving to New Mexico in 1998 to concentrate full time on his novels. Author of dozens of published short stories, he has also written for more than fifty newspapers and magazines, and is a frequent contributor to *Boys' Life* and *True West*. His Western novels cover a wide range. *The Lonesome Chisholm Trail* (2000) is an authentic cattle-drive story, while *Lonely*

Trumpet (2002) is an historical novel about the first black graduate of West Point. *The Despoilers* (2002) and *Ghost Legion* (2005) are set in the Carolina backcountry during the Revolutionary War. *The Big Fifty* (2003) chronicles the slaughter of buffalo on the southern plains in the 1870s, while *East of the Border* (2004) is a comedy about the theatrical offerings of Buffalo Bill Cody, Wild Bill Hickok, and Texas Jack Omohundro, and *Camp Ford* (2005) tells about a Civil War baseball game between Union prisoners of war and Confederate guards. "Boggs's narrative voice captures the old-fashioned style of the past," *Publishers Weekly* said, and *Booklist* called him "among the best Western writers at work today." Boggs lives with his wife Lisa and son Jack in Santa Fe. His website is www.johnnydboggs.com.

Center Point Large Print
600 Brooks Road / PO Box 1
Thorndike, ME 04986-0001 USA

(207) 568-3717

US & Canada:
1 800 929-9108
www.centerpointlargeprint.com